Also by Brenna Yovanoff

THE REPLACEMENT

SMOULDER

PAPER VALENTINE

FIENDISH

BRENNA YOVANOFF

SIMON & SCHUSTER

First published in Great Britain by Simon & Schuster UK Ltd, 2014
A CBS COMPANY

First published in the USA in 2014 by Razorbill,
a member of Penguin Group (USA) Inc.

1 3 5 7 9 10 8 6 4 2

Simon & Schuster UK Ltd
1st Floor, 222 Gray's Inn Road
London WC1X 8HB

www.simonandschuster.co.uk

Simon & Schuster Australia, Sydney
Simon & Schuster India, New Delhi

Simon Pulse, and colophon are registered trademarks
of Simon & Schuster UK Ltd.

A CIP catalogue record for this book
is available from the British Library

PB ISBN 978-0-85707-817-9
E-Book ISBN 978-0-85707-819-3

Printed

Askews & Holts	

For Maddy,
who was there.

PART I
DIRT

THE LAST DAY
CHAPTER ONE

When I was little, everything twinkled. Trees and clouds all seemed to shine around the edges. At night, the stars were long tails of light, smeared across the sky like paint. The whole county glowed.

Back then, my life was mostly pieces—tire swings and lemonade, dogwood petals drifting down and going brown in the grass. Cotton dresses, bedsheets flapping on the line. An acre of front porch. A year of hopscotch rhymes.

On the hottest days, I kicked off my shoes and ran out to the middle of the low-water bridge. The air was warm and buzzing. The creek raced along under me, bright as broken glass.

I jumped rope with my cousin, who was older and shiny. Shiny like an opal ring or a ballerina, and Shiny because it was her name. She hooked her pinky in mine and swore how when we were old enough, we'd run away from Hoax County and live in a silver camper on a beach somewhere. We'd be best friends forever.

Later, when everything went dark, I tried to think how the bad thing had started, but the pieces wouldn't come. No matter how I walked myself back through that last day, there was always a point where time stopped. A sheet seemed to loom in my mind, and no matter how I pressed my nose against it, I couldn't see past.

There were things I knew. I knew my mama had been making skillet chicken for dinner, because I remembered running out to the garden to pull some onions for the gravy, and how when I crawled down through the vegetable patch, the place under the tomatoes smelled like hay. It was warm and sweet, and for a while, I just sat smelling it, singing the first line of "Farmer in the Dell" over and over because I couldn't remember the rest, and counting my numbers.

The vine above me had four little tomatoes all hanging in a row, and in the middle, there was a fifth one. It was like the others, except not. Because instead of silkworm green, the fifth was gray—heavy as an elephant and made of stone, growing in the garden like a living thing, and I laughed because it was a miracle.

I was too little to think a miracle could be anything but good.

Later, it seemed that the whole world began and ended with that tomato. Not with the voices of men, or the way every room in the house got hot. But with that one stone marvel in the garden. With the clean white sheet in my head, and a silver needle pinched between someone's fingers. Hands that reached to close my eyes and a whisper like a spell. *Hold still and sleep. Wait till someone comes for you.*

But no one came.

In the canning closet, the air got hard to breathe. Jars broke open. Cherries splashed my face and arms, hissing on the bricks, but if it was hot, I couldn't feel it.

Then everything got quiet and that was worse. The shouting stopped and the fire burned out. I thought I might be the only person left in the world.

Before, I'd never been scared—not of deep water or falling off the swing set, or any of the other things that kids from town cried about. And never of the dark.

Dark was my best time. In summer, when the sun went down and the moths flapped against the screen, I sat in my mama's lap on the back porch, looking out at the tupelo trees, wearing my blue-fairy nightgown and holding my flannel bear. Mama wound the key in its back and sang along— *Oh my darling, oh my darling.*

Sometimes it doesn't matter how dark the world gets. You can be saved by the smallest thing. I played the Clementine song, turning the key again and again, winding up the memory of her voice until the music turned slow and jangly and the flannel bear wore out like a sock.

The closet was in the back corner of the cellar, and I had never liked to go down there. The floor was made of concrete and the air smelled swampy. Spiders lived behind the closet door and in the cracks between the shelves.

Now it was the only place in the whole world I was even really sure of.

The farm where we lived was on a shallow little branch of the Blue Jack Creek, and the water fed the stands of willow trees that grew around the house. Before, my mama had always kept them in their place, but now they stretched out, reaching in the dirt. They pushed until the wall caved in. Roots grew over my body.

The shoulders of my nightgown let go and my elbows poked through the sleeves. My hair got long, snapping its rubber bands. Sometimes I could feel my bones growing.

Every little stitch and seam told me I was changing, leaving behind my old, baby self, but when I tried to think how I must look, the picture wouldn't come. The more I tried to see it, the harder it was to see anything but that white sheet, and then the voice would rise up in my ear, getting louder, echoing around me. *Hold still and sleep.*

It was easier to turn toward it, to follow it down into a jumble of dreams—hills and creeks and hollows. Trees to climb, fields going on forever.

I fell headfirst into a sinkhole of pretty things, and the world inside your eyelids is just as big as the one outside.

THE GIRL IN THE CELLAR
CHAPTER TWO

The voices came from a long way off, and at first, they didn't mean anything. They were just mutters in some broke-down cellar, and I had long since stopped being Clementine in the canning closet.

In my dreams, I was Clementine running through the grass. I was alone, or else with a boy. I couldn't see his face, but I knew him from some other time, or maybe I'd only just invented him. We raced across an open meadow, toward a tree covered in blue and purple flowers, which meant it wasn't real, but I ran to it anyway.

Or I might have been someplace else. Maybe sitting in my own living room, listening to the TV and stitching pictures on a quilt square with my mama's embroidery thread, or standing on a lawn somewhere, watching crowds and colored lights—a party of white tablecloths and paper lanterns. I just couldn't remember if it was a place I'd been to once, or a life happening far away, or something I was only now making up. I'd been living on dreams so long it was hard to know if any one of the fifteen things happening inside my head was real.

Then someone spoke, closer than any of the ghost-people at the party, than any of the voices in my dreams.

Nothing down here but dry rot and trash.

A boy's voice, with an accent thicker than was common for Hoax County. Almost thick enough to cut.

He sounded bored with the trash and with the dry rot. Bored with the whole business—maybe even with himself—and hoarse like he'd been shouting.

Also, though, he sounded real.

In the moldy dark of the closet, I opened my mouth. The sheet and the sharp, warning voice were there at once, ordering me quiet, saying *wait* and *sleep*, but I'd already been waiting for so long. I was done with that. On the other side of the door were real people and I was going to make them hear me.

I tried to shout, but it was no good. My throat was too dry to make words. My arms wouldn't move to pound on the wall. I stood in the dark, with roots tangled in my hair, bits of glass sticking to my skin, still holding the windup bear. The flannel was squishy with groundwater, and I squeezed hard, digging my fingers into the clockwork. The song came whining out, broken from how many times I'd played it. It only clanked one line, *Oh my darling, oh my darling,* before grinding to a stop.

I could hear feet kicking around through junk and broken glass, too many to be just one person. Then they stopped, and the whole place got so still it hurt my ears.

The breathless silence went on so long I thought I would

nearly go crazy, and then the first boy spoke again, close to the wall. "Did you hear that?"

Someone answered from farther off, and I could hear the way the words rode up and down, saying *no*. Saying *what are you talking about* and *I don't hear anything* and *let's leave, let's leave.*

The roots had all grown over me, twisting around my arms and between my fingers, and the sweetest sound in my life was the ripping noise when I pulled my wrist free.

I wrenched the bear's key a half turn, a full turn. Then the clockwork caught, singing out its broken song, tinkling in the dark.

Oh my darling Clementine, thou art lost and gone forever, dreadful sorry Clementine.

And I waited.

"I'm telling you," said the first voice, close to the wall. "There's something in there."

Yes. Yes, there's something—here, I'm here. Please come find me, I'm here!

But no one answered. I could feel myself sinking, running out of hope. Already half-willing to let go, to fall straight back down into dreams.

Then came the dry *shush-shush* of someone running their hands over the wall, feeling along the bricks.

"Check this out. I think there used to be a door. Here—Cody, help me get it clear."

There was a scraping noise like chalk on a driveway, and I told myself it wasn't how it sounded, it wasn't someone pulling out the bricks, because if I let myself believe in rescue and it turned out I was wrong, I would sink right down in the cold black dirt and die of the despair.

But the scraping got louder. The voice in my ear had stopped telling mc to wait.

There was a crash, a burst of light against my eyelids, and the bricks fell away in a storm of noise and dust. My heart beat harder, and now he was in the canning closet with me.

"Oh my God," he said, and then his hands were on mine, so warm they nearly hurt. He grabbed my wrists, peeling back the willow roots, yanking so hard my whole body jerked.

I tried to help him, but I could barely move. He was touching my face, steadying my head as he unwound the roots in my hair, tearing me away from the wall.

Then I was falling. I knew I should catch myself, but my bones felt loose and unstrung. It had been an age since I'd taken a single step, and my legs wouldn't move. My eyes wouldn't open.

"Jesus," he said, catching me around the waist. "Would one of you *help* me? Get her arms!"

No one came to get my arms, though, and he dragged me out himself. I could smell his shirt and his hair, like leaves and summer and fresh air.

He went stumbling back with his arms around me and we fell hard on the floor. The bump when we landed seemed to knock something loose. My fingers spread wide and then made fists. My arms and legs began to tingle. When I turned my head, he seemed to glow against my eyelids, and I knew he must be the hero of the story, just like in all the books.

This is *ever-after*, I thought. This is the *happily*, the *end*. This is the prince who saved me.

I lay in his lap with his knees digging into my back and waited for him to kiss me and break the spell. Instead, he scraped his thumb across my mouth, wiping away the dirt. The rush of fresh air was almost too much to take. I coughed on it, trying to remember how to breathe without choking.

"Holy hell," someone said from over in the corner. "Holy everloving hell. Fisher, what have you *done*?"

He said it loud and quick, sounding so scared that for a second, I was sure they'd leave me there, lying in the cellar with all the bricks and broken glass.

"Give me your shirt," was all Fisher said.

"Are you crazy?" said one of the other boys. I thought there were two, but their voices were enough alike I couldn't tell them apart. "I'm not messing with that. You do it, Luke."

"No way I'm letting anything of mine touch anything like her. Fisher, you don't know what she *is*."

Fisher didn't answer, but there was a shuffling noise above me and this time when he touched my face, it was with a wadded-up cloth. It felt like cotton, warm from the sun, and it smelled like him.

"Who are you?" he said. When he leaned down, I could see him printed on the inside of my eyelids, a bright mess of colors like a paint splotch in the shape of a person. "How did you get here?"

I tried to answer, but my voice felt ruined. I wanted to tell him that I was Clementine DeVore and he was scrubbing my face too hard and this was my cellar and my memory was a clean white sheet and what was he doing here in my cellar, but all that came out was a sigh.

One of his friends spoke then, slow and soft. "Fisher, this is just too freaky."

"I know," he said, holding my face between his hands.

"Well, how do you know she ain't some creep down-hollow?"

Fisher crouched over me, still scrubbing my forehead and my cheeks. "I don't, so just shut up. God, look at all this soot."

I tried to turn my head, but he had his palms pressed hard against my cheeks. The shape of him was a warm blur on the inside of my eyes, twinkling with gold.

"Hold still," he said. "You have to hold still. There's busted glass everywhere."

"Look at her eyes," said one of the other boys under his breath. "If that's no fiend, I don't know what is."

The word was ugly, and the way he said it was worse.

"I'm not deaf," I said, and my voice was dry and scratchy, more grown-up than the one I remembered, but it was mine. "And I don't know how your mother raised you, but mine taught me it was rude to go throwing around a word like *fiend*."

The three of them got very quiet. I could feel their stillness in the air, the way they had all stopped breathing.

12

Then Fisher laughed, a short, barking laugh. "Looks like she's got more manners than you, whatever she is."

He turned away from me, like he might be about to stand, and when he did, the light around him faded.

"No," I said, before I could even think about it. "Don't go. Come back where I can see you."

"You *can't* see me," Fisher said. "Your eyes are shut."

But he leaned closer, putting his shirt against my face again, and in one long breath, I was nearly swallowed up by all the things I'd lost. I remembered days spent laughing in the knotweed down by the creek, nights out in the fields and the woods, skimming through the long grass like a ghost, a blanket spread over the ground and Shiny, my Shiny, with her fast, flashy laugh and her finger hooked through mine.

"You smell like a picnic," I said, struck again by how strange my voice was—like a picture doubling over itself.

"And you smell like mildew." His voice was rough, but for just a second, I thought I could hear him trying not to smile.

He was checking the lace at the edges of my nightgown, sliding his fingers along the insides of my cuffs. He pulled the collar away from my neck, following it around until he found a lumpy knot of cloth that had been pinned there since the world went dark, a strange weight against my collarbone.

"What are you doing?" I whispered, but he didn't answer until one of the other boys said it too, sounding small and scared.

"What is that? What's she got around her neck?"

13

Fisher tugged at my collar, unfastening the knot. "I don't know, but it looks like one hell of a trickbag."

The third boy spoke from farther off, and if I'd thought he sounded scared before, it was nothing compared to how his voice wavered and cracked now. "Then don't *mess* with it. You don't know what kind of craft is on that thing."

Fisher laughed that short, dog-bark laugh again and put the twist of cloth into my hand, closing my fingers around it. "The kind that can keep a girl shut up in a basement for God knows *how* long, and she lives."

"*Shit*, Fisher! Just—what are we going to do?"

"I'm taking her down to the Blackwood place."

Right away, the other two began to argue, talking over each other. "No, no way. You can't go messing with hexers and fiends. It's no business of Myloria Blackwood's that we found some crooked girl down in some burned-out house."

Fisher slid his hands underneath my back. "It's Myloria's sister that lived out here, and by my count, that *makes* it her business. So I'm taking this one down there, and if you're going to help, then help. If you're not, you can find your own way home."

Without another word, he scooped me up, one arm hooked at my knees and the other around my waist. When he lifted me, the shoulder of my nightgown split wider. The air felt damp and cool against my skin.

"Here," he said, jostling me higher against his chest. "Grab on around my neck."

"Why don't they like me?" I whispered, getting my arms

14

up, feeling around for his shoulder. "What's wrong with me? I never did anything to anyone."

Fisher was quiet for a second and when he answered, he sounded strange.

"It's not your fault," he said. "They're just nervous about how your eyes are sewed shut."

THE BLACKWOOD HOUSE
CHAPTER THREE

Fisher carried me out of the cellar.

At first, I was so overcome by the rush of sunlight and good air that it was hard to think of much. But even as Fisher reached the top of the stairs and stepped down into the yard, my wonderment was fading and I needed, more than anything, to look around.

I wanted to see the pastures behind the house, speckled blue with morning glories, and my special corner of the garden where I was allowed to dig, and the tupelo tree that shaded the porch, and if the little green birdhouse I'd painted to look like our own house was still hanging in its branches.

I tried again and again to open my eyes, and the harder I tried, the more decidedly I knew that Fisher had been telling me the truth.

"Well, that's a vexing thing," I said, and I'd meant it to sound brave, but all that came out was a whisper. "They really are sewed shut."

"I think once the thread's out, they'll be fine," he told me, but he was quiet a minute before he said it. The way he stopped to pick his words only made me sure that things were very bad. "You'll be fine. Just hang on. I'm taking you to someone who can figure out who you are and where you come from."

I wanted to tell him it wasn't that complicated, that I came from the cellar, from right where he'd found me. That this was my home.

"My aunt Myloria," was all I said. "That's what you mean. You're taking me to Myloria Blackwood."

He didn't answer, but hitched me higher in his arms and walked a little faster.

The only way I knew what direction we were headed was by the sun on my face—the patches of shade as we moved in and out of the sycamore trees that grew along the ditch. I could tell by the crunch of his boots that the driveway out to the main road was grown over with weeds.

His arms were warm and he held me tight enough that I could feel him breathing. My face was against his shoulder and he hadn't put his shirt back on. His skin was slick against my cheek, and even when my neck started to hurt, part of me was perfectly fine to keep smelling the warm, dusty smell of him.

But there was another part that wanted to get down. The way his arm moved when he walked was rubbing the side of my face. My legs ached now. My feet were tingling like they'd been crammed into church shoes for too long.

When we finally stopped, Fisher bent and laid me down on something metal. It was smooth as a piece of hard candy, warm from the sun. I felt around for the edges with my fingertips

17

and understood that I was lying across the hood of a car.

I could hear him nearby, crunching around in the weeds, jingling keys and opening doors. Then he scooped me back up and arranged me in the passenger seat.

As soon as he'd dropped down in the driver's seat, there was a low rumble, coughing and snarling, getting louder. The engine roared and we lurched forward, then the whole world seemed to fall away and there was only the wind, whipping by with fantastic speed, tearing at my hair. Almost too much air to breathe.

The drive took a long time, or else no time at all. The darkness of the canning closet had made me confused about things like time, like I couldn't feel it passing or count the minutes anymore.

When Fisher parked and hauled me out of the car, I tried to tell myself that I only liked the feel of him because it was so good to not be walled up in a canning closet, but it was other things, too. He smelled like green and sun and goodness, and there was plenty to like about the way his shoulder fit against the side of my face.

Then he was jostling me higher, pounding on someone's door.

We'd been waiting long enough for Fisher to start shifting his weight from foot to foot when a voice spoke from somewhere deep inside the house, sweet and strange and familiar. "Who is it?"

"Eric Fisher, ma'am. I've got something that you're going to want to see."

For a moment, there was nothing. Then the voice called back, "Come on in."

As soon as Fisher stepped inside, the light behind my eyes got darker. His boots echoed on the floorboards as he made his way through the house, and then someone else was with us.

Her footsteps were light, and she smelled like roses and mint and the warm, dusty smell of attics. "Oh, my word."

For a second, no one said anything else.

Then the woman let out a long breath and stepped closer. "Who is that?" she said. "What happened to her eyes?"

"Don't know, but I'm pretty sure she belongs to you. Me and the Maddox boys found her down in the DeVore house. Is there someplace I should set her?"

For one strange second, the woman seemed to disappear. No movement or breath, no sound at all.

Then she spoke from across the room, loud and shrill. "And you saw fit to bring her *here*?"

Fisher stepped farther into the room and laid me down on something hard, covered in a cloth so rough it felt like a potato sack. "I had to bring her somewhere. What did you want me to do, leave her? Anyway, the Maddox brothers are way too superstitious to go around making trouble. They probably think you'll witch them or something. They won't say anything."

From across the room, Myloria spoke in a whisper. "Eric Fisher, I do not want this creature in my house."

But her voice seemed to fall apart in the middle. She

19

sounded so afraid that it made me frightened too, and I squeezed my hand tight around the little cloth bag.

Fisher stood over me, resting his hand on the top of my head. "I don't think it's got much to do with what you want," he said, and the rough little tug when his fingers got caught in my hair was like the shiver when a cat licks your hand. I was just so grateful that someone in the world could stand to be near me. "I'm not concerned with what you all are doing out here—that's your business—but I'm pretty sure she's one of your people."

The way he said the last part was as final as *goodbye*. Suddenly, all I knew was that I didn't want him to go, and at the same time, I understood he was already walking out, and when he did, I'd be alone with a woman who could barely stand to be in the same room with me.

When he left, the house felt hollow, like the air after a thunderclap. We were alone—so alone that the whole kitchen seemed to echo.

Out in the yard, the car started up, roaring away in a storm of engine noise and gravel. Then, silence. In it, I was suddenly so afraid that I was still in the closet—that I had always been there and would never be anyplace else. I fumbled with my hands, reaching for the bricks, already half-convinced I felt the roots wrapped tight around my wrists. The stillness was so bottomless it made my chest hurt.

Then, Myloria moved closer. I could feel her standing over me, but couldn't see her edges through my eyelids the way I had with Fisher. When I tried, all I got was a broken clatter, fuzzing at me like a TV, but I couldn't tell if that meant something special about her or something special about him.

She made a low, unhappy sound—a breathing out. Then she bent over me and began to pick away the glass from around my eyes. Her hands were cool, and very careful, like she was worried I'd try to bite her. Next there was a cold pressure, followed by two hushed snips, soft as whispers. I tried to hold still, but her fingers were tickling my eyelids. They left a nagging itch, deep in my skin, and then I understood. She was pulling out the threads.

The first thing I saw when I opened my eyes was a burst of light so warm and red it could have been the sun or someone's beating heart. I stared up at it, waiting for the room to come clear.

Then I blinked and the light above me was just a water-spotted lampshade made of red paper and dried flowers. In the middle, one flickering bulb swung gently on a plastic cord.

I was lying in a dim little kitchen. The curtains were pulled and only a sliver of light showed between them. At the sink, my aunt Myloria stood with her back to me.

Her hair was so dark it was almost black, arranged in a messy knot on top of her head. She had on a checkered halter top that tied at the neck and a pair of men's undershorts with an ivy pattern. Her back was bare, so covered in tattoos that her whole skin seemed to be crawling with a tangle of blue-green snakes. Every inch of her was skinny, skinny, skinny.

21

I braced my hands on the table and sat up. "Myloria?"

She turned. Her collarbone showed and she had shoulders like a skeleton. Her face was beautiful, but in a sharp, unhealthy way, all jaw and cheekbones.

"How do you know my name?" she said, and now her voice was a long way from sweet. "What were you doing in my sister's house?"

"Don't you know who I am?" I whispered, gazing around at the peeling wallpaper and the chipped porcelain sink. The faucet was rusting, and underneath, there was a wet-looking rag tied around the bend in the pipe.

Myloria stared back at me—a blank, awful stare. I didn't know what to do or say. I was dressed in a raggedy nightgown, sitting on a kitchen table, and my elegant, glamorous aunt now just looked used-up and hungry.

"I'm *Clementine,*" I whispered. "I'm your niece."

She looked at me like I'd told her I was the president. "How *dare* you. How dare you come into my house and dishonor my sister. How dare you profane her memory."

Her voice shook. I understood that people only talked about dishonoring someone's memory when that person was dead.

The weight of it sat in my chest like a stone. I knew that it should hurt. And it did, but it wasn't a breathless, skinned-raw hurt. It dug and bit at me. It ached.

I'd spent so many days—years—in a fog of sadness for my mother, knowing with a slow, ugly certainty that she was gone, but I hadn't really known it in my heart until now.

Myloria stood with her arms around herself. In one hand, she still held a little pair of gold-colored sewing scissors.

"Don't you remember me?" I whispered, and it sounded pitiful.

But she didn't have to say a word. It was all there in her eyes. She didn't.

"Please, you *have* to. I used to go around with Shiny all the time. I used to sleep over in the summer and make waffles and lemonade in your kitchen!"

"You're a devil and a liar," she said in a thin, shaking voice. "But you can't work your tricks on me. My sister never had any children."

I didn't know how to argue. The fact that I was sitting there wasn't a thing that needed to be argued. I was looking across the kitchen at my own aunt, and still, she was acting like I didn't exist.

"Where's Shiny?" I said. "Is Shiny here?"

Myloria only backed away, toward the other side of the room where an ancient round-cornered refrigerator hummed softly and a dark, narrow doorway led out of the kitchen.

I swung myself off the table, keeping my hands out to steady myself.

"Shiny!" I yelled. "Shiny, are you here?"

Myloria stood in the corner by the refrigerator, still clutching the scissors. "Stop! Stop it right now! Don't you even talk to her!"

I was about to yell again when a voice answered from the dark little hall behind Myloria. "What in the hell is going on?"

23

A girl was standing in the doorway. She had high, savage cheekbones and a face like a movie star. She looked like Myloria—not Myloria now, but a memory I had. Her hair was dark and glossy, making wild spirals all the way down her back. Her eyes were like two hot black cinders. Everything about her seemed graceful and long-boned, all wrong against the crooked walls and the cracked plaster.

For a long time, she just studied me. Then she said, in the flattest, slowest voice, "My God."

Her voice was terrible, like someone at the edge of a high cliff staring down into the wondrous nothing.

"Shiny?" I said. But I sounded slow and full of doubt.

The girl in front of me couldn't be my cousin. My Shiny was eight years old. My Shiny was bossy and bratty, but sweet, too. She made dolls out of cornhusks and set them floating away down the creek in summer and tied grasshoppers and cicadas to strings for me so I could fly them like tiny buzzing kites. My Shiny was a little girl, and I'd missed all the minutes and the years between then and now.

She nodded, but there was an emptiness in her eyes that filled me with despair. I'd been saved from the dark, only to come home to a world that didn't even know me. I had no people, no family. Nothing.

Then, with a high, breathless scream, Shiny launched herself across the kitchen and threw her arms around my neck, heedless of the state of my nightgown, or the glass stuck to the front of it, or the way I was covered in soot.

Her hair smelled bright and sticky like hairspray, but she

24

smelled like candy, too, like the times we used to walk into town for saltwater taffy from Spangler's. Like the memory of a smell, or maybe even the actual thing, and nothing that had happened all morning mattered at all, because her arms were fierce and warm, and her cheek was pressed against mine.

With a shaky breath, she let me go, holding me at arm's length. "Oh my God, this is real. It's really *real*."

Over in the corner, Myloria only hugged herself tighter, shaking and shaking her head. "Bastiana," she said. "Go to your room."

Shiny took her hands off my shoulders and turned to face her. "What is *wrong* with you? This is your *family*."

Myloria stood against the wall, looking like someone had slapped her. "This is some kind of ugly business, baby. We're looking at the worst kind of craft, and you act like you can't even see it, like you don't know the trouble it will bring, people spreading all kinds of lies and gossip, so happy to talk their heads off over any crooked doings in this house."

Shiny tossed her hair out of her face, looking ferocious. "I'm not an idiot, Myloria, but we are not throwing her out. This is my cousin."

Myloria drew herself up, tall and frail. "You have no cousin."

Shiny gave her a scorching look that seemed to last a lifetime. "I have been telling you for ten years that Clementine was *real*—that she was a real person—and now that she's right in front of you, you still want to go around acting like I

25

made her *up*?" She turned her back on Myloria and reached for my hand. "Come on, let's get you fixed up. And ignore her. She'll be better in a minute."

"How do you know?"

Shiny sighed and looked away. "Because she mostly is. And if she isn't, sometimes I just have to pretend she will be."

Her hand was so warm it was almost hot, tugging me along. The little cloth bag was still sitting in the middle of the table and I reached for it, not trusting it, but not wanting to let it go, either.

SHINY
CHAPTER FOUR

Whereas the kitchen had been shabby, the hall was entirely ruined. It was papered in a striped pattern that might have been nice once, but was now burned black in huge smudges, peeling down in strips. The floor slanted under my bare feet and the paint had blistered up from the baseboards and started to flake off in ragged scales, like a snakeskin.

I followed Shiny through the house, wondering how anyone could live in a place like this. Doorways interrupted the burned walls now and then, but all of them were boarded up.

We turned a corner that led nowhere except to the end of another useless hall. There was a heap of cardboard boxes sitting piled in the corner, and Shiny dug through them. They were full of old clothes, and not old like the shirts at the back of my mama's closet. They were old like the antique store, or like something straight out of the movies.

Shiny pulled out a rumpled green dress and tossed it at me.

"Most of this stuff used to belong to Grandma Emmaline and hasn't been in style since about the dust bowl, but it should fit all right," she said. "But first, you are a pure mess. Before you do anything, you need to get washed."

The bathroom was at the far end of the house from the kitchen, little and dark, like everything else. There was no window, only a deep, old-fashioned bathtub and a pink toilet. No mirror and no sink. The tub had long-toed animal feet and took up nearly the whole room in a way that tended to suggest it hadn't always been there. That this had once been a powder room, but someone had dragged the tub in from someplace else and hooked it up where the sink used to be.

The blue-fairy nightgown was impossibly small, stuck to my body like another skin. Both the shoulder seams were out and the lacy hem that used to brush the floor only came down to my knees. Shiny wrestled with the zipper, yanking so hard the plastic teeth tore apart. Then she ducked out of the room and left me to deal with the state I was in.

I ran the faucet and washed. My arms were covered in ash up to the elbows, like I had on smudgy gray gloves. My hair was one big knot, but with no mirror or brush, it was hard to work out the tangles. I wrung it under the faucet until the cherries and the soot washed away and the water ran clear.

There was a towel hanging on the edge of the tub and I dried off, trying not to think too much about how I was a completely different person from the one I'd been. Every time I caught a glimpse of my body, it was like looking at a stranger.

I changed into the green dress, which buttoned down the front and had a bow at the neck like a sailor's. The top was tight, with barely room to move, and I knew that I was going to need what my mother had always referred to as *support garments*, if she had to refer to them at all.

When I left the bathroom, Shiny was waiting for me. She led me back to the kitchen, through the crooked door where I'd first seen her, and into a cramped, narrow room. It wasn't much more than a closet, with a rickety little bed pushed into one corner, and the rest of the place taken up by a giant water-stained dresser.

The walls were plank instead of plaster, and hung all over with wind chimes. They were nailed straight to the bare boards and tacked haphazardly to the ceiling. Among them, Shiny seemed like the only useful thing, and everything else was completely silly.

It was strange and dizzying to stand and look at her, when the last time we'd been face to face, she'd still had messy pigtails and a missing tooth. The way she looked at me, I knew she was feeling the same, like I was something that had been stored away, and now that I was unpacked and out in front of her, she could only stand back and count all the ways that I had changed.

"How is it you remember me, but Myloria can't?" I said.

Shiny leaned against the dresser, chewing on her thumbnail and scowling. "If I could tell you that, I'd feel a lot better, if you want to know the truth. She's right about it being craft, for sure. And there are tricks for keeping secrets or messing with someone's memory, but I've never known one strong enough to just paper over a whole person. That's something more serious than I know about."

"Then how can you be certain it's really me at all?" I said, wondering how to ever trust a world where my own aunt could forget me. "I mean, what makes you so sure?"

Shiny laughed, tossing her hair over her shoulders. "Sure that you're my cousin? I'd have to be crazy to forget. I missed you every day," she said. "I used to just sit out back in the tire swing and think of your face, like if I forgot a single thing, even an eyelash or a freckle, something bad would happen. I feel like I've been waiting for you my whole life."

The way she said it was so raw and fierce it showed in her face, and I felt a rush of gratitude to know that someone had been waiting for me after all.

She leaned closer. "You still look right, you know. Or at least, how I'd have thought you'd look. Except your hair—now *that* is really something."

"What do you mean?"

She turned me by the shoulders, steering me in front of a heavy mirror propped on top of the dresser. For the first time in forever, I looked at myself.

A part inside me wanted to cry or scream, or just do something to show how awful it was to be lost for so long and then come back looking nothing like myself.

At first, I couldn't do anything but stare—at my hands on the top of the dresser and the wide, unfamiliar shape of my mouth and my cheeks, and my eyes, the way they gazed back at me, full of hurt.

After a minute, though, I began to pick out things I could almost recognize.

I looked less like myself and more like my mother, with her high, smooth forehead and her chin. My nose had grown from a button into the long, straight one common to the Blackwoods, but my mouth was big and soft like a stranger's, like it belonged to someone else, and no matter how far I tried to open my eyes, they stayed heavy-lidded. Half-closed. The skin around them was dotted with little scars.

What Shiny had spoken was the absolute truth. I looked right, more or less, for someone belonging to the Blackwood family. And also, the strangest thing about me was my hair.

When I was little, it had been a plain dog-brown that promised to darken to mahogany, the same color that Shiny's was now. Instead, it had gone red. Not an unfortunate carroty red like the O'Radley girls had, or even beauty-parlor red. My hair was the deep, bloody red of cherries, black at the roots and getting brighter as it went, nearly glowing by the time it got to the ends.

"What happened to it?" I said, holding my hands away from myself, like I was marked with something dirty.

Shiny came and put an arm around me. "Hey, hey, don't act like that. It's not so bad. It just needs to be brushed out."

I didn't know how to say that it wasn't the color or the tangles making me seem wrong. It was my broken voice and my scarred eyes and my strange new body. And my cheeks and my chin and my grown-up nose. I stared at my reflection, trying to get friendly with the fact that I wasn't myself anymore.

"Okay," I said finally, after I'd looked and looked and it had changed nothing. "Okay, you can help me fix my hair."

Shiny got out a comb and had me sit on the edge of the bed. She settled down next to me, holding a matted handful straight out from my head and clucking to herself. Her nails were painted a deep, sticky purple.

"Well, this is a devilish state of affairs," she said as she went to work on the tangles. The comb bit at my scalp, yanking my head back, and at first I thought she was talking about my hair.

Then she leaned around me, peering into my face. "You want to tell me where you've been this whole time?"

"In my house," I said. "Buried in the cellar."

She stopped combing. "All this time? Since you were seven?"

I nodded.

"Well," she said after a second. "You're definitely not seven anymore."

"No," I said, looking down at the front of the dress. "Definitely not."

She laughed a breathless little laugh. "I mean, not in your head, either. You're like a real person."

It was true. I could feel the difference between now and then, a plant that had outgrown its pot, and now the roots were forcing their way between the cracks.

"I knew things," I said, trying to put a name to the dreams that weren't dreams but more of a cross between visions and memories. "Sometimes I lived on old pictures, like looking through a photo album, and sometimes, it was more like I flew out into the real world and floated there. I saw things. I was part of the world, but not *in* it, if that makes sense."

Shiny's face made it plain that it didn't, but she nodded anyway, frowning to herself. Then she went back to work on my hair.

I held as still as I could and looked around me. The bedroom was impossibly small and like a carpenter's mistake, growing straight off the side of the main house.

I winced, grabbing at the back of my neck to keep her from combing me bald. "I don't remember this place."

Shiny shook her head. "*She* had it built a few years ago. When I finally just about lost my mind and told her that maybe wandering around at all hours was good enough for her, but I needed a bedroom. So, she went out and paid a bunch of the O'Radleys' cousins two hundred and forty dollars to build me *this*."

The room was decorated with a little rug and had a window at the back, but I couldn't help thinking it wasn't a lot bigger than the closet I'd been buried in.

"It doesn't seem like much," I said.

Shiny let her hair fall over her face and looked away. "'Not Much' is kind of the name of every damn day around here. Things are—well, they're not how you remember."

But in truth, it seemed that what I mostly remembered were

only the recollections of a little girl, overjoyed by dragonflies and Fourth of July sparklers. Every other fact and feature was missing, covered up neatly by that clean white sheet.

"Where does Myloria sleep?" I said finally, because it seemed better to say anything than to let Shiny keep sitting there with her hair in her eyes and her shoulders slumped. Better than to keep dwelling on all the things I'd lost and could not get back.

"Are you kidding?" She started picking at my tangles again. "Myloria doesn't sleep. All she does is wander around like a crazy person, vague as hell and scared of everything."

I considered the Myloria I'd known when I was little, tall and proud, full of flash. "She didn't used to be."

Shiny shrugged and looked away. "And the dinosaurs didn't used to be dead. Do you know that your hair is like trying to put a comb through wire? It's breaking off the teeth."

She set the comb down, and then there was a strange tickling feeling at the back of my head. She was running the tips of her fingers over my hair, but the knots were so matted and thick I could barely feel it.

When she spoke, her voice was smaller than before, and kind of lost. "It used to be so soft, like a bunny."

I reached for the dropped comb, touching the gaps where the teeth had snapped off. "Shiny, how long have I been gone, exactly?"

She sighed and took her hand away. "You mean how long has it been since the Coalition for Purity flipped their shit and started burning out all the old families before My-loria or your mama or any of the church people could stop them?"

I nodded, running my finger along the broken comb.

"Pretty near ten years."

"Oh."

"I thought you were dead," she said, keeping her chin down, fiddling with the corner of the crazy quilt.

"I guess I should have been, right? A long time ago, I should have been."

Shiny nodded. The light shining between the boards of the room made thin golden lines on her face. "I thought you were dead, and at the same time, it was like you were this invisible friend I'd had. I believed so hard that you were real, while everyone else just forgot you were ever alive."

I reached into the pocket of my dress and held out the tattered trickbag that had been pinned inside the collar of my nightgown. "This might have something to do with that."

Shiny studied the bag, but made no move to touch it.

"Rae Dalton knows a thing or two about trickbags," she said finally. "And she knows a thing or two about you. She'd be one to ask."

I remembered Rae—her small, easy smile and her hair twisted into five fat braids, the ends fastened with plastic ponytailers shaped like gum balls. She was one of the clean, well-tended in-town kids, but her parents would visit with my mama over the sorts of things that other folks would only frown and whisper about, and they brought her out to play sometimes. I had liked her. Maybe not in the fierce, frantic way I'd liked Shiny, but Rae had been my friend.

"If this kind of craft is too big for anyone to explain," I said, "if it's too powerful or bad, does it mean that I was put away by fiends?"

All my life, I'd heard stories of the fiends that had settled Hoax County, but even in my family, where most folks were born with the power to do things, the fiends themselves were half a fairy tale. Now, sitting on the bed, holding Shiny's broken comb, I was suddenly sure that if I could be shut up and forgotten so completely, it must be the work of something too huge and powerful to be accounted for by anything else.

Shiny looked absolutely scandalized, though. "What? No, are you crazy? Why would you say a thing like that?"

"When they took me out of the wall, one of the Maddox boys—Luke, I think—he said that bringing me to you and Myloria was messing around with crooked people. 'Hexers and fiends,' he said."

"Luke Maddox is an idiot. The Blackwoods may be crooked as they come, but he wouldn't know a fiend if it punched him in the dick."

I laughed at that, a hard, rasping laugh, like a crow shouting over a button, and Shiny laughed too, tossing her hair back over her shoulders.

I watched her, thinking how strange and glorious it was that I could be sitting on this wobbly little bed with my cousin, when just that morning, I'd been so sure that I was going to spend the rest of my life in the dark and never be anyplace else ever again.

Shiny must have been thinking it too, because she reached over and gave my hair a tug.

"Not to be indelicate," she said, with a long, knowing look that was mostly about my chest. "But we should probably go down to Spangler's. You've got a whole little situation going on right around here."

I crossed my arms and leaned away from her. "I know."

"So we'll go into town, get you a bra. I'm supposed to meet Rae, anyway. We'll get it sorted out about your piece of craft."

＊　＊　＊

Out in the front hall, Shiny stopped to dig around in a Florida Orange crate by the door. She yanked on a pair of beat-up cowboy boots over bare feet and was scrounging me up some sneakers when Myloria came shuffling in.

The way she looked at us was like she was seeing something else—not Shiny and Clementine, but Shiny and the ghost of something monstrous. Her eyes were pink, like maybe she'd been crying.

"Where are you going?" she said, sounding stuffed up in the head, and also like she was scared we might tell her.

I started to explain about Rae Dalton and the trickbag, but Shiny stuck her elbow in my side and said, "Nowhere. Just showing Clementine the town."

I wondered whether Myloria might argue over that, or say it was off-limits, but she didn't. The way she studied my face was grave, like she was really seeing me for the first time. "You say you know me."

"Yes," I said.

"And Bastiana, she remembers you from way back."

"Yes."

The way Myloria spoke was careful and slow. I could see her wanting something from me—needing something—but I didn't know how to give it to her. Her eyes were red and wet, and I crossed the hall and reached for her hand. There was a split second where I was certain she'd pull away. Then she let me take it.

Her hand felt fragile and cold in mine and she leaned closer, like she was whispering a terrible secret. "You look so much like my sister."

I nodded, because her voice was sad, and it was true. When I'd stood at the mirror in Shiny's room, it had nearly been my mama's face looking back at me.

"But you're not her," Myloria said, leaning so close that the messy wisps of her hair almost brushed my cheek. "What are you?"

"I'm her daughter," I said, so afraid that she would shy back from me again, call me a liar like she had in the kitchen.

Her eyes were so sad I could barely stand it and she held my hand like she was clinging to a past I could never quite know. Sisters and mothers were different people. I thought that I had never seen someone look so undone.

"You be careful where you go and who you talk to," she said finally. "And stay well away from the boys hanging around Carter's Garage. Town is town, and they'll leave you be for the most part, but those ones are not good boys. And don't go around mentioning yourself to anyone if you can help it."

Shiny was standing by the door, picking off her nail polish. "And just how are we going to explain where she came from, if we can't mention her?"

Myloria hugged her elbows. She didn't look much braver than before, but she put her shoulders back, like she was pulling herself together. "This whole business is a bad one, but I'm not so sure that whatever trickery is at work here doesn't work a little in our favor. If the craft is as strong as I think it is, and Eric Fisher and his Maddox boys don't go shooting their mouths off about digging her out of what's left of the DeVore house, I don't imagine we'll have to explain at all."

It took a second to realize what she was saying—that I'd been put under a spell so strong that no one in the world would remember me. And for all the questions I might be able to avoid, it wasn't reassuring. The other part was even less so, as it seemed to depend a lot on Fisher being right and the Maddox boys being too scared to say a word against me.

Even Myloria looked doubtful, like maybe she was considering that, but none of us went so far as to remark on it.

"You look nice," she said finally, as though it were an afterthought, or like someone remembering their line for a play a beat too late.

I knew I was supposed to tell her thank you, but the

words felt wrong. She was still watching me like she expected me to go wild and tear up everything, and anyway, I didn't even really know what it meant for me to look nice anymore. When I was little, nice was a pink dress and a pair of shiny shoes. Now I was just some strange, grown-up girl, with matted hair and someone else's clothes.

"You be good in town," she said, and then glanced at Shiny. "Because I know this one won't."

Her voice was almost too thin to hear. I wanted more than anything to make her back into the aunt that I remembered, make her not be scared anymore. Not just of me, but of everything.

TRICKS
CHAPTER FIVE

The front of the Blackwood house was nearly as bad as the inside. The porch sagged where the boards had begun to rot, and everything felt squishy. There was a jar of sun tea at the top of the steps, the Lipton bags floating like giant soggy beetles.

Shiny clomped past it and down into the yard, kicking at some of the milkweeds that were taking over the flowerbed. I started to follow, then turned back to look at the house.

Most of the top floor was gone, and where it wasn't, the boards were burned nearly to charcoal. The only spot that hadn't been touched was the kitchen corner of the ground floor. There, the windows still had their glass and the paint was a watery yellow instead of just charred.

"It's ruined," I said, and my voice was dry and ragged. "Oh, Shiny . . . it's awful."

She twitched her shoulder and looked away. "Fire will do that. This place went toe-to-toe with the reckoning and didn't even creak, but a few cans of gasoline, and there it went."

I waited for her to tell me the story of the fires that had

taken our homes, or at least say what a "reckoning" was, but she turned and started across the yard and the only thing was to go after her. For a second, though, I just kept staring at the house.

The flowerbeds were choked with weeds, and a dirt lawn wrapped around the front, ending a good hundred feet before the road. The porch roof was strung all the way along the eave with wind chimes and tin cans clanking against each other.

Standing there at the bottom of the steps, I had a funny kind of double vision, like I could see the shape of the house as it had once stood, big and yellow, three stories against a tick-gray sky, with hollyhocks and sugar-pink peonies growing in the yard. I remembered playing in the shade of the porch, lying in the peony beds, looking at the way little clusters of ants swarmed up the stems, and for a second, it was like coming back to the Blackwood house of my memory, as though I'd never left it.

Then the picture went fuzzy and I looked away. It didn't matter what the house had been when it was whole. It wasn't that anymore.

I followed Shiny out to the end of the driveway, where the turn-off was marked by a faded board nailed to a post. All it said was BLACKWOOD and then under that, WEEPING ROAD.

Ordinary folks might be disinclined to call a place *Weeping*, but this was the lowlands, and Myloria's house was set even closer to the creek than mine had been. In another county, they might call the whole place just that—the lowlands—or else the bottoms. Around here, though, everyone called it the Willows, after the thickets that grew along the creek, and with that in mind, *Weeping* didn't seem quite so strange or so unlucky.

Out on the road, the air was damp and hazy. Shiny walked with a purpose, like going into town was nothing, when I'd never even been allowed to walk down past the gate by myself. I followed her, trying to work out if the pale shimmer that hung over the fields was really the air or just my eyes. The day was sticky, and cicadas screamed in the trees.

We'd only gone a little ways up the road when we came to a house. I knew it, but like everything else, it was changed.

People down in the Willows tended toward the wild, the headstrong, and sometimes toward the trashy, and Greg Heintz was all three. More than once, my mama and Myloria had stood comfortably in our kitchen, mixing medicines or peeling peaches and talking about Greg and the devilment he went in for—his nasty way of chopping down trees and trapping rabbits and squirrels and all living things.

The Heintzes' gate was right up by the ditch, but the house itself was set far back from the road. It was small and narrow, with a covered porch, but even as ramshackle as it was, there were no missing walls or broken windows or burned places. It was hemmed in by trees, not nice ones like Myloria's beeches, but mostly loblollies and red cedars.

Greg lived there with his half a dozen mangy dogs and his daughter, Davenport, who was a shade younger than

Shiny and a shade older than me. She'd been the kind of girl who always looked blurry and a little bit tangled, and even though she lived directly between my house and Shiny's, she hadn't been allowed to play with us. That wasn't such a remarkable thing, though. To the best of my recollection, Davenport hadn't really been allowed to play with anyone.

Now the house looked smaller and shabbier than ever, and under the big cedars near the gate was one of the oddest sights I'd seen in my life. Instead of weeds or grass, the whole yard was just a big dirt patch, filled with a collection of coops and pens and cages.

There were so many that at first I thought it must be some kind of farm. After all, sometimes farmers did keep rabbits and birds, and there were a fair few in the cages. But there were other things too, and they were not the kind of creatures you ever raised for eggs or meat.

The whole place was built from scrounged boards, all painted a peeling, bubbly green that flaked off and ran to black in places. I stopped in the road, tasting metal in my throat. I knew the color and the burned, blistered paint.

The Heintz zoo was made from pieces of my ruined house.

I climbed down through the ditch and came all the way up to the chain-link fence. On the other side, the animals crouched in their cages, staring back at me. There were doves and quail and a scraggly possum, some baby raccoons and a white peacock, but those were nothing—they were almost normal—compared to the weasels and the foxes. There was a speckled bobcat in a wire run, and a coyote, and there in the back corner of the yard, a bony-ribbed creature too big to be anything but an actual cougar. It crouched in the dirt, glaring out from under a tin-roofed lean-to like it wanted to tear me down.

Up close to the fence was a badger in an ugly little hutch that had been hammered together with pieces of my own front door. I'd never seen a badger anywhere but in books, and its face was broader and shrewder than I'd pictured. It peered out at me with small, bright eyes. Not pitiful, but patient, like it was just waiting for the right moment to break out and get going.

I stared over the mismatched roofs of the zoo and toward the house. With a start, I realized that a girl was watching us from the porch, slumped on the bench swing with her pale hair in her face. She raised her head and even from the ditch, I could tell that it was Davenport, as see-through and wispy as ever.

Behind me, Shiny made an ugly noise. "The weird-as-shit apple does not fall far from the crazy-tree."

"It's not her fault," I said, because the way Davenport sat huddled on the swing was as sad as any of the animals in their cages, and I could think of nothing worse than having to live in the middle of it.

Shiny just shrugged and turned away. "Her dad is plain out of his mind. Shit like this should be illegal."

"*Isn't* it? Illegal?"

"I don't know. I guess maybe, but it doesn't matter.

It's not like anyone ever comes out here and does anything about it."

"Why not?"

"Well, it's his business, wanting to own every kind of creature around. And anyway, to do something, they'd have to go up on his property, and no one's going to risk that. He *will* shoot you."

I knew that was probably true—folks in the Willows could be very particular about their land—but still, it seemed to me that some things were ugly enough that fixing them was worth trespassing. I didn't tell Shiny that if I had my way, something was going to be done about it.

We turned our backs on the house and started walking. The county road that led into town was number 5, but everyone called it the Crooked Mile, though it was more wiggly than crooked and quite a bit more than a mile. We walked along the gravel shoulder, because even though it was faster to take a straight line through the woods, I'd had it hammered into me from birth not to step in other people's pastures.

The way into town was marked by bridges. The Blue Jack Creek wound down through the hills and hollows, snaking back and forth across the lowlands and the road, all the way down to the county line. The land around the creek was mostly pasture, marked by nothing and nothing, with one rickety water tower rising in the distance.

As we got closer to town, the road got paved and the woods got thin. We crossed the last bridge, past a faded tin sign that said WELCOME TO NEW SOUTH BEND: HOME OF GOOD PEOPLE AND GOOD WATER.

Town itself was ten blocks long, low and slow and sleepy. You could walk from one end to the other in less than a heartbeat. As we went, I tried to see the place as it had been, but it was older and deader than the town in my mind. Everything was smaller than I remembered.

I read off the names of the streets we passed, Chester and Peyton and Main—names like old songs or people I'd known once. At the corner of Broom Street, a pair of ribby dogs loped slowly down the sidewalk. Their shadows made long slashes on the pavement.

A truck went rattling by with a stack of metal poles laid out in the back, and on top of that, a big roll of canvas, striped like a circus tent.

Shiny saw me looking after it and said, "That's the public works crew. They'll be setting up revival tents and all the bake sale tables and the booths for Green Week." Then she stopped and squinted at me. "Do you remember Green Week?"

I started to nod, but it wasn't really true. Mostly, I remembered a bobbing rainbow of balloons and the warm, sugary smell of cotton candy. No revival or anything green.

She shrugged. "It's mostly just like a fair, you know? A carnival. There's a big camp meeting on Friday night, but no one goes to that, and some games and rides and a funnel cake stand."

We crossed the road and turned down Main Street. So

many of the stores were empty now, with boarded-up doors or missing windows—a hardware store and a bar and the Tracy Ann Boutique, where Mrs. Ralston had sold perfume and magazines and smoked long, skinny cigarettes that turned her fingers yellow. Now it was nothing but empty shelves.

Farther down, though, things were more lively. Men in dusty shirts were unloading boxes and sawhorses from flat-bed trucks.

Behind them was another long stretch of deserted buildings, but someone had been hanging up a set of huge painted canvases on the fronts of these ones, at least. All along the block, the canvases hung down almost to the sidewalk.

Most of the paintings were everyday scenes—bright, pretty gardens and flowery orchards—but the one hanging over the old train depot was disturbing. In it, a dark, proud woman with long hair and a hard face was in the middle of cutting a man down from a bony winter tree. He had a rope looped around his neck and the woman stood on a little step-ladder, sawing at the knot with a buck knife. She wore a dark green dress, and at her feet, a whole mess of vines were climbing up the bottom of the ladder, twining around her legs.

I was inclined to stop and look, but Shiny hurried past like she had someplace to be, so I turned and followed her.

In front of Carter's Garage, a bunch of boys were sitting out on the metal bike rack, looking bored and sunburned. They were a few years older than us, hard to tell if they were boys or men, and I didn't like to get too near, but Shiny strode past like they weren't even there, although one of them whistled loud enough to make me jump.

"Hey, crafty girl," he called, with his hand on the front of his jeans. "I've got a piece of craft for you and it's a doozy!"

Shiny whipped around so fast her boots left scuff marks on the sidewalk. "You couldn't find your piece with a jack-light and three hands."

She was smiling, but there was an edge in her voice that made me think the smile was mostly for show. Her hand had moved to the pocket of her cutoffs.

I stood beside her, wishing we'd leave, but she didn't move as he pushed himself away from the wall and came rambling over. He had a loping, uneven gait, like he'd just gotten off a horse.

"Shiny Blackwood," he said, and I did not like his grin, not one bit. "You've got a nice little walk on you. I've only got two hands, though—maybe you can lend me one of yours."

Shiny sighed and pulled out a silver cigarette lighter. "You do not want to test me, Michael Faraday, so step away while you still have your eyebrows."

And for a second, it seemed like he *would* step back, but the other boys had followed him and were elbowing each other. I knew that whatever happened next would be less about what he felt like doing and more about saving face.

He smiled, moving toward her with his hands held out. "Aw, Shiny, don't be like that."

"I will be however I *want* to be," she said, hammering down on each word.

He was nearly on top of her now, but Shiny wasn't giving him an inch. Then, without warning, his hand snaked around to land square on her bottom.

She sucked in her breath.

The moment seemed long. It seemed so long it was impossible. Something white-hot was happening in the air around her. Her smile was a fixed, blazing thing that burned through her eyes and shone in her skin like starlight. I wondered how he could possibly stand to be so close to it.

Then she flicked the lighter.

It was hard to say where it started. It was like the air between them went up in flames, burning in an orange sunburst, and he yelled and stumbled back. The wall of fire climbed toward the sky and then went out, leaving a trail of smoke that floated over them in a wash of dry, scorching air.

"I hate this place," Shiny said, turning on me with an expression so ruinous and black that I leaned away from her. "Some days, I would not be sorry if it burned right to the goddamn ground. Some days, I'd happily to do it myself."

Behind her, I watched Mike Faraday and the others take off rambling down toward the end of the block, trying hard to look like they were only going because they felt like it.

I knew all kinds of stories about people from the old families who had a special way with fire. I had just never known a person to actually be able to do it in real life. Certainly no one in my own family.

"Shiny," I said, and even to myself, I sounded awed and out of breath. "That was amazing."

She just shook her head and stared down the sidewalk like it might still be worth her while to go stalking after the boys and really light them up. The air around her smelled like matches, and I was glad when she finally turned her back on them and headed for the park.

Union Park was square and grassy, taking up nearly the whole block. Over by the picnic shelter, a bunch of women in capri slacks and sleeveless blouses were gathered, hanging green and white crepe paper and laying out covered dishes. The sight was familiar, and although Shiny and I had never been invited to attend church picnics even when we were little, it heartened me to see that at least some things hadn't changed.

Shiny cut across the lawn to the war memorial, where a skinny black girl in a yellow sundress sat on the little wall in front of it, holding a big wicker bag with a wooden handle. Her hair, which had been rolled into fat twists the last time I'd seen her, was cut so short now that it stood out an inch from her head. She was fiddling with it, twisting a piece between her fingers.

As soon as we got close, she slid down from the wall. "Punctuality is not an empty virtue, Shiny Blackwood."

She was a little shorter than me, which made her a good deal shorter than Shiny, with tiny wrists and narrow shoulders. The wicker bag looked nearly as big as she was.

Shiny waved her off. "Punctuality is for people with reliable transportation. You remember my cousin, Clementine?"

The question sounded so casual that suddenly, it wasn't casual at all, and Rae came closer, taking tiny, careful steps.

51

"Well, sure," she said after a moment. Her voice was unexpectedly low, like the sound of a bell. "Of course I do. You don't just forget a person. Although, to be fair," she said, turning to me, "I can't say that I'd have known you on the street. But that's mostly the hair. And also that I've not seen you in a very long time. Would you like to say where you've been?"

Her way of talking was slow and precise, almost like a grown-up. Or at least, someone playing a game about grown-ups. She was standing with her bag hooked over her arm and her head cocked, like a cat will watch a pot simmer on the stove.

"I was hidden down in the cellar," I said, wondering if it would ever get easier to say the circumstances aloud. If it was possible to ever stop feeling like I was waking up into some kind of new and bewildering dream, going from nothing to everything all at once. "For a long time. Kind of like in a story."

Rae frowned, then reached out and touched my arm like she was feeling for an edge or a seam. "Well, that *is* a situation."

Beside me, Shiny was looking grim. "And it's worse. Even now that she's out, Myloria still doesn't remember her."

Rae's eyebrows went up. "She doesn't recognize her at all, not even as family? Well, I supposed it could be that hair."

Shiny shook her head. "What I'm saying is, Myloria thinks Clementine never existed, and that's got to be some pretty serious craft, to keep working even once it's broken. Show her, Clementine."

I pulled out the trickbag and offered it to Rae. The little knot of cloth seemed very shabby suddenly, not nearly remarkable enough to account for the hugeness of what had befallen me.

Rae only leaned closer and then took it, looking shrewd. "Now, *that* is something. Let's find someplace we can lay this out."

She led us over to the playground, where a red plastic play-tunnel, with a curve in the middle and round openings all along the side for windows, stretched between the jungle gym and the slide. She tromped up the ladder with her bag slung over her arm.

"Well, come on," she said when she'd reached the top and Shiny and I were still on the ground. "I'm not doing this out where just anyone can see."

Shiny and I followed her up into the play-tunnel, scrunching our knees to fit. Rae was already sitting cross-legged, picking at the knotted string, then dumping the bag onto the sandy floor.

At first, it was hard to say what we were looking at. The insides of the bag were just the kind of odds and ends that always seemed to wash up in the back of a junk drawer or get lost under sofa cushions.

Rae hunched over the little heap of knickknacks. "Now there's a funny thing," she said, but she said it strange and slow, like she was talking to herself.

She was studying a plastic baby doll head. Just a bitty one, about the size of a shooter marble, but I could tell its eyes were meant to open and close when you laid it on its back. They didn't, though, because they were glued shut.

"Ick," said Shiny. "More like *creepy*."

"That's from the Tiny Tot doll," I said, touching the plastic head, covered all over with coarse, slippery hair. "I had one from Spangler's."

Rae was sorting through the junk, moving each piece around like she was working a jigsaw puzzle. There was a cut-up playing card—just the middle part of a suicide king, knife jammed into the side of his own head. Stuck to it with yellowy Scotch tape was a scrap of paper that said *Danger Begets Caution*, with a bunch of tiny stars and crosses drawn around it.

The whole assortment made very little sense, but Rae seemed to be arranging everything into some kind of order, so I could only surmise that it meant something to her. She sat with her mouth pursed and her knees up, squinting at the pile.

The thing she seemed to find most disagreeable was nothing but a little white bone, dry and old, picked clean, but when I reached for it, Shiny swatted at me like it was dirty.

"What?" I said, snatching my hand back.

Rae shuddered. "That's a black-cat bone. They throw it in a pot and boil it with sticks and things, until all the meat and skin is off. It's twice nasty, but some of the old-school hexers swear by it."

The idea was more horrible than I could contemplate, and I was in full sympathy for them not wanting to touch it. I didn't want to touch it either.

The last thing in the bag was a curl of hair, tied in the middle with a little piece of thread.

I reached for it. "That's mine."

Shiny scowled, rubbing the curl between her fingers. "This was *never* your hair."

I grabbed it from her, letting the ends brush against my hand. "It is so. It feels just like it, and it's even the same color as it used to be."

Shiny leaned against the wall of the tunnel, shaking her head. "That's not how your hair was when you were little, though. It was dark, sure. But it was all fine and soft."

The way she said it was so unbearably sad I could only fidget with the coarse little curl and touch her cowboy boot with the toe of my sneaker.

"Okay," Rae said finally, watching me dust the back of my hand with the lock of hair. "So here's the thing. It's clear enough this wasn't originally made for you—the king of hearts is all wrong for a girl, and that's not your hair. But someone gave it to you anyway, and that is *crazy*, giving away a trick this valuable. I mean, you can't even pay money for something like this. And that's not even the weirdest part."

"What, then?" I said. Everything about everything seemed pretty weird.

Rae held up the scissored-up playing card. "Well, this is for protection from any kind of harm. But this—" she pointed to the cat bone, but didn't touch it. "This is to contain a harmful thing. It's like they couldn't decide if it was a spell

55

to protect or a spell to bind, but whatever the intention was, they both mean the same thing. Someone really wanted you locked up."

We were sitting quiet in the tunnel, contemplating the contents of the trickbag, when suddenly from down below, there was a shrill, bright cry. "Yoo-hoo! Girls!"

Rae peered out one of the little windows and then ducked down fast. "Oh, good God, here comes trouble."

"Shit," Shiny whispered, grabbing the pile of junk and stuffing it back in the little flannel bag.

"What? What are we doing?"

Shiny shoved the bag into my hand. "Wanda Tuttle. Don't look or she'll come over here."

But it was too late. A tall, fluttery lady was already coming across the playground to us with her frilly blouse frilling and her high, honey-brown hairdo wobbling all over the place.

"Shiny Blackwood," she called in a voice so dripping sweet it hurt my ears. "What are you all doing up there in that playhouse? Not getting into trouble, I hope!"

Shiny rolled onto her hands and knees and poked her head out of the tunnel. "No, ma'am. Just enjoying some shade."

"Even so, why don't you be a dear and come on down. I'd just hate to hear that anyone had been getting into any sort of mischief, or God forbid *drugs,* around where the babies play. And is that Rae Dalton up there? Rae, honey, I'm not going to have to tell your mother you've been hanging around with *folks,* am I?"

Rae peeked out of the tunnel and shook her head, hugging her wicker bag.

We sat very still in case Mrs. Tuttle might go away, but she stood at the bottom of the jungle gym, heels sinking into the sand, waiting.

Finally, Shiny and I clomped down the ladder, Shiny slipping in her boots and me trying not to let my dress get away from me, while Rae crawled out the other end of the tunnel and slid neatly down the slide.

As soon as all three of us were standing in front of her, Mrs. Tuttle turned to me and stuck her hands out like she was planning on grabbing me by the face. "And who's your little friend?"

Shiny stared back without changing expression. "This is my cousin. Clementine. DeVore." She said my name like it was a strange, heavy thing, almost an accusation.

Mrs. Tuttle studied me and let her hands drop. "Well, I have to say, I wasn't aware that Magda DeVore had children. We're all still just so sad about the accident, of course. Those old houses are a tragedy waiting to happen, with all that bad wiring."

Rae made a noise under her breath that sounded like *hunh*.

Shiny was more direct. She looked Mrs. Tuttle in the eye. "That and a can of gasoline."

"Well," Mrs. Tuttle said, looking away. "I wouldn't know about that. It's been real good to meet you, Clementine. I hope you enjoy your stay and y'all stay out of trouble."

Then Wanda turned and prissed herself back into the

57

picnic shelter with her tidy friends and their tidy casseroles, heels sinking precariously into the sand.

For a minute, none of us said anything. Far away, a train whistle sounded, long and steady, getting fainter.

Shiny stood in the shadow of the jungle gym, so still it looked like she was shaking. Her whole skin seemed to be buzzing, ready to fry anything that brushed up against her.

Then she took a deep breath, letting it out between her teeth.

"What was *that*?" I said, reaching to touch her arm, then snatching my hand back. The air around her felt hot as the air over an open flame.

Rae gave me a kind look. "That's Wanda Tuttle."

"She's the *mayor*," Shiny said in a hard voice. "Back before the . . . *before*, when Aunt Magda was still on the town council, Wanda was just Councilwoman Tuttle, but after the fires, she ran for mayor on this bullshit campaign of unifying the town after our *tragic accident* out in the Willows, like she doesn't hate us crooked folks just as much as the rest of them do."

Rae stood balanced on the edge of the slide with the wicker bag against her chest, biting on her bottom lip like she was sorting through all the things she had on her mind.

Then she stepped down and said, "Look, don't mind Wanda. I'm not sure she means well, but I don't think she means to be hateful, either. She might not like craft, but she's got no love for vigilantes like the coalition, and that's something."

"Not enough," said Shiny. "Not even close."

Rae considered that. Then she gave a curt little nod. "It's been better, and it's been worse, but no matter who's in charge, this whole town is just one long-ass war between folks who can work craft and ones who can't."

Shiny crossed her arms and stared off toward the picnic shelter. "It's not a war, it's an occupation."

I wanted to reach out and take her hand, like I would have back when we were little, but that was such a long time ago, and next to me, she felt dangerous to touch.

PART II
HEAT

THE FISHER BOY
CHAPTER SIX

I watched my feet as we left the park, not knowing how to feel right in my own skin. My town was not a place I'd ever been inclined to feel wrong in. Now I couldn't tell if things had been so much different before or if I'd just been too young to know better.

Rae wandered along next to me, twisting a piece of her hair like she was deep in thought. "So," she said finally. "Do you have any idea what you could have done to make someone want you gone?"

The question gave me a sinking feeling and I shook my head. "I mean, I was just little. I couldn't have done anything bad enough to warrant the kind of craft it would take for Myloria to forget me. Rae, you should have seen it—it was like I'd been erased right out of her head."

"I've got to admit, I kind of thought that when Shiny said Myloria didn't remember, she might have just meant Myloria was being Myloria."

Ahead of us, Shiny stomped along at a reckless pace, her boots clopping on the pavement. I still had a yen to stop and look at all the paintings, but she strode past like she'd seen them a million times before, and it occurred to me that she probably had.

We passed under one of a girl dancing in a dove-colored dress with a raggedy frill of lace around the collar. Her arms were held over her head like a ballerina, her hair flying out in a pale halo around her head. Her hands were long and fierce looking, almost like claws.

At one end, a pair of girls stood side by side. Their faces and haircuts were different, but they looked alike, dressed as maids and holding a giant silver plate. In the middle of the plate, a man's head sat in a puddle of blood. His eyes were turned up toward the top of the canvas, horrible and sad.

Rae had been watching me closely, and now she caught me by the elbow and pointed. "Your grandma Emmaline did those. The ones of quilting parties or orchards and that herd of spotted ponies down at the end are all from the Ladies' Auxiliary, but if it's weird and dark, that's how you know it's a Blackwood painting. That one's supposed to be Salome, like from the Bible."

"If she's from Bible times, why's she wearing a housedress?"

"Well, the stories are from Bible times, but the way she painted them, they're also pictures of the humors—all the different crafts a person might get up to depending on their blood. I guess Emmaline wanted them to look like they were from around here, like someone you could just walk up to on the street and say hey to."

I raised my eyebrows, trying to imagine a situation where

you'd want to say hello to the beautiful, clawed creature dancing over the head of John the Baptist.

Rae smiled and let go of my arm. "Hoax County has a regular love/hate relationship with the humors. This place used to be thick with hollow craft and old families. These days, folks aren't too pleased about any of it, but since Wanda's been mayor, the town council hangs the banners every year anyway, just to show how they're so damn *tolerant*."

I considered how Wanda had treated Rae in the park, like she was an entirely different creature from Shiny. "They seem to tolerate *you* pretty well, anyway."

"Well, there are a lot of different kinds of craft. Your grandma was all about dirt, just like Myloria and your mama, and half the Blackwoods as far back as anyone remembers. Dirt is real. It's the living, breathing body of the world, and sometimes real things can scare people."

"Isn't everything real?"

Rae frowned a little and touched her bottom lip. "Oh, no. There's all kinds of things that aren't. Or at least, they don't start out that way. Is having an idea the same as having a trumpet vine?"

"No, but you could have an idea of a trumpet vine and plant a seed, and then it would grow into one."

"See, that's the difference. With dirt, the craft is real to start—the seed and then the vine. The sort of thing I favor starts out pretend. That doesn't mean it isn't power. Just that my way is fiddly. It takes longer. And when you do quiet, fiddly things that take longer, people aren't so scared of you."

I nodded, but the explanation only made the barest sort of sense. For my mama and Myloria, there had only ever been dirt—reading people's leaves, mixing pinches of yellow pollen in their hands and sending them away with little bottles of snakeroot in oil, while I drew pictures of birds I'd seen and lay under the table with the dog.

I asked Mama once if she was like a doctor, but she said no. She said a doctor was someone who learned their trade from books. The things she knew couldn't be written down, only told to you by the ground itself.

I wondered if what Rae was talking about was the same— if she pulled her knowledge directly out of the air around her.

As we walked, I began to pick out the other Blackwood banners hanging along the street. The colors made them easy to spot, all dark and wild—blues and blacks and purples, and there on the front of the empty grocery, a woman so taken up by white light that you couldn't see her face. Her whole being was eclipsed by a glow that seemed to be bursting out of her skin in one bright, fast lightning bolt.

Rae looked across the street to where I was looking. "Fool's light," she said. "That one's a strange one. It's the humor that makes all the others kind of just . . . go faster."

Then she pointed up ahead to the biggest banner, hanging down over the whole front of the empty bank building and showing nothing but a giant star on a black background, painted so fast and so sloppy it looked like it was exploding off the canvas in a spray of colors like a firework.

"See there?" she said. "That star's for the humors. Those

veins of blue at the bottom are the creek. The red splashes are for fire and then dirt is the green, and yellow above that on the other side for air. And all the white there at the top is fool's light. That star used to be the town symbol for pretty much everything good and right around here."

"And what about now?" I said. The star looked crazy and jagged and powerful, but nothing about it made me feel very good.

Ahead of us, Shiny snorted. "Now it's nothing but a fancy seal for them to print on the letterhead at the courthouse."

We were coming up on a long brick storefront with a big hand-painted sign, and I was glad to see that Spangler's Sundries and Dry Goods was still open, at least.

Inside, the air conditioning was making a lot of noise to very little effect. The whole place was hot and grimy, full of matched separates in wild prints. I gazed around, remembering afternoons I'd spent crawling on the floor under the racks of blouses and skirts, watching feet go by and counting the pairs of ladies' shoes.

Behind the little counter, Bonnie O'Radley leaned beside the register. Her hair was as red as it had ever been, and her face was freckled and bored as she flipped through a rumpled magazine.

I bounced across the store to her before I could help it. "Bonnie!"

She just stared back like she didn't know me from Adam.

I stood with the counter between us, trying not to look crestfallen. "It's Clementine."

Her eyes stayed empty, though, and I felt my shoulders sag. It was one thing to be a stranger to grown-ups like Myloria and Wanda Tuttle. The nature of being a kid was that you were half-invisible anyway. But to be a stranger to Bonnie, whose mama had watched me almost every Wednesday and who had played tea party with me under the kitchen stairs, that was something different.

Rae came over and set a hand on my arm. "Clementine's visiting. Up from Louisiana for the summer."

Telling lies seemed wrong, but right away, Rae's story smoothed the line between Bonnie's eyes and she nodded politely. "Well, I hope you enjoy your stay."

I nodded back as Rae settled her elbows on the counter and the two of them began to discuss the best colors of nail polish in a mild, breezy way. After a minute, I turned and followed Shiny through the store.

We made our way to the ladies' section, where Shiny pulled a tangle of brassieres from a plastic bin and then sent me into the little dressing room to try them.

I got into the first one all right, but couldn't figure out how to get it fastened. Everything about it was the worst thing ever. Finally, I just did the hooks and then wiggled it up where it belonged, slipping my arms through the straps.

The wall mirror had a chunk of glass missing in the corner and I stared at it, because the other choice was to stare at myself. Everything was wrong.

When I was little, I'd see ladies on TV and think how

I'd be grown one day and look like that. I'd just never really believed it.

The bra was itchy with lace and the band dug into my back, pinching in weird places.

"How is it?" Shiny yelled through the door, so close she could have been shouting in my ear.

I tugged the front part, trying to get everything to sit right. "Shiny, this is the most uncomfortable thing I've ever worn."

I could hear her laughing through the door like she was trying not to. "I'm sorry—I know. That's kind of just how they are, though. I mean, you get used to it."

I pulled off the price tag and put my dress back on, then followed Shiny up front to the register. She handed the tag to Bonnie, along with a plastic package of socks and one of underwear, and a wooden hairbrush that looked unlikely to have much of an effect on my hair.

I was worried how we'd pay for everything.

I had no money, and from what I'd seen of the Blackwood house, Shiny had none either, but Bonnie never even touched the register. As I watched, Rae reached into her wicker bag and brought out a little knot of cloth that at first glance did not look much different from the one I'd been buried with.

She set the trickbag on the counter and said, "Two weeks' worth of being near irresistible to Matt Allen should cover it, I think."

Bonnie didn't say anything, just looked away. She cupped

the trickbag in her hand like a secret, and then began to put all the socks and underwear into a plastic sack. We left the store with my new things, and Bonnie still taking care not to look at us.

Outside, it was getting more crowded. Across the street, a bunch of men with heavy boots and tool belts were hammering up a half-built stage. People stood watching, mostly little kids with sticky faces, but a few older boys slouched around too, bottom lips stuffed with chaw, spitting on the sidewalk and looking bored.

I caught sight of the ones who'd tried to gang up on Shiny earlier. Now they'd been joined by a bunch of other rough-looking boys, all wearing work boots and worn-out jeans.

Shiny glared at them, shaking her head. "All puffed up like they own the place. They wouldn't act so big if their friends could've seen them a minute ago, practically running down the road, they were in such a hurry to get away."

Rae waved a bored little hand. "They're just sassing around, trying to make Eric Fisher think they're pretty."

"Fisher?" I said, and my voice sounded all wrong, not just because my throat was hoarse, but because the word itself was so tight and shrill and unnatural.

Shiny glared at Rae and shook her head. "Do not even talk to me about Eric Fisher."

"Who is he?" I said, studying the pack of boys.

"Just a plain jackass, with a fancy old witch of a grandma who runs every organization and charity club and town meeting."

70

I'd been worried I wouldn't know him. That now that my eyes were open, I could pass him in the street without a clue, but it was easy to see the one she meant.

He was standing with his back to us, not all that much bigger or taller than most of the others, but with a way of carrying himself that made him seem like he owned everything around him.

The evening was still hot, and his undershirt was damp enough that through it, the ghost of a tattoo showed. It started at the bottom of his spine and traveled up to where his hair curled against his neck. The shape was narrow and mysterious, like a black snake creeping up his back. The longer I stared, the harder it was to tell what the picture was supposed to be.

"What's so bad about him?"

Rae gave me a kind look. "He keeps a few too many of his secrets . . . well, *secret*, for Shiny's tastes."

Shiny tossed her head so that her hair flew around her shoulders, all fading sunlight and dust. "And what makes him so special that he doesn't have to mind what anyone says or does around here?"

Rae shrugged mildly, rummaging in her bag. "Well, he *is* special."

I stood shading my eyes, looking after him. "Special how?"

Rae fished out a lipstick and snapped the bag shut. Her face was cool and blank and didn't give away a single trick. "He has a particular skill with living things."

Shiny made a scoffing noise. "Maybe with some of them. Not so much with people."

It wasn't the truth, though. All the other boys seemed to flock to him, ready to laugh at whatever he said, all looking to him for his opinion as soon as they opened their mouths.

Rae twisted up the lipstick and dotted it on. "Let's say he's got a skill with living things, but the boy doesn't like to advertise."

Shiny's scowl deepened. "If he was from the Willows, people'd be calling him every kind of crooked and hellbilly just like the rest of us, just for walking down the street, but get raised by Isola Fisher, and everyone treats him like a prince!"

Rae shook her head. "You know that's not the truth. If he didn't pretend so hard that his blood was straight, they'd be after him in a heartbeat. He'd have it just as rough as you, so don't go around acting hard done-by. You could lay low too if you wanted, but you *don't*, and you can't have it both ways."

Shiny gave an ugly snort, but didn't answer.

"All I'm saying is, if you want to get after someone for keeping their head down and making nice, then get after me."

But Shiny only laughed and slung her arm around Rae's shoulders. "Naw, you're my little witch-girl. You know that. Besides, if you didn't make nice, we'd never sell a single trick."

On the other side of the square, Fisher was telling some

sort of joke or story. He looked very tanned and kind of wild in the evening light, with his head tipped back and his grin wide, and I told myself that the only reason I was paying him any mind at all was because you were supposed to thank people. You were supposed to show your gratitude when they'd done you something nice.

I stepped down off the curb. "Well, I'm going over there to say hello."

Shiny grabbed my arm. Her breath smelled like warm bread and bubblegum, but under that was a tight, perilous smell, like the air of a stormy afternoon, right before the lightning starts. "Excuse me, you *what*? Did you not just have the pleasure of meeting Mike Faraday?"

"Fisher dug me out of that cellar and brought me home to you. Without him, I'd still be down there. I don't know how *you* were raised, but I was raised to say thank you."

"Do what you want then," Shiny said, letting me go. "But I am not going over there to stand around with him and play neighbors."

"You don't have to," I said.

Already, something in me was finding it a struggle not to turn and look. It was hard to keep my back to him for very long.

The air around Shiny had gone hot as blazes and her eyes were flickering. "Then I guess what you're saying is you can find your own way home?"

Rae didn't say anything, only cut her gaze at me. Her expression was mild, but her opinion was clear. No matter how evenhanded she might be, she did not think much of Eric Fisher.

There was something more to it than thanking him, though. A nagging whisper had taken hold of me, like the closer I got to him, the less frantic my heart might feel. It was there in my chest all at once, tugging me across the street, telling me I wanted to stand near him.

When I came up to the pack of boys, I was careful to keep well away from Mike Faraday, who eyed me with his lip stuck out and his hat pulled low.

The rest of them, I didn't mind so much. I knew half their faces in blurry ways, and some of them had changed so little in the time I'd been gone that I could even put names to them. I saw Matthew Allen and Tony Watts, who had a crooked tooth and a dent in his chin, and Brandon O'Radley, whose hair was just as red and as curly as his sister's. The rest were strangers, but the kind of strangers who had only to offer a name or a shared recollection and then you would know them again.

Two were gangly and blond and looked fair enough alike. I wasn't sure, but I pegged them for the Maddox brothers, who'd wanted to leave me in the cellar. I was *entirely* sure a minute later, when they caught sight of me and both flinched like I'd tried to bite them.

Fisher still had his back to me. He was watching the men from the public works crew raise the walls of the bandstand and didn't turn or look in my direction, but I was fairly certain he knew that I was there. That he could feel my very

74

presence with the same insistent, nagging itch that I could feel his.

I reached out, barely brushing his arm. "Hello."

When he turned to face me, he did it slowly. His eyes were a dirty shade of hazel, too light to be called brown, but not quite gray or green either, and he had a hard-boned face, with flat cheekbones and a square jaw. His hair was shaggy and almost black, but his complexion was fairish, burnt, and freckled. He was a whole mess of almosts, of mismatched pieces.

The other boys all watched me without a word. I could feel them looking, and maybe Shiny hadn't been able to do much about my matted curls, but I was very glad to be clean of soot at least, and wearing my new bra.

Fisher stared down at me. His hair fell over his forehead, hanging in his eyes. "What do you want?"

The way he said it was so rude that I had to wrestle with an urge to step back. "I wanted to say hello. I thought I should let you know that I was grateful to you for coming out to the Willows this morning and finding me. But maybe I just shouldn't bother explaining friendly gestures to you, seeing as you're not friendly."

"That's 'cause I'm not your friend," he said. "I don't even know you."

I stood looking up at him, no idea what to say. It seemed impossible that someone could do the best thing anyone had done for me in a long time and then tell me not to count them as a friend.

Around us, the other boys all stared daggers at me but didn't say a word. Mike Faraday stood against a streetlamp, with a lump of tobacco in his cheek and his arm hooked around Tony's neck, watching me. There was a black mark on the collar of his T-shirt where Shiny had scorched him.

I was beginning to understand, deeper than I ever had, that the crooked side of things could be a hard place to live. Shiny got along by flash and hellfire, and Rae by dimples and smiles and making nice, but neither of those seemed to fit quite right with my own disposition. I didn't know which way was mine, but I knew I'd have to find it soon enough.

"You must have had *some* good reason to come calling for me," I said to Fisher, talking up at him like there was no one else around. "I mean, since we're not friends and all."

He raised his eyebrows and didn't look at any of the other boys, but I could almost feel him weighing their opinions, like everything he said, he was saying it for them. "That's a little bold, assuming that I came for you."

"I'm not assuming, I'm just saying. After all, if you weren't there for me, then what were you doing in my house?"

He laughed, but it was dry and not at all friendly. "I don't know if you know this, but there's no house out there to be in."

I was quiet a minute, trying to decide what new, grown-up Clementine did when someone was short with her. I felt relatively sure that she did not put up with it and so I stepped closer. "I don't know if you know *this*, but that is not an answer."

He turned away so that his hair hid his eyes. I couldn't tell if he wouldn't look at me because he found me not worth looking at or if he was worried I might see something he didn't feel like showing.

"Do you not want to talk about this in front of your friends?" I said, trying to sort out what was happening on his face.

"Get away from her, Fisher," said one of the Maddox brothers suddenly, like he'd only just now worked up the courage. "Get away if you don't want her to hex you in a minute. You saw how she was down there—all stitched and shut away. She's got to be crooked as they come."

Fisher stood with his hands in his pockets. His shoulders were hard and the look he gave the rest of them was unimpressed. "I didn't see shit but a dirty little redneck girl that had got stuck down in a caved-in cellar hole, and we pulled her out. So don't go blowing this up into some kind of thing."

It was the second time that evening that someone had lied for me, and I wasn't at all sure why he was bothering. Rae was my friend—it only made sense that she should try to help me—but Fisher had been very clear that he was not. All at once, I didn't believe him.

The way he was watching me was a bit too fixed, and I could feel the flush hit my cheeks, but I didn't look away. My mother had always told me never to be bashful or drop my eyes, and so I stared back at him. When I squinted, I could almost see the blur of light that had shone around him in the cellar, and I thought that no matter how steadily he looked at me, the truth was, I scared him a little. Just maybe not the same way I scared the Maddox boys.

The moment thudded between us like a heartbeat and I had an idea that any dare or challenge I gave him, he would take it. Maybe he'd do it to prove something to his friends, maybe just to make them nervous or think that he was brave. I didn't care.

"I'm going down to that zoo on Crooked Mile," I said. "Do you want to come?"

For once, he didn't have anything smart to say. He shook his head, looking disgusted. "What do you want to go someplace like that for? It's completely cruel."

"I know. I'm going to go let the badger out."

He raked his hair out of his face and squinted. "Serious?"

"Do I look like I'm lying?"

His eyes were softer now. When he smiled, the shape of his mouth made my blood go hot.

He glanced back at the other boys, who watched us with their hats pulled low and their hands shoved deep in their pockets, gumming on their chaw and spitting brown streams of it onto the sidewalk.

Across the street, Shiny and Rae were looking at me with their heads cocked and their arms folded, but I was out in the world now. I could find my own way home. The night was coming on, and I was ready to do something wild.

When Fisher smiled again, it was sharp and fierce. "Okay," he said. "Okay, let's go."

THE ZOO
CHAPTER SEVEN

I'd thought we might be going to walk, since that was how Shiny and I had come into town, but Fisher paused at the corner of Main and Chester and steered me across the street.

It was just starting to come down dark, and the streetlamps were flickering on. His car was sitting by the curb, nearly glowing in the light that shone above it.

When he'd driven me out to Myloria's, the car had sounded so loud and vicious I'd had an idea that it wanted to pull loose from the road and tear up the whole world. So I'd known what to expect, and still, I had not expected it. It was jewel-blue with a white stripe, all long shark's nose and hungry body and a saucy little flip at the tail. The words TRANS AM were printed across the back, tiny flowers of rust flaking around the edges.

"Where'd you get it?" I asked, marveling that someone my same age could own something so fancy.

"Used to be my dad's," he said, throwing himself into the driver's seat. "Now it's mine."

I got in on the passenger side. "Oh. Did something happen to him?"

Fisher didn't look at me, just shrugged and jammed the key into the switch. "If disappearing in the middle of the night when I was five counts as something happening."

He said it like it didn't matter, but when I blinked, I could see the strange trails of light again, shining around him in the dusk.

Under me, the vinyl seat was smudged with ash and dirt, and it was peculiar knowing it had come from my own bare legs—that just a few hours ago, I'd been sitting in the same seat, with my eyes stitched shut, feeling the sun and the air on my face for the first time in years.

Then Fisher turned the key and it was hard to think about anything at all. The engine roared as we swung away from the curb, aiming down Chester Street and out of town.

We drove with the windows down, dust flying up around us, and the back end of the Trans Am squirreling on the gravel whenever Fisher put his boot on the gas.

We stayed quiet, not because there was nothing to say, but because the road was loud and the night was mysterious and electric. Then we turned out onto County Road 5, toward the Willows, and Fisher killed the engine and the lights.

"The zoo's farther down," I said in the sudden quiet, squinting through the windshield at the road.

He nodded, coasting onto the shoulder and setting the brake. "I don't know about you, but I see no reason to go announcing ourselves to the whole neighborhood right before we start turning the animals loose."

Then he got out and shut the door, and I got out and followed him.

At the zoo, nothing was moving. The sky had darkened to an inky shade of blue and the packed dirt yard was sunk in shadow. Up at the house, all the lights were out.

"Are they in bed already?" I whispered, mindful of what Shiny had said about Greg Heintz shooting at us. Growing up in the Willows had instilled in me an understanding that if there was one thing you weren't supposed to do, it was walk right up into someone else's yard without being invited. And it was probably worse if you were planning to steal their badger.

Fisher shook his head. "It's early, still. They're probably in town, watching the tents go up like everyone else."

We let ourselves in through the gate and followed the long, weedy driveway up to the house. We walked without talking, but now and then, Fisher lost his footing on one of the hard ruts or slid a little on the gravel. I had an idea that maybe he couldn't see in the dark as well as I could, but I didn't know if that was because his eyes were bad in the dark, or because mine were very good. I thought I might just be more used to it than most people.

We crossed the yard to the low chain-link fence that wrapped around the zoo, and Fisher reached over the top of the little gate and unlatched it.

Inside, the rows of cages went on and on. As we picked our way along, we passed something with a huge humped back that looked like a raccoon, or maybe a groundhog. It was sitting with its face turned to the corner so all that I could make out was a mass of thick brown fur.

Fisher stood in the middle of the zoo with his shoulders set, like he was about to explode at any second. His mouth was hard, but as soon as he saw me looking at him, his face went blank again.

When I kept looking, he glanced away. "This place is sick."

"Why does he do it?" I whispered. "Keep them like this?"

Fisher shrugged. "It's just how he is, collecting anything he can get his hands on, storing it up, selling shit to people who need it."

"Like what? Animals, you mean?"

Fisher shook his head. "Other stuff. Moonshine, guns with no numbers on them, stuff you don't need to know about. Living things, though—I guess he likes to keep those for himself."

I was a little offended that he should be telling me what I did and did not need to know about, but the list he'd given me was all kinds of unlawful, dangerous in ways I didn't even fully understand, and so I just nodded.

We wound our way through the zoo, past the cages of ducks and possums and rabbits. I was headed straight for the badger, but Fisher stopped at one of the dove coops, looking in through the mesh. "These guys could come out too, if they want."

There was a metal bolt on one side of the door, but even just running my fingers over it, I could tell it was useless.

Rusted shut. Whoever was in charge of the doves just poured the feed in through a slot at the front and changed out the watering tray from time to time. Looking at the scum of feathers floating on top, it seemed to have been awhile.

Fisher didn't even bother with the door. Instead, he hooked his fingers in the wire and yanked. Wood creaked and then the staples popped out in a silver spray all over the ground. The whole side of the coop peeled away in one big sheet.

When he went to throw it away, the edge of it sliced across his arm, leaving a neat row of gouges, like the dotted line in a book of paper dolls. He hissed and dropped the screen.

For just a second, there was nothing but that patch of torn-up skin. Then blood rose in round drops all along his arm. In the moonlight, it looked black.

He wiped the blood away, and when he did, I nearly gasped aloud. His skin was closing as I watched, sealing up as easily as it had torn.

Almost without thinking, I grabbed his wrist, pulling his arm up close to my face, but the marks were gone. There was nothing left but that smudge of blood, already drying. In my hand, his skin felt rough and warm and I let him go so fast it was like I was flinging him away. "How did you *do* that?"

"What?"

I stared up at him. "You must be out of your mind, saying *what* at me! You just cut yourself open and now there's nothing."

The power to heal was a power of the dirt, and I thought

83

of Rae saying in her prim, clever way, *He has a particular skill with living things*. What I had just seen was a lot more than that, though. This was no run-of-the-mill dirt-work like Myloria and my mama had liked to do, but pure, undiluted craft. This was the living, breathing body of the world.

For maybe five seconds, neither of us spoke. Then I moved closer. "What *are* you?"

Fisher didn't answer right away. In the light from the moon, his face looked ghostly and far away. After a minute, he laughed, but it wasn't a good sound. "That's a pretty personal question."

"Well as that may be, I think it's one worth asking. Are you trying to tell me that that what just happened is *normal*?"

"Let me put it another way. That's a pretty personal question coming from a girl who survived being buried alive. What are *you*?"

At our feet, the birds were marching out of their ruined coop in a wobbly line—quail and pheasants and doves. They trooped past like they barely minded that we were there, and waddled off toward the middle of the yard, too stupid to know that they were free. The white peacock came last of all, pecking along the ground.

"I'm Clementine," I said, watching the birds scratch aimlessly in the dirt.

But I said it to the darkness. To no one.

Fisher was already walking away, heading deeper into the zoo. After a second, I kicked the screen out of my way and followed him.

We wound between coops and hutches built from wire and the rotting salvage boards that used to be my house. There was something wholly satisfying about watching Fisher break them all to pieces.

The badger was at the corner of the yard closest to the road, locked inside its small scrap-wood cage.

Fisher stopped in front of it. "This is who you wanted, right?"

I nodded, peering in at it, just a white stripe in the dark.

"Well, let it out, then," he said.

When I tried the padlocked door, though, it wouldn't budge. I got down on my knees and started pulling at the latch. The ground under me was rocky and shot through with tree roots.

"Hurry up," said Fisher, glancing toward the house. "They're not going to stay gone forever."

I held the lock with both hands and closed my eyes. The inside was complicated, all little pieces of metal. I stared into the heart of it, looking for the part that would make it open.

The way I felt when my eyelids came down was like every dream and vision I'd had in the caved-in cellar, like I was crawling outside myself and into something greater. Shiny might be fierce and forthright, and Rae might know the delicate truth in objects, but I had a trick or two myself, and I knew how things worked.

"Can you break it?" Fisher asked in a voice so low it was barely louder than the sound of his breathing.

"No," I whispered back. "But I see how it opens, sort of.

It has these . . . things—they go up and down and let another thing turn. Do you have something skinny, like a wire or anything?"

"No. But we don't need one. Move."

It took less than a second to see what he was going to do, and then I scooted away on my butt so fast the backs of my legs scraped the gravel.

His boot swung right past my face, leaving a long, glowing afterimage. He hit the frame with his heel and the hinges tore away from the wood as easily as the staples on the bird coop had done.

The door clattered into the yard.

The badger trundled up to the edge of the cage and sniffed curiously at the opening before stepping out into the night. It stood over me where I sat in the dirt, a hulking shape against the starry sky.

"Leave," I whispered, but for a second, it just stood above me with its paws on my leg, sniffing the air around my face. I could feel its claws on my skin, leaving dimples where they pressed down. "You're out now. Just leave."

Fisher gave a short, barking laugh. "Looks like you made a friend."

The badger didn't move until I put my hand against its side and gave it a push. Its fur was bushy and not soft. It prickled against my hand, leaving a dark, oily smell. Then it turned and lumbered off into the dark.

Fisher was already yanking open an old rabbit hutch, turning free a mangy fox with a torn ear. He took care to stay in front of it, steering it away from the milling flocks of birds and toward the back of the property.

When every cage had been broken into and every animal set loose, Fisher turned and made a beeline for the tin-roofed shed at the back of the yard. It was set apart from the others, with a set of rusty bars across the front. The air around it was thick with the smell of something mean and hungry. The cougar crouched in a corner, staring back at me with eyes like kerosene lamps.

"I'm turning that one loose, too," Fisher said.

I shook my head and took a step back. "Isn't it dangerous?"

He raised his eyebrows. "Well, *yeah*."

I stared at him, but didn't know what to say to explain how the idea was crazy, so I didn't say anything.

"Look, if you're worried about it, go stand over there. No reason everything else should go free and that's got to stay locked up. If we're going to do this, we're going to let out everything."

I took a step toward the gate and then, when it became fully clear that he was going to open the door, I took another.

Fisher slipped back the bolt and eased the door open.

For the first few seconds, nothing happened. The cougar sat crouched in the corner. Then, with its ears stuck flat back against its head, it slunk out, glaring around the yardful of empty hutches.

I stood perfectly still as it crept past me, holding my breath, but it didn't turn or come closer. Suddenly, it took off toward the back of the property, moving close to the ground. With a last backward glare, it bounded across the yard, then scrambled over the fence and away into the dark.

Fisher turned to look at me. "There, nothing to it. Now, what are you so scared about?"

"I didn't feel like getting bit is all. But I think *you* must have some kind of death wish. Or maybe you just heal up so fast you don't care."

He laughed at that and tossed his hair out of his eyes. "You don't really lie about how you feel, do you."

I shook my head. "I don't have any reason to."

We stood looking at each other in the long, jagged shadows thrown by the trees. Above us, the moon shone down into the yard, making patterns of light and dark.

His expression was complicated, and I had a sudden idea that he was going to ask me something else, something private, and if he did, I wouldn't lie.

He opened his mouth, closed it again. The moment stretched on and on.

I was about to tell him to just go on and get it over with, when someone else spoke out of the darkness by the cedars— a tiny, fretful whisper. "You shouldn't be here."

The nearness of the voice nearly made my heart stop, and we both whipped around. A pale shape stood in the shadow of the trees, looking ghostly. Then Davenport Heintz stepped out into the yard. Her feet were bare and she was carrying a metal bucket. Her hair seemed to glow almost white in the moonlight.

Fisher and I stood in the middle of the ruined zoo, staring at her.

"What in the hell do you think you're doing?" she said, clutching the bucket. "Are you *crazy*? Do you think—"

Then, up at the little frame house, the porch light went on.

The glow was yellow, spilling down into the yard, and I saw on Davenport's face that we were about to be in a whole lot of trouble.

She darted past us and pointed toward the gate. "*Hurry*, before he sees what you did!"

But even as she said it, her father was already shouting down from the house. "Davenport, is that you? If someone's up on my property, in about three seconds, you will be very sorry."

For a moment, all three of us stood perfectly still. Then Davenport opened her eyes very wide, pointing to the gate again and mouthing the word *gun*.

Fisher and I didn't wait to be told twice. We took off running toward the road, pounding down the driveway, away from the house and the empty cages.

I was halfway across the ditch when there was a terrible shriek, like a rabbit caught in a snare, and I stopped to look back.

Greg Heintz was silhouetted in the light from the porch. He was ten years older than when I'd seen him last, tall and slope-shouldered, but I knew him, just like I knew everything about the Heintz place was wrong, wrong, wrong.

He was down in the yard, standing with his back to the road. He had Davenport by the hair.

As I watched, he shook her hard, then leaned down to bellow in her face. "What are you thinking, setting the critters free?"

"I didn't," she said in a thin, pitiful voice that floated to me across the yard.

He gave her another shake and her hands flew to her scalp, but she didn't cry out, even when he dragged her toward the ruined zoo, her hair wound in a knot around his fist. She was bent over at the waist, stumbling along behind him. It seemed to me that she must dream a thousand times a day of running away.

They disappeared through the little gate into the dark, but even as they did, I could still hear him shouting. "Where in the goddamn shitfire hell is my cougar?" he roared in a voice that echoed through the trees.

My mouth was dry suddenly, and when I turned to Fisher, my voice came out in a numb little whisper. "How can he do that to her?"

Fisher shook his head, and I thought that if he answered me the same way Shiny had explained about the zoo, if he told me that this was just what a man did in his own house, with his own things—if Fisher said that, I would lose my mind and scream.

But he didn't. Light glowed behind him in a pale circle, making it hard to see his face. I looked for the haze of colors that seemed to spill out of his skin sometimes, but I couldn't tell if the glow around him was just the Heintzes' porch light or if it came from my own eyes.

"Come on," he said finally, taking me by the elbow and turning me toward the road. His voice was low. His hand left a warm spot on my arm.

We walked without saying anything, down the road, past the broken beech tree that marked the edge of the Heintz property, and I realized Fisher was leading me in the direction of Myloria's.

"What about the car?" I said, glancing over my shoulder.

He shook his head. "I'll come back for it. You're just down the road and it's no good making a bunch of noise for Greg to hear."

Then he stopped walking and caught my arm, yanking me around to face him.

"Clementine," he said. His voice was low and suddenly, I was very nervous about what he might say. "You never did tell me how you wound up behind that wall."

"My mother died and someone burned my house down."

I expected him to do any of the polite, regular things— offer his sympathies or say how terrible it was. But he didn't. He stood in the road, looking into my face. Just watching me.

The dark was closing in, making me doubt my own presence, and I needed to know that I was here with him and not still down in the closet. Not someplace else altogether.

The way he was looking at me seemed too full of secrets. Like he already knew me.

"Did you ever dream of me?" I said suddenly, even though it wasn't the kind of question you were supposed to ask.

"I don't know what you're talking about," he said, but he glanced away when he said it.

I pushed my hair out of my eyes. "I'm talking about dreams. Any sort of feelings or visions—just something that might have told you how to find me."

According to Rae, the spell that had hidden me in the cellar had been powerful, made to keep anyone from ever setting me free. Now the more I thought about it, the more it seemed nearly impossible that Fisher could have stumbled upon me by chance.

He didn't say anything. The night was warm and still. Far away, an owl called out in its sweet, ghostly voice.

Nothing showed on his face.

I touched his hand because he was standing so still it was like he was too scared to move. I wanted to protect him from whatever was making him hold his breath.

"What are you so afraid of?" I whispered.

He only jerked away like he'd been stung. "Nothing." But he kept his face toward the ditch when he said it.

"I think you're lying," I said.

He shrugged, but it was slow and tired. "Think all you want. I don't care."

Around us, the frogs and crickets sang their sad night-time songs, filling the air with their cries. I didn't think that last part was true, but I didn't say so.

"Thank you for coming out to the zoo with me."

He laughed at that, his harsh, unguarded laugh, and shook his head. "Do you *always* just do whatever you want?"

"No, but I do what I think is right."

He looked at me, that strange unfathomable look, painful around his eyes and blank everywhere else. "That's an upright way of thinking, but around here, it can get you in an awful lot of trouble."

"I know how bad things can get," I said. "I'm not a total fool."

Fisher didn't answer. The look on his face was like he was wanting something—wanting and wanting until I was sure that nothing in the world could fix it.

Then he hunched his shoulders and turned away, shaking his head.

I'd thought he might walk me all the way to Myloria's door, but when I started up the driveway, he didn't follow.

I left him standing in the road with his hands in his pockets and his head down. When I looked back over my shoulder, he was only a white smear where his shirt stood out against the black outline of the trees. Everything else had already sunk back into the dark.

✳ ✳ ✳

In the house on Weeping Road, all the lights were out.

I made my way through the maze of halls and into the back bedroom, keeping my hand against the wall, but it was only habit, a trick from when I was little and would crawl out of bed for a drink of water. I knew the shape of things now, knew the stained paper and the scorched walls by heart, like they'd been printed on the palms of my hands.

Shiny must have lost her patience with town, because she was already in bed, cozied up under the blankets even though the night was warm. The room was full of the slow sound of her breathing. As I stepped inside, the chimes on the walls rustled and jingled to themselves, like a friendly little breeze had blown through. Then they stopped.

I stood for a minute and listened, thinking how strange it was to be near another person. To really hear her. The room was dark—almost willfully dark. It made my breath turn hoarse, but strange enough, I felt at home there too.

I peeled out of my dress and sat on the floor. Shiny had left me an old T-shirt and a pair of flannel shorts, along with a rolled-up camping mattress and some mismatched sheets and blankets.

The room was so narrow there wasn't much but a little space between the bed and the wall. I unrolled the camping mattress, then shoved the whole production underneath the bed.

There was a dusty suitcase in the way and I had to push it down to the foot before I could crawl under.

Up top, Shiny didn't move. Her hand hung over the side of the bed, phantom-white in the moonlight. I lay on the mattress pad, which was too thin and full of lumps to really be comfortable, but after my willow roots and my pile of dirt and my ten years' sleep, I wasn't feeling picky. I pulled the blankets up, shivering a little. It had been so long since

I'd slept in a bed, even a makeshift one, that I'd almost for-gotten the way the sheets always felt a little damp at first, clammy against my legs.

The space under the bed was dusty and cramped, and I was suddenly deathly afraid that if I woke up in the dark, I would think that I was still underground.

When I closed my eyes, there was only the feeling of a great nothingness pushing in on me, getting closer. I was suddenly so sure that I would wake up to find this entire day had been just a dream and in my real life, I was still down in the cellar hole, forever and ever.

Then I reached my hand out, sliding my fingers along the floor, reminding myself that there was a whole wide world out there. That I could always get out again.

THE CREEK
CHAPTER EIGHT

Even before I opened my eyes, the air hit my face in a damp wave, reminding me of where I was and what had happened. Outside, the cicadas were whirring, and I could tell the day was going to be a hot one.

Shiny was already up, standing at the mirror and running her brush through her hair like the world was a hateful place and her reflection most of all.

I got up too and buttoned myself into another of the ancient dresses. I'd have rather had some pants, but there were none in the box. I considered seeing if I could borrow some of Shiny's, but it didn't take more than a glance to know that all her things were likely to be too tall and too skinny.

I sat on the bed, looking at the chimes that covered the walls and dangled above us, still now, in the quiet room.

"What are these for?" I said, reaching to touch a tin star that hung with a whole galaxy of other tin stars. "Don't they belong outside?"

Shiny set down her brush, but didn't turn around. Her voice was strange and flat. "They're supposed to make noise if any kind of demon or spirit walks through."

"Do you think that's likely?"

But I was remembering the way they'd jingled softly the night before, light and cheery, like someone was in the room waiting for me. Like they were welcoming me home.

Shiny shrugged. "Every old family's supposed to have a fiend that wanders through the house once in a while to check on them. Whoever was their first link between their craft and the regular world. The Blackwoods are so deep in relations with fiends, though, we've probably got more like eighty."

"If they're supposed to watch over us, why bother with all the chimes?"

She leaned over the dresser, examining herself in the foggy mirror. She twisted her hair into a knot on top of her head, then let it fall again. "Because if someone's going to be wandering around in my house, I want to know they're coming. *So*. Did you have a good time ditching me for Eric Fisher?"

"He's not as bad as you keep acting like."

Shiny rolled her eyes like I'd said something so backward it hurt. "Don't even give me that. He's ten times worse than any of those raging assholes he hangs around with."

"Really," I said, in a voice meant to show just how unconvinced I was. "You think Fisher is so much worse than someone like Mike Faraday."

"Mike and them, they're just doing how they've always done, being ugly like they always have. But Fisher? He goes around pretending he's just like them, so redneck and regular. He tries to act so ordinary in town, like he belongs there, but his family is just *full* of the old blood, and he's as wild as they come, always running off to Wixby Hollow. And no one even gets after him for it! They pretend like it's not even true."

For a second, I just stared at her.

It was commonly held that every piece of craft in Hoax County came from down in the hollow. It was supposed to be a wild place, full of strange plants and hell dogs and fiends with glowing eyes and more power than a person could even properly conceive of—foreign things, bound by the hollow like creatures in a book, or else bound to the families that served them. The hollow drank its craft from them, and all the old families got theirs from the hollow.

But even though the mouth of it was directly behind my mama's house, I had never been there. My mama was happy enough to use the plants that grew there to make tonics and medicines, but she was scared of the animals and of the fiends, and had never let me go past the fence that divided our back-yard from our neighbor Harlan Beekman's pasture.

I turned to face the mirror, working my fingers through my tangled hair, already knowing I was never going be able to do a thing about it. "Now you're just telling stories at me—he can*not* be going down there."

Shiny was putting on her eyeliner now, drawing a hard purple smear along the base of her lashes and waving around her free hand the way people did when they were spouting gossip. "He can and does. Anyway, he's just as crooked as the rest of us, and everybody knows it. Everybody knows that's why his parents got out of town."

"What does that mean, got out of town?"

"Just that Randall Fisher got married to one of the Wallace sisters—Marcy, I think—and they had Eric, and then one day, they ran off. Spirited him away to Alabama or somewhere, and no one hears a word. Then one August, *she* comes slinking back alone in the middle of the night and leaves Fisher with his grandma. He was about nine, I think, and it was the biggest scandal in years. Them running off was bad enough, and Isola was about ready to just blame the whole thing on a bad gambling debt or something—save face and pretend none of it ever happened, and then his mom brought him *back*, and him being how he is? I mean, no wonder Isola hates him."

I nodded, thinking of how careful he'd been to seem plain and regular in front of his friends. "So, you're saying he's like Mama and Myloria then?"

"Oh, no way. The things people say about him, his craft is the real deal—none of this powders-and-pills bullshit that the Blackwoods are so in love with, but full-on, to-the-hilt magic." Shiny was brushing her hair with a vengeance again. "Anyway, now he goes around acting like the prince of Hoax County. Like being left on his grandma's doorstep is something so great. Whatever," she said, making a thin, purposeful line with her mouth. "That boy is the devil."

"Well, I'm going to kiss him."

It was the kind of thing she used to say about boys when we were little, sitting out under the apple tree in a tent made out of sheets. She'd say, "I'm going to kiss Andy Buckner," or whoever, and then she'd slap her hands over her mouth and we'd both laugh like crazy people, and sometimes she would and sometimes she wouldn't, but the thrill was all in the saying it.

Instead of laughing, though, she just put her hands on her hips and looked at me, this long, judging look that said my store of common sense was about what she'd figured. "Clementine."

"What?"

Shiny sighed. "You can't just go around deciding to kiss boys. You have to be smart about stuff like that. You have to make them work for it."

"Why?"

"Well, because . . . *because*." Her eyes flashed, and I remembered all the ways we'd been like best friends, but now none of that was evident in her face, and it was like I didn't even know her.

Suddenly, I had a clear recollection of my mother's voice, low and singsong, making a game of it once when Shiny was having one of her bad spells. *There was a little girl who had a little curl, right in the middle of her forehead. When she was good, she was very, very good. But when she was bad, she was horrid.*

I sat on the bed and looked up at her, trying to figure out the thing that had changed since last night. "Why are you being so mean today?"

Shiny glared at me. "Because you ditched me! I'm your *family*, and he's just some down-hollow creep who likes to pretend so hard that he's not. He's nothing to you."

It bewildered me that she could say that like it was some kind of fact. How you went about knowing if a person was something to you. I couldn't help the way I wanted to stand close to him. I couldn't help that when I closed my eyes, I sometimes saw the world through someone else's, or that it was like he found me even before he came to find me.

I slumped against the wall, remembering the dark silence of the cellar, and suddenly, even the tiny room seemed like too much, because my hair was tangled and there were blisters on my pinkie toes from Shiny's sneakers, and I was so ungodly hungry.

"Will there be breakfast?" I said finally, scooting up to the edge of the bed.

Shiny sighed and sat down next to me. "Probably not. Myloria isn't really bothered about things like that—food and clothing and keeping things clean."

Even just saying it seemed to take the fire out of her, and we sat side by side, daunted by the empty kitchen and my fascination with a boy whom Shiny believed to be everything wrong in the world.

"We could go down to the creek," she said finally. "See if we can catch some bass or catfish."

I nodded, but I was not entirely optimistic. We'd played at fishing when we were little, tying lines onto crooked sticks and letting the ends dangle in the water, but it wasn't like we'd ever caught anything.

Shiny was already heading toward the door. "Come on, we'll drop in over one of the lower bridges by the county line. The holes are really deep there and the channel cats come in close during the day."

In the front hall, she took down an old-fashioned fishing basket that had clearly seen better days. The bottom looked like it might fall out at any second.

Outside, she got down on her hands and knees, feeling around under the front steps. She pulled out a plastic margarine tub and I watched with interest as she tucked it into the basket. Then she got up from the ground and led me around the side of the barn.

A truck was sitting in the grass behind the hay crib. It was very old and very rusty and very white and green, with a big bald spot on the hood where the paint was fading off. Shiny slipped into the barn and came back carrying a gas can. She popped the cap and slopped some into the truck tank. She did it fast, with her foot propped on the tire and her shoulder braced.

I watched her wrestle with the can, balancing it on top of one knee. "Can't you just go into town and fill up at the pump? I *know* Carter's has a pump."

Shiny flipped the gas cap closed and set the can in the bed of the truck. "I am not going to waste a single dime on fuel just to burn it up on my way back out to this hellhole. I buy a couple gallons, take it home, and just pour it when I need it."

When the gas was in the tank and the fishing gear was in the bed, she opened the driver's side and hopped in. Seeing her sitting up there in the cab was like seeing a wish come true, but something in my throat hurt anyway.

We had talked about this, made up stories about it, but now that it was here, it just made something ache in my chest. I'd missed so many things, and every bygone holiday and birthday left a kind of hole that couldn't be fixed, even sitting in the cab with Shiny beside me, remembering the wild plans of two little girls who'd once hooked pinkies and sworn to drive away.

We headed down the Crooked Mile, away from town and toward the county line, to the widest, deepest part of the Blue Jack Creek.

The truck hit every rut and pothole like it was looking for them, and the radio didn't work, but I was too pleased to be riding around the back roads with my cousin to even care. The truck was high as a house, and Shiny drove like she was getting away from somewhere.

We crossed the low-water bridge, rumbling over the creek, and when I looked down, I saw that there were people in the water, wearing all white and standing waist deep. The way they raised their hands and looked to the sky was so reverent it made my neck prickle. Their faces were pure and peaceful, lit up with a powerful kind of devotion.

"What are they doing?" I said, nearly leaning out the window to see better.

Shiny hardly even glanced over. "Oh, they're just getting dunked. A lot of the folks outside town do it at the start of summer so the devil won't get at them."

I leaned my elbows on the window, watching the preacher tip them back and dunk them under. Their white robes billowed in the water and stuck to them like wrinkly skins as they came up again. One by one, they waded back up onto the bank, looking eerie and beautiful, like creatures in a fairy tale.

I pulled my head in and turned to Shiny. "Are you dunked?"

She laughed like I'd said something clever and shook her head. "Are you kidding? That is not for people like us, okay?"

"Do a lot of people do it?"

Shiny tossed her head and gave a little shrug. "Naw. I mean, Rae's family's Baptist, but the in-town kind, not dunkers. And some of the folks in town aren't anything at all. Or else, they traded out one thing for another. Like the Fishers are originally supposed to be from Moravia, I think. In the beginning, they might have been some other kind of religion altogether—Jewish, maybe—but now I'm pretty sure they're Pentecostal."

"What are we, then?"

Shiny just shrugged and stared straight ahead. "Wicked."

The way she said it was like she was sounding angry so she didn't have to sound sad, and after that we rode in quiet, rattling along through the open fields and into the far bottom of the Willows.

The longer we went without talking, the less sure I was of my own true whereabouts, and I started to think about the cellar again. The cab of the truck was feeling smaller and smaller, and I had to keep reminding myself that I was going fishing. I was out in the world and we were going to get ourselves something to eat, and that was almost enough to make me feel free.

"Hey," I said finally, looking around the empty road. "Do you think you can you teach me to drive?"

Shiny raised her eyebrows. "I guess. But just out here. I don't want anyone giving us a hard time because you haven't got a license."

She pulled up to the shoulder and switched places with me, leaning across the seat to point out the positions on the shifter. "Okay, now the Ranger's a three-speed, and it is really awful for upshifting, so you have to just hope, pray, and stomp down the clutch like you mean it. Do *not* try to baby it, or it will know you're scared."

The steering wheel felt warm and cracked in my hands. When I was little, I'd always figured the pedals and the gears had their own special kind of magic, but now, with the engine rumbling through the floorboards, I could almost see the parts that made up the clutch, feel the tug of the drive-shaft moving to turn the axel. When I stalled out the first time, I could almost see what had gone wrong.

The second time, I knew it was coming before it happened, but I still didn't get the clutch down quick enough to beat it. The truck coughed and died, rattling to a stop.

Third time was a charm, though, and I took us rocking and shuddering along the shoulder of the road and then pulled out into the lane.

The truck was finicky and hard to turn, but driving

made me feel better. Like things were governable. Like I could fix on a solid thing in the world and have it do what I wanted.

When we reached the county line, Shiny had me park in the little dirt turnoff at the top of the bridge and got out. The creek was low and lazy in its banks, and Shiny's truck was the only thing around.

She opened her tackle basket and took out the margarine container. Up close, the smell coming off it was so bad that I covered my face with both hands. "*Oh*, what *is* that?"

She laughed and reached into the bed of the truck, tossing a fishing pole at me. "Spoiled chicken livers. Catfish are so nasty it's like their idea of a treat."

She offered me a hook and a piece of liver and I followed her down along the bank, where the weeds grew thick and tangled and the ground sloped away.

Shiny stood over me, watching as I made a mess trying to get the liver on the hook, before finally taking pity and doing it herself.

Then she scrambled down the bank and pointed out into the creek. "You're going to cast into the middle, over there where the water looks dark. I'll go a ways farther down, and you stay here up by the bridge."

"Why?"

"Because the big ones are all down in the bottom of the creek bend, and you won't hold one if you catch it."

"How do you know?"

She gave me that long know-it-all look she'd been doing

since we were little, and it made one part of me feel safe and homey, and another part feel plain furious. "I just do."

I sat on the top of the weedy hummock nearest the bridge. The water was slow and clear, and I sat with my feet tucked under me, watching the crawdads skitter around in the shallows. Farther out, my bobber floated over a dark, uneasy shadow. The day was warm and mostly still, and there was an empty mason jar lying near the edge of the water, caught in the weeds.

We'd been sitting for maybe twenty minutes when my line gave a jerk, so hard it almost took the pole out of my hands. In less than a second, the creek had gone so wild it looked like it was boiling, and then I saw the fish, shining like gunmetal, rising out of the water and thrashing down again.

Shiny gave a shout, and then came crashing through the weeds behind me.

"Hold it," she said, her voice buzzing like an electric current.

"It's too strong! I think it's getting away."

"*Hold* it," she said again, sounding nothing at all like Shiny and everything like a girl with fire in her blood. "Keep the line tight—no, don't pull on it! Just play it, play it!"

I worked the reel, letting the line run slack and then catching it before it could spin all the way out, but the fish was wild, making the water churn up in a white froth. I saw a flash of spiny tail, and then it splashed under again.

Shiny marched straight down to the edge of the water

and peeled her shirt over her head. She did it in one fast yank, like there was nothing strange about skinning off her clothes on the side of the road. She had on a black bra with flowers embroidered on it and there were a pair of wings tattooed on her back, right over her shoulder blades.

Then she was in the water, splashing down off the bank and wading out.

She looked tall and tan following my line and when she got to the end, she ducked and grabbed the fish in both hands, then hauled it, flopping and wriggling, up onto the bank.

I dropped the pole and ran over to her.

Shiny sat down hard on the dirt, holding the catfish in her lap. The wings rippled on her back when she moved. I wanted to reach out and touch them. They were the most delicate thing I'd ever seen, each feather perfect, like every line of the picture had been loved into existence. Under them, the rest of Shiny was sharp and brown and kind of lonely.

She stuck out her chin and clamped her fingers around the fish, never minding the spines. Its skin was a slick, awful green—an impossible green—with slimy whiskers and dull, milky eyes. The ends of her hair were wet, sticking to her arms.

She was about to stick her fingers in the fish's mouth and twist the hook out, when suddenly she yanked her hand up to her chest and we both froze. Its mouth was full of long, jagged teeth. Row upon row of them, and every one like a needle.

The fish twisted and flopped, mouth opening and closing, and we sat looking down at it. Suddenly, the green skin seemed much greener and much, much wronger. Shiny had taken out her buck knife now but was holding it the way someone would hold a stick of butter, like she'd forgotten what it did.

"Shiny?" I said, sounding much calmer than I felt. "I don't think I've ever seen a catfish with teeth like that."

"No," she said in a soft, faraway voice, and put the point of the knife against the back of its head. "No, I don't think anyone has."

The fish thrashed, reaching with its needle teeth, trying to take a piece of her hand, but she squared her shoulders and held it steady. Then she drove the knife through the slimy green skin between its eyes.

Afterward, we both breathed out. The fish lay on the bank, oozing a little.

Shiny shook herself, then wiped the blade clean on the grass. Her face was empty and cold, like a stone girl's.

"Dig a hole," she said. "Now."

I ran across to one of the willows and got down on my knees, scrabbling in the dirt with my hands. The ground was soft and black, getting under my nails, and as I dug, I remembered something that until that instant had been tucked safe behind the sheet in my mind. It was a squirming, awful thing that left a hard knot in my throat and a taste like pennies in my mouth.

My mama, out in the garden, ripping down the strange

stone tomato I had found and burying it, looking stricken in the evening light. I dug faster.

Over on the bank, Shiny was chopping up the fish. She cut away the fins and the head, then began, in fast, hard jerks, to skin it.

When I'd dug a hole as deep as my shins and Shiny had pulled the fish nearly to pieces, she gathered what was left and dumped it in the ground. Her hands were pink with blood and slime.

We stood together kicking dirt over the top of it, and then, when it was buried, covering the hole with rocks and brush till there was nothing to show that such a wrong, vicious thing had ever been there.

THE DEVORE HOUSE
CHAPTER NINE

When we climbed back in the truck, we were both shaking a little. Shiny swung out of the dirt turnoff, jouncing out onto the road. Her foot was heavy on the gas and we didn't talk. My heart was still beating like a wild thing, and I didn't know of a single thing I could say.

"What are we going to do?" Shiny whispered after much too long. "I don't think we can tell Myloria."

But the very idea was impossible. I didn't even know where I would start. Tell Myloria *what*? That we had buried a catfish? That it had happened to be monstrous one? And even if we told her, what would she say to that? What could she possibly do to change it?

Shiny was driving fast, looking more frightened than I'd ever seen her. "Do you think we put it deep enough?" she said, gripping the wheel tight with both hands.

"Deep enough for what?"

"To keep the craft in. That fish was touched by the hollow, and the only way to keep it from spreading is to put it straight back in the ground."

"I think so," I said, reaching across the seat to her,

although I truly had no idea.

We were quiet after that. Shiny seemed very focused on driving, but she still blew right past the sign for Weeping Road.

"Shit," she whispered and kept on going, heading up past the Heintz place, where the shoulder got wide enough to turn around.

Greg Heintz was out in the yard, wearing a red feed cap and looking sunburned. He was nailing the wire mesh back onto the side of the dove coop, but he looked up as we drove by. I didn't see Davenport anywhere.

The zoo was in bad shape, empty and leaning every which way. The cages Fisher had kicked apart looked worse in the daylight.

"Shit," Shiny said again, slowing the truck to a crawl. "What happened *there*?"

I sank down in my seat, chilly from the way Greg Heintz was looking at me. His eyes were a clear, ringing blue that seemed to bore directly into me, so hard and flat they looked like coins. The way he watched us go by was like he was seeing some far away, dark part of me, some nastiness that hadn't yet been accounted for.

"Me and Fisher let the animals out," I said in a low voice, facing forward.

The look Shiny gave me was ruinous. "What in blue hell would you do *that* for?"

"Why *wouldn't* I? No one *else* was going to."

"Clementine, I don't know how to make you see, but

there is a *reason* people leave him alone. Greg Heintz is mean, sure, but plenty of people are mean. The main difference is, he is also crazy."

"And just because he's crazy, he gets to do whatever he wants?"

"Listen to me. He doesn't follow a single law if he can get away with it. He has shot people for hunting on his property. Back when things got bad with the reckoning, he was the one who dragged that goddamn Coalition for Purity out of hibernation. They still have meetings to this *day*. The last thing we need is him paying more than a passing attention to us. You can't go around messing with just anybody because you don't like how they're behaving!"

I didn't answer. There was that word again—*reckoning*— but I still didn't know what it meant. I had no say about how Shiny chose to do things, but I wasn't about to put up with ugliness like the zoo just because someone was crazy.

At home, we straggled into the kitchen, where Shiny slumped at the table with her hands against her forehead. Sitting there, she looked about the same way I felt, but still, I couldn't see the point in starving over a fish, so I went through the cupboards to find something for lunch.

I got down some beef jerky and crackers, and ate a scoop of peanut butter out of the jar. It wasn't much, but I felt better afterward. Shiny just stared out the window, running her hands through her hair. Finally, she pushed her chair back and stood up, so I put away the peanut butter and followed her into the bedroom.

She sank onto the bed with her back to the wall and her pillow held against her chest. After a second, I sat down next to her.

"It's going to be okay," I said. "It was just one fish."

She shook her head. "The last time I saw anything like that catfish, it was the reckoning."

"Shiny, I don't even know what that is."

"The day everything broke loose from Wixby Hollow, and the coalition came down here and torched our houses and there was nothing we could do. It's the day Myloria stopped being worth a damn."

Shiny's arm was pressed against mine. Her skin was very hot and so I leaned away. "What did they do to her?"

She hugged her pillow tighter. "Just took or killed or ruined everything we had and now she's afraid that if anyone even gets an idea she's still using craft, they'll come back and do it again."

"Oh," I said, because it was the only thing I could think of. Suddenly, the hole we'd buried the fish in didn't seem nearly deep enough.

Shiny bowed her head, squeezing her eyes shut. "You know how termites will eat up a board until there's nothing left? I think it was like that. The reckoning went through like plague, infecting everything, and people were just willing to do anything to put it back where it belonged."

"Like set fire to anyone known to have anything to do with craft."

Shiny nodded. "The only ones who didn't get the gas-can

treatment were folks like the Daltons, who keep their talents low and don't do more than sell advice or make a trick sometimes."

I nodded. It was a remarkable thing, what Rae had done in the play tunnel at the park, just taking something mixed-up and mysterious and sorting out its meaning. But what she had done was a world away from Shiny's blowing a plume of fire in Mike Faraday's face.

Rae had a gift for understanding and for solving problems, but Shiny's kind of craft was extraordinary. A little frightening, even.

And still, it seemed preposterous—out of the question—that someone could be so frightened they would actually want to *hurt* her. To hurt me.

"Just how scary was the reckoning?" I said. "Scary enough to make people want to get rid of us? I mean, what did it look like?"

She shook her head. "Like—I don't know—like impossible things. Bad dreams. Sometimes it's hard to even know what really happened. It was all so crazy, and I was little. I try to remember and then think I must have imagined half of it."

She took a deep breath and hugged herself like she was trying not to shiver. "There were birds everywhere, falling out of the sky. Some of the trees got gnarled and turned black, and others were tossing around all over the place, smashing out windows like they were alive. I saw animals coming out of the woods and they didn't look like any

115

animals I knew of. It was like the whole world had just . . . sprouted teeth."

"Are you saying the reckoning was like craft, but stronger?"

Shiny nodded. "Not just stronger, though. It was like the world was getting mixed up. Flowers were turning to dust everywhere. The top of the birdbath caught fire like it was full of kerosene instead of water. The creek looked like black paint and smelled like poison."

I tried to picture it, to live that day like she had lived it, but all I could see was that one wrong tomato, the day the stone things and the growing ones had stopped being separate and there were no rules about anything anymore.

"So the whole town got taken over by craft, and it all just happened one day, like for no reason?"

Shiny leaned forward and shook her head. "I think it was slower than that. After, people started talking about all the little things they'd seen, days or sometimes *weeks* before. I think it started slow—so slow people hardly noticed. And then just got faster."

The catch in her voice made me look up. "And now you're worried about that fish."

Shiny nodded. "That fish," she whispered.

I reached across the quilt and patted her arm. "Maybe it's not anything. Maybe it's only that catfish are ugly."

"Or maybe it's the reckoning all over again."

I shook my head. "How can that be? That doesn't even make any sense."

116

"It does," Shiny said, and now her hands were both over her mouth. "It *does* make sense."

"How, though?" I said, and I'd meant it to sound calm, but the longer she wouldn't look at me, the raspier my throat got. Suddenly, my heart was beating almost too hard to stand. "*How*, Shiny?"

She raised her face to mine and her mouth was trembling. "Because I keep going around and around it in my head, and as much as I don't want it to be true, someone had the sense to lock you away last time. Someone made it a *point*, and now there's a crooked horror of a fish lying in the ground down by the creek and the only thing that's changed since yesterday morning is you."

The words were like a slap, and we sat in the tiny room, looking at each other. I was holding my breath, waiting and waiting for her to take it back, and when she didn't, I stood up.

"Clementine."

With an awful knot in my throat, I dragged the old suitcase out from under the bed. It rattled messily and when I opened it, the bottom was full of screwdrivers and chisels and loose nails. I left them in and began to pack the camping blanket and the sheets, folding them carefully at first, and then piling them in willy-nilly. I dumped in the mess of clothes I'd taken from the cardboard box, then the broken comb, the hairbrush, and all the socks and underwear that Shiny had gotten for me at Spangler's.

She stood in the corner of the room with her arms around

117

herself, watching me pack. "Clementine, wait. I didn't mean to go running off like a crazy person. What are you going to do? You can't just *leave*."

I shut the suitcase and fastened the clasps.

"Clementine—come on, don't! We'll figure this out."

I straightened and stepped into my canvas sneakers that used to be hers.

"Clementine, please!"

I picked up the suitcase, tools and all. I could feel them sliding down into the bottom of the suitcase the way sugar sinks to the bottom of a glass.

I gave her a quick, shaky kiss on the cheek and walked out.

✻   ✻   ✻

I walked fast down the driveway and out to the Crooked Mile, but I couldn't walk faster than the thoughts that circled in my head, telling me I was the thing that had brought ruin to the Willows. That I was nothing but loss and destruction and death, and without me, my pretty green house would still be standing. Shiny's life would be whole and bright and better. My mama would still be alive.

I walked with my head down, afraid to look around me, afraid that anything I laid eyes on might somehow be changed by the very strength of my gaze.

The road and fields and ditches all seemed so normal, though, and the more things stayed the same, the more my heart loosened in my chest.

Down in the cellar hole, time had been endless, a snake

clamped onto its own tail. A bad dream could last a lifetime, but already, the panic was leaving me. The breathless, scrabbling fear that had gripped me in the bedroom didn't grip me now, and I began to think that maybe when you were out in the world, feeling things in your body, in your waking mind, you couldn't feel them forever.

I was better by the time I crossed the Foxhill Bridge, and much better the closer I got to my mama's house and to the hollow. If I couldn't be wholesome or harmless, at least I could stand in my mother's garden and feel like I belonged there. I could go home.

As soon as I came up the weedy driveway, though, it was clear that Fisher hadn't been lying about the state of things, not even a little. There was no house to be in.

Nothing was left but the foundation, burned black in feathery streaks, and even after all this time, nothing grew in the scorched dirt around what had once been my house.

The ground crunched under my feet, glittering with melted glass and bent nails. Whatever they'd been trying to burn out, they had gotten it—every last brick and board. Everything but me.

I left the suitcase on the edge of the foundation, and started down the concrete steps into the cellar. Most of the brick and the lumber had been hauled away—by Greg Heintz, to build his hateful zoo, by anyone else who needed scrap—but there was still a fair amount of trash lying around.

I kicked my way through it and over to the canning closet. The spot where Fisher had dragged me out was an explosion of loose bricks, but the rest of the opening was still walled up, covered with a thin coat of cement. Unless you got very close and knew right where it was, the doorway looked just like the rest of the cellar.

Peering inside the closet gave me an uneasy feeling. My toy bear was lying on the dirt, so wet and moldy it hardly looked like a bear at all anymore, just a rotting lump of flannel. I left it where it was and climbed back out, picking up the suitcase and toting it around the side of the house.

The yard had all gone to weeds and tangles, making it hard to tell where the woods started, or even exactly where my mother's garden had been. The squash and strawberries were gone, but here and there, tomato frames still stood, weather-gray and overgrown with knotweed.

I stood in the tall grass, feeling small and strange and lost. I didn't know what I'd been expecting, but I'd been expecting *something*. Some kind of secret or revelation, but I had stood there in the cellar, right at the place where it had happened, and there were no answers. Nothing to prove that the decision to lock me away hadn't been the right one.

Then from far off, I heard the roar of an engine. The sound cut off and the whole place was still again. From the garden, I could look down the driveway and out to the road. A car had pulled up on the shoulder and even from where I was standing, I could tell it was the sweet candy-blue of Fisher's Trans Am, but I didn't see him anywhere around.

I circled the foundation and stood at the spot where the back porch had been, so that I had a clear of view of the pasture. The grass was long and someone with wide shoulders and dark, shaggy hair was walking down toward the hollow. I grabbed the suitcase and took off after him.

"Hey," I yelled.

Fisher didn't even look around, just headed for the back paddock, where the meadow grew long and where Harlan Beekman kept his stud bull, which was a thundering, vicious thing that hated kids and dogs and anything else dumb enough to wander into the field.

Harlan himself was a huge, scowling man, with a great denim-covered belly and a mess of bristles that crept down his neck and up around his jaw. His eyes were small and deep-set, and his eyeteeth were sharp, so that on the bottom they stuck up like tusks, giving him a passing resemblance to a razorback hog. For all that, he was a kind man, and a good one, but he would light you up for stepping into the bull paddock.

I started to run, throwing the suitcase over the top of the fence and wriggling through the wire, crashing through the witchgrass after Fisher. "Hey! You can't go back there. Harlan will ruin you!"

Fisher glanced over his shoulder, then stopped walking and rubbed the back of his neck. "Harlan Beekman's been dead for two years."

All my life, Harlan had owned the pasture behind our house and most of the land around it. He'd been protective about it, and particularly about the thick stands of trees that marked the top of the hollow.

The news of his death hit a tender spot in my heart that wasn't sad, exactly, but more like sore. He'd been old, and I'd been little, but still, it seemed wrong that someone so comforting in his dailiness could simply stop existing.

Fisher shook his head, misunderstanding my look. "The land deed fell to the town chamberlain. My grandmother's been looking after the property ever since. I'm *allowed* to be here."

I nodded, but it was clear he didn't care what I thought about his right to be there. He didn't waste any time before turning away again. His back was broad and indifferent, moving away from me, leaving me there like we'd never broken into the zoo together, never stood in the road. Never watched each other shyly in the dark and then looked away.

I picked up the suitcase and called after him. "You have to tell me how you knew where to find me!"

Fisher stopped walking. This time, when he turned around his face was put together. It was no expression at all. "What?"

"How'd you know? How did you know there was a door there?"

"I know what a goddamn *door* looks like. Now, do you want to tell me what you're doing out in Beekman's back pasture with a suitcase?"

I wanted to tell him what Shiny had just told me—that I was the reason my mother was dead. I was dangerous and terrible. I was smack at the heart of the worst thing that had ever happened in Hoax County.

122

But all I said was, "I ran away from Myloria's."

"Really."

The suitcase was heavy and I hitched it up. "Well, I guess I mostly ran away from myself."

He nodded, like that was the first thing I'd said this whole time that actually made sense. "Sometimes, that's all you can really do."

Then, without another word, he hopped the fence and started toward the trees, in the direction of the hollow.

"You can't go down there," I said to his retreating back.

"Too bad," he answered, not bothering to look around. "It's where I'm going."

I'd never been down in the hollow, not even on a bet or a dare. I'd grown up with it nearly in my backyard, but it was drilled into me that no one was ever supposed to go past the fence for any reason.

Fisher had no such misgivings. He walked right out to the rocky bluff and disappeared over the edge.

Wixby Hollow was a place where craft was in the very ground—in the air and in the water—and only the roughest and the most reckless people went there. If I followed Fisher down, I'd be walking into someplace wild. I might see hell dogs and monsters. I might see the fiends that lived there. But I would be someplace that held those fiends inside it, and down there, whatever power I had brought out of the cellar might be held in check and the Willows would be safe from me.

I climbed the last fence and went plowing through the

weeds to where the bluff dropped off. The brush was so thick I couldn't see the bottom, and I didn't like the way the hill was littered with rocks. I was half-tempted to leave the suitcase sitting under the trees, but I didn't like to lose track of the only piece of property in the whole world that I sort of owned.

The way down the bluff was steep and slow going. There was no path that I could see, but Fisher had done it like it wasn't any trouble, so I took the suitcase in both hands and followed him, down into the place where the trees grew almost on top of each other and the branches were so tangled that they blocked out the sky.

THE HOLLOW
CHAPTER TEN

The ground at the bottom of the hill was squishy with moss and standing water. The Blue Jack Creek forked off all through the county, sending hundreds of tiny streams creeping out into the stands of birchwood and sprawling across acres of cow fields.

A branch of it wound down through the hollow, clear and shallow. When I stood too close, the dampness soaked out of the ground, straight through the canvas of my shoes.

I crouched at the edge of bank, watching as water bubbled up into the muddy gouges left by Fisher's boots. The white of his shirt still showed in flashes through the trees and I followed, picking my way through the brush.

The farther we went, the harder it was to be quiet.

Under me, the moss was full of strange little tendrils poking up like fingers, catching at my ankles. The trees had turned knobby and wild. I moved carefully, watching for anything that looked like craft or like Shiny's stories of the reckoning, but as far as I could tell, the hollow mostly just looked like any other green, tangled place.

Ahead of me, Fisher had stopped on the edge of the water

and was poking around in the weeds and bog moss like he was looking for something.

I stumbled down the bank and ran after him, splashing through the stream. "Fisher, wait."

He glanced back, then turned to face me and threw up his hands. "What are you *doing?*"

I stopped, holding the suitcase up out of the water with both hands. "Following you."

"Well, don't," he said.

I shook my head. "Don't act like you're the only one who can be back here. I'm allowed to walk down through my own yard."

"It's not your yard. The hollow doesn't belong to anybody."

He was looking at me with that strange, steady gaze, and suddenly, something in his eyes made me think that he was very lonely. Even just seeing it there made me lonely too.

"I don't know what to do anymore," I whispered. "All I wanted for so long was to get free. I thought if I could just get out of the cellar, everything would be better, but maybe it's not. Maybe that bricked-up closet was just where I belonged."

I tried to sound matter-of-fact, but it nearly hurt to be so honest. I waited for him to nod or argue or maybe even tell me he understood, that he knew exactly what I meant.

His own craft was something wondrous, but most people were not at ease in the presence of miracles. I thought if anyone would understand, it would be him, but he didn't say anything.

"I'm not sure I belong out in the world," I said, finally. "I think bad things might happen when I'm around, and if that's true, then maybe the hollow is the safest place for me."

Fisher was still watching me in that blank way that made him impossible to read. "I'm sorry you feel like that, but I don't think you're going to belong down here, either. It's not that kind of place." His voice was low, and lonelier than his face.

"Let me come anyway," I said. "I won't be any trouble, and I'll keep out of your way. You don't have to worry about me getting scared."

That made him press his fingers into his eyes and tip his head back. "Believe me, I know. Okay, look—just stay close to me and don't go bothering anything."

The walk down through the hollow was like the drive we'd taken to the zoo, quiet and purposeful. Every now and then, Fisher would stop and poke around in the moss by the water, but he always straightened up and then moved on.

I was crunching along after him, pushing branches out of my way, when a pale fluttering caught my eye and I stopped. A pencil drawing had been nailed to one of the trees. The paper was rumpled, waterstained from being left out in the woods, but the picture was clear. It was of a little old woman with dark, wicked eyes and a jagged razor-slash of a mouth.

I stood with my hands against the tree trunk, flat on either side of the drawing. "Why is there a picture of an old lady hanging way out here in the woods?"

Fisher stopped and studied the drawing. "That's my grandma," he said finally, sounding less surprised than I would have imagined.

"Well, why's there a picture of your grandma out in the woods?"

He shrugged. "It's some old kind of craft. Supposed to be a way to keep someone from using on you—draw their picture and nail it up someplace no one will find it." He leaned closer, running his fingers over the paper. "Someone thinks she's working them."

"And is she?"

He laughed a sharp, ringing laugh that echoed in the trees. "Oh, probably."

Then he yanked down the drawing and shoved it in his pocket.

"Why'd you take that, if someone put it there to stop her from working them?"

"Because if Isola's working someone, they probably deserve it."

The winding path beside the water finally led out through the bottom of the hollow and into a wide, sunny meadow, full of wildflowers and a kind of thick, silky grass that made me want to lie in it. The stream had run itself out, ending in a clear trickle that seeped out into the field.

It was a quiet place, full of bog moss and clusters of tiny purple flowers. I walked out into the sun, leaving Fisher still kicking around in the soggy ground by the water. He was businesslike about it, but if his boot uncovered a box turtle or a lady's slipper plant, he was always careful to step around it.

"What are you looking for?" I asked, watching from the edge of the meadow.

"Nothing. Just, sometimes I collect agates and certain kinds of flowers for my grandma. She uses them for . . . stuff. And if you buy from someone who deals in those kinds of things, it's pretty expensive."

I nodded, wondering what kind of people would risk coming down here just to deal in rocks and leaves.

Across the meadow was a big, gnarled dogwood tree, sitting alone on a little rise with wild roses and black-eyed Susans all around it. I wandered over, dropping the suitcase under the tree and sitting on it. The place was familiar. Like home, in a way that I hadn't known a place so wild and strange even could be.

"I know this tree," I said, looking up into its branches.

Fisher stopped kicking around in the moss and came across the grass to me. "I thought you'd never been down here."

"No, I know. But in the cellar, I wasn't always just . . . myself. I had a lot of dreams. Sometimes they seemed almost close to true. And this tree, I've seen it. In the dream, though, the flowers were all the wrong colors."

He studied me, almost like he was waiting for something. When I watched him back for too long, though, he looked away.

"It's nice here," I said. "How come no one in town ever wants to come down?"

He didn't answer right away, just stood over me in the shade of the dogwood tree. He was leaning against its trunk with his hand up, so that his fingers were hidden in the leaves. "Some people do. The Beekmans always did, and I'm pretty sure Greg Heintz makes his whole living off selling sticks and rocks and anything else he can carry out. Not a lot of people would admit it, but more than a few will keep a hollow charm for luck or protection. More than you'd think, for sure."

I sat with my back against the tree trunk, looking around the clearing. "And you don't worry about the fiends?"

For the first time since we'd come down the side of the pasture, Fisher smiled a true, honest smile.

He held up the arm he'd cut on the dove cage the other night. "Do I look like someone who worries about much? Anyway, they're supposed to be pretty private. They keep to themselves unless you have a question or a problem. And even then, you have to bring them stuff."

"Like presents?"

"Blood is what *I've* heard, and a steel spoon for them to drink it."

I wrinkled my nose. "That's disgusting. Have you ever seen one?"

"Naw," he said, but he said it with a shrug, like seeing a fiend would be no big deal. "I bet they're not as scary as people think, though. Nothing else down here really is."

He ran his hand through the leaves above us, almost like he was petting them. And that was when the miracle happened, like the miracle of how his skin had closed up.

Like nothing I'd ever seen. When he touched the branch, flowers began to sprout from it. One minute, there weren't even buds. The next, the tree was teeming with them, starting at the place where his hand rested and spreading out along the branches, sweet-smelling and creamy pink.

In that moment, I understood that everything Shiny had told me about Fisher and everything I had guessed was the absolute truth. It wasn't only people out in the Willows who came from old families. Who had pure craft running in their blood.

He smiled at me, but it was a slow, uneasy smile, like I might be shocked at him, or frightened. Like I might run away.

I stared up at the impossible clusters of flowers. They looked like any other dogwood flowers that might grow around any other stream. I reached up to feel the rough, flaky texture of the bark, but my touch didn't do anything. I squeezed a petal, and it was soft and smooth, turning to paste between my fingers.

I considered him, trying to make sense of what he'd just shown me. "Did you *make* this place?"

He nodded, then shook his head. "It's not like that. It's more like it listens to me."

When he said it, his eyes got faraway, and he looked past me, like he was looking for something to make the explanation easier.

His bottom lip was very soft, and suddenly, I wanted to touch his face. But when I raised my hand, he ducked and turned away. I thought I had never seen anyone look so wholly ashamed over something so amazing.

The air in the meadow was clear and there was no colored halo around him, but it didn't matter. Now that we were in the hollow, I caught glimpses of him everywhere—doubt and frustration and shyness—when out in the everyday world, his moods were hidden, like he was keeping himself behind a wall.

The black-eyed Susans around his feet were leaning, drooping sadly against his legs. They had a look about them like they were hanging their heads.

"It's pretty," I said. "You should make nice things more."

Fisher leaned closer, watching me in a careful, sidelong way. "You're not surprised? Or scared?"

I twirled a picked flower between my fingers. "No, not much."

The sky brightened and Fisher reached for one of the dogwood branches, pulling it down close to his face. He blew gently, making the petals scatter. They floated away from us, white against the tremendous blue of the sky. I waited for them to lose their balance and fall back down on our heads, but instead, they simply floated higher, higher until they were gone.

"Now you're just showing off," I said, but I couldn't help smiling at the way grass rippled merrily around us.

Fisher shrugged. "It's how things work for me down here. I mean, it's not even a real trick—just, everything about me is stronger."

"It must be nice, having that kind of power."

"Can't you do anything?"

I stepped away from the tree and tried to look fierce. It

was hard though. My mouth kept wanting to laugh. "I can do a *lot* of things. I'm not helpless."

"That's not what I meant. Like, if somebody cut you, though, what would happen? Are you like me, where you'd heal up?"

"No, I'd still bleed."

"So can you do any sort of charms or tricks, or read the future in a bowl of milk or anything? Like, there used to be these guys out in the hills—the Farriers—and they could melt just about anything by touching it with their hands. Or, even your cousin is crazy tough. At the bonfire a few years ago, I saw her pick up a stray log and chuck it back in like it was nothing."

I sat back down on the suitcase and pulled my knees up, looking over the meadow, thinking about all the things there were to figure out—locks and clocks and engines. The three-speed gearbox in the Ranger, and the sprawling hallways of Myloria's house.

"I can understand how things work inside. And sometimes I see the colors around—" I stopped though, because I was starting to feel like maybe the light I saw around him was something private. I was starting to wonder if maybe it wasn't the kind of thing meant to be seen at all.

So I started over, even though my mother had warned all my life never to tell lies. "I see colors around people, how they look inside when something worries them, or when they're upset or happy."

The look Fisher gave me was long and lazy and amused. He had me sort of trapped under the tree, standing over me with his feet planted on either side of the suitcase, but I didn't really mind.

He smiled, leaning closer. "Colors like this?"

His voice was husky. Above us, the dogwood flowers were changing color, going from white to deep cherry-red, so dark it was almost purple. Bruised. It was a red I'd never seen blooming on any tree I could remember. A red so impossible it nearly matched my hair.

"How did you find me, really?" I said. "I saw the cellar door and it was covered over."

"I heard you."

I shook my head. "I think you knew before that, though. Before I ever turned the music box key on that bear, you knew you were going to find something."

"I heard a sound," he said again. "That's what I'm trying to tell you. Quiet and steady and just *there*. I think I heard you breathing."

"That's impossible."

He looked away, shaking his head. "Whatever. You don't have to believe me, but I'm telling you the truth."

And I could see from the liveliness of the hollow that he was. It was in the changing shapes of clouds and the bright, restless jewelweed springing up around his boots.

"Do you know about the reckoning?" I said, watching his face.

"Everyone knows about the reckoning. What's to know?"

"Nothing, just that I think it's why I was down there. Rae Dalton said that someone went to a lot of trouble to keep me shut up, like maybe they thought getting rid of me would save the town. I guess it even did."

Fisher looked at me like I had lost my mind. "You think you being buried in a cellar is what saved the town?"

"I don't know. But something changed. Shiny told me how it was—like the whole hollow just came out into the world. How do you stop something like that? You can't. But still, after I was put away, everything was fine." My voice sounded tired, suddenly.

Fisher wasn't smiling at all anymore. His face was blank, but there was something in his eyes that I didn't know the name of. I kept thinking of the wrong ones, shame or fear or secrets, but it was more like all of those at once.

"What's wrong?" I said.

But he didn't answer. He was looking past me, and whatever he was looking at had made his eyes go helpless and vacant.

Then I saw it too. The grass was dying, going yellow and brittle at my feet.

"What's happening?" I said, and my rusty voice made everything seem a lot more dangerous. "Are the fiends coming?"

"You have to get out of here," he whispered. "The hollow's acting up."

"What does that mean, acting up?"

"It means get out of here if you don't want to be food for creatures and hell dogs! Just go!"

I'd meant to say more—to ask how the place had changed so fast, why his hands were shaking—but I was cut off by a long, grating howl, like the sound a flywheel on a tractor made when it spun too hard and too hot, dry and shrill and furious. The sound echoed through the clearing, racing up my spine and shivering in my teeth.

"God*damn* it." Fisher grabbed me by the arm, yanking me up and pulling me along behind him in the direction of the shallow little stream and the bluff.

The suitcase swung crazily in my hand, slamming into my legs, and his fingers dug into my skin. I tried to squirm loose but he just moved his hand to my wrist, squeezing hard.

"Ow! Let—*go*!" I jerked out of his hand.

I thought he'd try to grab me again, but another howl ripped through the trees.

"*Go.*" He raked his arm in the direction of the bluff and the path back up to the pasture. "Run! Run that way and don't stop till you get back out into the Willows!"

"What are you going to do?"

"I'm going to make sure nothing follows you."

He turned once in a slow circle, then began to sprint all out for the dogwood tree. All the pretty red flowers had turned black, and as soon as he reached the tree, they crumbled and fell, getting lost in the grass. He grabbed hold of a branch and broke it off.

The sun seemed brighter suddenly, like a cloud had been lifted off the world. The howl rose out of the woods, closer and more ferocious. The ground was mushy, seeping into my shoes, and I knew I should run, but the way home felt all wrong and I hesitated.

Something was happening in the air around me and suddenly, I was scared. Everything smelled sweet and chemical, and underneath that, rotten. I stopped and looked back.

Fisher stood in the middle of the clearing, with the dogwood tree behind him. He swung the branch, testing it with both hands like someone holding a baseball bat.

When the first dark creature came slinking out into the sunlight, I knew that I should run—my head knew it and my feet knew it, but something in my chest said stay, and it was stronger than everything else. I stood at edge of the meadow, waiting, wanting to make sure that I wasn't leaving Fisher to be savaged.

They crept across the grass in a pack, moving low to the ground. The one at the front glared hungrily, ears pressed flat, lips drawn back from its teeth. It was the size of a beagle, or maybe a fox, sly and slinky and nasty. The rest of it was trickier to make out, even when it moved out of the shade and into the clearing.

The brighter the sun shone, the harder it was to see the shape of it. Stories of hell dogs never really told you what they looked like and now I understood why. The thing was so black that it seemed to be made of the shadows, or else of some soft, evil goo that changed and ran and melted like wax.

I stood holding tight to the handle of the suitcase, watching as they closed on Fisher.

His head was up and his shoulders back, and he gripped the branch like he was waiting, daring them to come on and do something. The longer he stared at the dog, the more solid it got, with a long, crooked muzzle and eyes that glowed a vicious, itchy red, flaring and pulsing so they seemed to burn like fire. Then, with no warning at all, it sprang, shoulders bunched and jaws wide.

When Fisher moved, it was quick and fearless. The branch arced high. Then came the impact, proof that the dark, oily creature was solid and real. When its back broke, the sound was dull and then sharp—thump of body, crack of bone.

It fell in the grass, crumpled and stinking. The others stepped over it like it was nothing, making a ragged circle around Fisher. He swore and then put down the second one, nearly spinning its head around.

When he showed his teeth, it was a smile that made him seem perfectly unholy. For the first time, he looked less like some in-town redneck with a flashy car and more like the descendent of whatever dark thing had graced his family with its old, fiendish blood.

I stood in the tangled weeds as he beat back the hell dogs. He was laying about himself with the branch, driving them back.

And then, he wasn't.

As many as he put down, more were sneaking out of the trees, closing in. They swarmed him as fast as he could shake them off, ripping at his clothes and his skin, cutting long gashes down his back. He didn't flinch or cry out, but *I* wanted to. I watched in a kind of slow horror as they clambered over him. In another second, they would bear him to the ground and tear him up if I didn't do something to stop it.

Then, in a fast, jarring flash, it was like every leaf and twig and blade of grass became very clear.

I swung the suitcase up by the handle. For an instant, it seemed to hang in front of me, taking up space, all corners and edges, flat planes of dusty leather. I could sense the shape of it but didn't look away from where Fisher stood, surrounded by snarling dogs, red soaking through his shirt.

Time seemed weirdly stretched, and I let the suitcase go. In the second that it hung there, I moved my hands to the corners and popped the clasps. The lid swung up and as the case fell, I caught it by the handle, dropping to my knees, the weight of it half-spinning me around.

All the clothes seemed to fly away, scattering over the grass. The dinosaur bed sheet trailed out like a flag, flapping wildly in the sunlight. I was already digging through the tangled mess to the bottom, where the tools lay, cold and sharp and waiting.

The ground around me was littered with dresses and underwear and with the bodies of the hell dogs, oozing their stinking blood.

In just a few minutes, Fisher had managed to deal with most of them, but he was staggering now, bleeding heavily down one arm. The two that were left bared their teeth and crept toward him.

He laid one out with a kick to the face, then slammed the branch down on the back of its head. Its skin broke and the black muck of its insides splattered over everything.

The last one was sly, though. It moved behind him and then, in one tightly coiled leap, went clawing up his back and over his shoulder, peeling his T-shirt open in bloody ribbons.

He yelled, but it was an odd, choked sound, like it had been jerked out of him, and then he was quiet. He thrashed and twisted, reaching around with his good hand, trying to scrape the hell dog off his back. It bit at him, tearing his shoulder in an awful, ugly way that had everything to do with pain. It sank its teeth into his arm and I began to run.

In a flash of double vision, I saw us in my head—laid out across the clearing like dropped toys. Fisher, with the branch in his hands, the blood on his back. The hell dog, slashing and clawing at his skin, laying him open.

I saw a girl with tangled red hair and a pair of wet, sloppy shoes, and in her hand, there was a crosshead screwdriver. The grass was poison-green. The woods around us were black. All the other colors were so bright they seemed to run together.

I had a sudden, sick understanding of the animal's body, seeing it, inside it. Its dark, awful bones, the heartbeat pulsing through it, slick and thick and throbbing.

When I stabbed it in the neck, blood jetted out, not red, but a black, slippery mess, splashing my arms and the front of my dress. It whipped around, snapping at my hand. Its eyes were wild and stupid and Fisher's blood was all over its teeth.

My next swing was aimed at its eye socket and I buried

the screwdriver to the handle. I yanked it back out and black ooze gushed over my hands.

The dog went limp and landed on the grass. Its legs were still twitching, but its sides didn't rise and fall, and its black stinking blood was all over everything.

Fisher stood in the middle of the clearing, breathing in huge gasps. He took two steps toward the naked dogwood tree, then sank to his knees, holding his shoulder with his good hand.

Blood was springing up all over his back, soaking through his shirt, running in bright streams from a gash in his arm. I dropped the screwdriver and crouched next to him. His eyes were closed and he'd begun to shake all over.

"Okay," I said. "Okay, you're okay. Hold still, I'm going to open your shirt so I can look."

I ran back across the meadow and fumbled around in the suitcase for some kind of garden shears or clippers. There was a rusty pair of sewing scissors, and I grabbed them and ran back to Fisher, holding the scissors in my fist like a knife.

I scrubbed at my hands, trying to wipe them clean on the dying grass, then slit his T-shirt up the back. I peeled it off him, revealing the full shape of the tattoo I'd seen the other day. It was the outline of a tower, black and crooked, traveling the length of his spine. Blood ran from a roadmap of cuts, covering the ink. One whole side of his body was smeared with a sticky layer of blood and black poison.

It smelled bad, and I squinted against the fumes that were

rising in hot clouds, burning my eyes. His skin was bruising as I watched, turning purple in huge smudges that feathered out over his back.

"You aren't healing." I said. "Why aren't you healing?"

He coughed, pressing a hand to his mouth, shaking his head, but didn't answer. He was gasping into his cupped hand like it was hard to breathe.

I cut up the bed sheet, rolling the fabric into pads, winding strips around his ribs and arm, and doing double bandages where the blood ran the fastest. My hands were jittering and the smell made me want to hold my breath.

"Do you think you need a doctor?" I said, knotting the sheet in place.

He shook his head, keeping his eyes closed.

"Maybe you don't know this, but you're bleeding a *lot*. I think you need to go to the hospital."

"No." His lips were chalky blue and his face looked gray in the weird, quiet light. "I just need to get home."

THE WAY BACK
CHAPTER ELEVEN

I dropped to my hands and knees in the yellowing grass, picking up my clothes. They were all over the ground and I shoved them into the suitcase.

Fisher was still on his knees, slumped sideways against the dogwood tree. His eyes were closed and he was holding his arm against his chest, breathing in long, harsh gasps. "Could you hurry up?"

His voice was tight and there was a numb, reasonable part of me that understood I was acting like a fool. That I didn't need to be fussing with the suitcase. That I was just wasting time. I slammed it shut and hauled it over to him.

He was trying to stand and mostly failing, but when I held out my hand, he waved me off, struggling up from the ground and using the tree to steady himself.

When he touched the trunk, though, the whole side of it went black and soft under his hand. A layer of rot was spreading from his fingers, crawling up into the branches, and I darted forward and yanked his arm away.

"Stop—you're killing it!"

For one second, his face was awful as he looked at what

he'd done. Then, like a board being wiped clean, his expression went blank and he only stood there, swaying a little in the shadow of the tree.

"Here," I said, and came in close enough that he had no choice but to let me help.

I half-expected that when he leaned his weight on me, his touch might send me to rot and ruin too, but it only left me breathless and a little off-balance.

With my help, Fisher stumbled across the meadow, toward the densest part of the thicket.

"That's not the way we came," I said, but he just kept on going.

I said it again, louder. "That's not the right way. The car's back in the Willows."

He shook his head, still staggering in the direction of the trees. "Doesn't matter now. This is shorter."

So I tightened my hold on the suitcase and let him lead me into the woods.

The whole hollow seemed to be coming undone around us. The grass was dying back along the ground, and it was getting dark much too fast. The blood had dried to a sticky mess all down Fisher's arm and soaked through the torn sheets. Along his spine, the tower stood out in a halo of bruises.

At first, it seemed like there was no path to follow. I didn't know how we'd ever find our way out. The hollow, which was only a narrow little gully from the top of the bluff, seemed to have grown to the size of a country, no way to know how to get through, or even where the edge of the forest was. It was unnerving that a space could be so huge, when from the outside, it was just an overgrown gouge between two cow pastures.

The deeper we went, the louder the woods got, creaking and groaning around us, sending leaves and broken twigs raining on our heads. The trees tossed and shook, swaying in gusty bursts, but there was no wind, and no storm clouds to explain the black sky. Every snap and rustle sounded like footsteps creeping after us through the woods, and I held the screwdriver tight, ready for the second those hungry red eyes came glowing up at us out of the shadows.

Suddenly, there was the sound of something crashing through the treetops, and the first branch hit the ground. The woods were coming down around us, limbs breaking like gunshots.

There was chaos overhead and Fisher grabbed me around the waist with his good arm, swinging us both out of the path and into the tall grass. We landed in a tangle, deep in the weeds. Over us, deadfall branches rained down, hitting the ground with huge thumps, sending up grass and mud.

We lay there as the splintered trees landed all around. My heart was beating so hard it hurt my bones, and I could feel the rise and fall of Fisher's chest. He was coughing, taking short, painful breaths. His whole body was shaking.

Then, as fast as it had started, it was over.

I hauled myself off of him and knelt in the weeds, feeling around for the suitcase handle, for anything to hold on to.

Fisher was struggling onto his hands and knees and swearing in a steady stream. He stumbled up and I followed him, kicking a path through the underbrush.

He was a few feet ahead, using his good hand to steady himself and striking for a place where the ground began to slope up. Suddenly he stopped, crouching against the bleached trunk of a fallen tree like he was waiting for something.

I crouched next to him, staring into the shadows between the trees. "What's wrong?"

In the dense thicket of the hollow, things were rustling. The light was so strange and dark it was almost blue, and I huddled there, listening to the sounds around us. My heart beat faster and I wondered if we were about to be food for some new ugliness, some other creature with long, dripping teeth.

And then, I saw the orange glow of flames. It moved through the trees in a ghostly rush and at the center, a woman, white as a snowdrop and wound in a ragged sheet, was running toward us through the woods at an all-out sprint.

Her arms were straight out from her sides like wings, the sheet flapping around her. She loomed down the slope at us, and then I saw her face, and I couldn't help it—I screamed. The woman only careened toward us, screaming back, a long nightmare screech that echoed through the woods. Her hands fluttered wildly and her eyes were two black, ragged holes. Her mouth was a burning oval of light, like looking into the glow of a basement furnace.

Then she was down the hill and past us, burning a trail like a white-hot comet through the trees. The woods went dark again and I crouched in the shadow of the beech tree with my heart beating hard and wild in my ears.

Fisher was hunched over by the turned-up roots of the fallen tree, leaning against it.

"Did you see that?" I whispered, pointing into the darkness. "What was that?"

"A fiend," he said, coughing a little, clearing his throat. "We just saw a fiend. Best thank Jesus she wasn't interested in us, and hope we don't see another."

The way he said it made my skin go cold. "How many are there?"

He shook his head. "No one really knows. They're always moving. The stories say they walk in and out of the world through the hollow the way a normal person would go through a door."

When he straightened, I slipped my arm under his on his good side and helped him toward the bluff.

I was half holding him up, leading him through the trees, when I saw her.

She was standing in the shade by a shallow little runnel of the creek, and at first, I thought she was a girl. Then she turned, and I saw her hands. They were long and gnarled, like the hands of the woman in my grandmother's painting of Salome. Her teeth were small, sharp, and animal.

She had on a gray dress with a wide lace collar and a square neck. The skirt hung wet around the bottom, making

147

the cotton a darker shade that faded pale halfway up her legs.

Her eyes were gray too, but a gray that seemed to bleed out into the white part, ragged around the edge like torn paper. The way she looked at me froze me to the bone.

"You don't belong here," she said.

"No," I said. "But we don't mean any trouble. We're trying to leave."

She came closer, with her head cocked to one side, leaving a row of tracks in the mud that looked web-footed. I tightened my hand around the screwdriver.

"Maybe so," she said. "But I'd wager this one causes trouble wherever he goes. He's got this whole place in an uproar and enough vigor in him to just about tear down the world."

I glanced at Fisher. His breathing was uneven, and when he looked up, his face was dirty-pale, like an old sheet. When he moved closer to me, he left a wobbly trail of blood sprinkled across the rocks. Vigor seemed like the last thing he had going for him.

The fiend watched, her eyes moving over his torn shoulder, her tongue darting to touch the corner of her mouth as the blood ran down his arm. "Give me some of that good red, and I'll tell you a fortune."

"I don't want a fortune," I whispered, suddenly so scared that she would tell me I was the thing that Shiny had said—the reason behind the reckoning—and then everything I was deathly afraid of would be true. It was one thing to fear and think and turn it over in my mind. It would be another to hear the words from someone else's lips.

As soon as I said it, the fiend's eyes went dark as bad dreams. "You called me out of the black like a genie out from someone's lamp, and now you don't want to know your fate?"

I shook my head. "We didn't call you."

She smiled a jagged, hungry smile. "Darlin', you've got enough wise old blood in you to call every fiend for a hundred miles. And they'll be here too in a minute clamoring to tell you your ending, so if it's someone else you're wanting, by all means wait. Otherwise, pay the charge, hear your fate, and I'll be on my way."

Next to me, Fisher cleared his throat. He was breathing in long gasps. "Whatever. Just do *whatever* she says so she'll leave us alone and we can get out of here."

The fiend turned her strange, blurry gaze on Fisher. "Give me some of that good red," she said again. "I'll tell you what you need to know."

Without a word, he reached over and took the screwdriver from me, smearing his bloody hand on the bit end. He held it out and the fiend took it from him. Then, with a smile as hungry as an alligator's, she licked the blood off.

Her tongue was long and pale, wrapping around the steel like a snake. She sucked her bottom lip and handed the screwdriver back to me.

"You're old-family wrong," she said to Fisher. "Crooked as they come, but that's no secret. I don't imagine any of the good folks up there in town ever wondered too hard or too close about what you were. I imagine they just let you be. But *you're* not one to let things be. You've got a whole mess of questions in you, and the answers have been slow in coming."

As far as fortunes went, it was county fair vague, but the way Fisher stared at her, she might has well have just looked straight into the bottom of his soul.

"Say your question," she said. "I know you want to."

He pressed his hand against his torn shoulder and said hoarsely, "Where is it I belong? Is it like Isola says, and I belong down here with you?"

His voice was so raw when he asked it that I wanted to drop my eyes, but the fiend only smiled, twitching her shoulder like the prettiest girl at a party.

"The look of you right now, I'd say you'd be a fool to want that." Her smile dimpled and then got wider. "I've known a man to give himself to the hollow from time to time. Crooked people come down here when they lose all reason and their blood gets the best of them. I've known them to go back to the land when they've got no place else that wants them. But that way's not for you."

I watched Fisher's face. I'd thought he might be grateful or relieved, but he just nodded, like a part of him had been hoping something else.

With sly, narrowed eyes, the fiend turned on me, tipping her head to the side. "And what about you, chickadee?"

"I don't want my fortune told," I said again, backing

away with the screwdriver held against my chest. The way she had seen so deeply into Fisher frightened me. "I don't want you to drink my blood."

She gave a stiff little shrug. "Then how about a piece of advice?"

I wasn't sure advice was any better, but Fisher had said to do what we had to do to get out of the hollow, so I nodded.

"It doesn't matter what you call yourself," the fiend said, waving a gnarled hand. "Any of these DeVores or DeWitts or Bedevils—some borrowed name your mama got somewhere, from whatever man she picked to be your daddy—I know a Blackwood when I see one. But not every crooked child is so obvious as *you* all. Take that Dalton girl. She's a clever one, and good at hiding her craft when she ain't using it."

"What has Rae got to do with any of this?"

"Just that there's five of you creatures up there in town now. Knocking around with craft in your blood and your bones. Five kinds of wrong, and that's one wrong thing for every point on the reckoning star."

"That's not advice," I said, trying to sound braver than I felt. "That might be a riddle, but it's not advice."

Beside me, Fisher made a groaning noise, but the fiend seemed to consider this. She stood in the shadows, under the canopy of leaves, and her hair looked very white.

"I know you think you're the one to start up this engine, baby," she said. "But you didn't do anything wrong. It's the light from the hollow—it's coming for you, leaking out slow right now, but it won't stay slow forever, so we got to do something. See to your blood, and I'll see to mine, don't you worry. Just see to your craft, keep it low when you can, and mind that reckoning star."

Then she turned, stepping down through the shallow water, into the woods, and out of sight.

I was of half a mind to run after her and demand that she be straight with me and stop talking in riddles, but Fisher was shivering in the dark spot under the trees, nearly colorless. I got his arm around my shoulders and we started up the hill.

❆　　❆　　❆

We made our way through the thicket, fighting through the brush until with no warning, we spilled out of the trees into a clearing that was all tall grass and fresh air and open sky.

We'd gone all the way through the dark, endless woods and come out into the bottom of Harlan Beekman's north pasture.

The black sky of the hollow had rolled back to a dusky blue, clear as a jewel and waiting for stars. The larks had all stopped singing and the night birds hadn't started yet. Everything was desperately quiet.

"How did it get so late?" I whispered, looking around the darkening pasture.

Fisher shook his head. "The hollow isn't like other places. It's got its own clock, and sometimes it eats time."

Now that we were out in the regular world, I could see the colors again, shining around him. A haze of pain glowed red, bright as fire and worse when I closed my eyes.

"Fisher?" I took a step toward him. "Can I do something?"

He kept his face away from me. All I could make out was the paleness of his skin, the dark, shaggy mess of his hair. I blinked and saw the bright shape of him against my eyelids, throbbing with a dull, orange heat. The pain looked electrical, all razor jags of red and black, loud and sharp and ugly.

He was hurting bad, but I didn't know how to stop it or what to do.

Once when I was little, we'd had a redbone dog who'd stepped on a piece of glass and sliced the bottom of her foot. My mama had boiled a needle and sewn it up, but the cut got infected anyway, and when I went to touch it, the skin of our dog's foot had been hot and tight. She'd tried to bite me, even though she'd known me since I was a baby. My mama told me that when things were hurting, sometimes it made them wild.

It seemed to me now that this was true of Fisher, that he might be wild. More wild than he was on a daily basis, anyway. He leaned forward again, holding his arm against his chest, breathing in long, trembling gasps.

When I reached for him, he stepped back like I'd slapped him, stumbling over his own feet.

"Please—" My voice sounded shaky and high-pitched. "Please, you're not okay. Just let me *help* you."

"Help with what?" he whispered, keeping his face turned away. "How are you going to help?"

I hugged myself, trying to sound sensible and like I had some sort of command over the situation. "Well you can't take care of yourself. You can barely walk."

153

He straightened, still holding his arm against his chest. "I'm cool, just dizzy for a second. Come on. I need to get home, mop up."

He hauled himself over the fence without hesitating, and I had an idea that maybe I'd been wrong, that maybe he didn't need a doctor, didn't need my help or anything at all. Then he staggered and went pitching face-first into the road.

I chucked the suitcase down in the weeds and scrambled over after him. He was on his hands and knees, making a hoarse, moaning noise by the time I got there.

"Are you okay?" When I said it, I didn't sound like myself—not even like my new self with the rough, scratchy voice. The words were thin and shrill. I sounded scared.

Every time I blinked, I saw the shape of him printed inside my eyelids, covered in twists of green and black squirming through a red fog.

This time, he bowed his head and let me reach for him. When I slipped myself under his good arm, he slumped against me, leaning what felt like his whole giant weight on my shoulder. For a second, I thought we were both going to lose our balance and fall into the road or the ditch, but I held him up, trying not to let the curve of my arm touch the places on his back where he was torn up the worst. The poisonous smell of the hell dogs burned my nose, but I didn't lean away.

I left the suitcase where it lay, half-hidden in the pasture.

The walk into town took a long time—the kind of time where it's hard to know how much is passing, because every step felt like an hour, and I knew without him ever saying so that it hurt just to keep breathing.

Broom Street, where he lived, was as wide as a river, lined with oaks and sycamore trees. The pavement was less worn than the roads lower down, and the houses were nicer than anywhere else.

At the very end of it, a white house rose out of the dark, three stories tall and situated atop a little hill. It was surrounded by slippery elms and giant oaks, and the slopes of the roof were wickedly steep. It looked grand, but uneasy— the kind of house where a witch would live.

As I stepped onto the paving-stone path that led to the porch, we were met by the frantic, tooth-jarring sound of dogs baying. Then a whole pack of them came pouring around the side of the house

"Get back," Fisher muttered. "Get away."

The dogs yelped and whined, but when he clucked his tongue at them, they all ducked their heads and slunk back toward the porch.

We stumbled up into his yard with our arms around each other and our legs shaking. The whole space around the front door was covered in china rabbits and angels, flocks of tin chickens and gnomes that sat around the front walk like a bunch of fairy-tale creatures.

On the porch, I put my hand on Fisher's arm and peered up at him, trying to get a look at his face. In the yellow splash of the porch light, his skin was chalky, and then he jerked away, turning so I couldn't see his eyes.

"I'm coming in with you," I said, reaching around him for the door.

"No." He moved to cut me off, keeping his back to me. "I'm fine. Just go home."

I stood on the porch and waited to find out if he meant it. Or more likely, if he'd fall or faint or stumble. All I knew was that if the same drawn, stoic look had been on my face, it would have meant that I was scared. That I was hopeless and hurt and didn't want to be alone. The way Fisher wore it, though, he made it seem like nothing.

"You can*not* come in," he said again. "There's nothing you can do to help, and if my grandma sees you, she will lose her mind."

Then he went inside and shut the door.

PART III
BREATH

DIRT MAGIC
CHAPTER TWELVE

Any other place, any other night, I might have let it go—sat down to wait, or just gone home. Fisher was hurt too badly to leave him, though, no matter what he said, and I stood on the lawn under the oak trees, trying to know what to do.

Overhead, the sky was black. The stars were hazy, a million miles off, and the sounds of night birds were low and mournful, making my skin crawl.

All around me in the bushes, things were rustling. I stood hugging myself, gripped by a chilly conviction that the hell dogs or the burning woman or some other wicked, awful creature from the hollow had gotten out and followed us into the world.

After so long it seemed like forever, a light came on at the top of the house. I stood hugging my elbows, looking up at that bright yellow square. All the other windows were dark.

I considered climbing the porch, knocking on the door, and asking his grandmother to let me see him. Then I remembered the pencil-drawn face we'd come across out in the woods, with its stone-black eyes and its ruinous mouth. If Isola in real life was half as grim as in the drawing, she might come down to see who was rude enough to call at this hour, but she was not going to be likely to let me in.

No, the only thing left to me was that one little window and that one burning light. I could feel him there, his nearness trembling in the air around me. He was in that attic room, with the window open and the curtains back, the lamp balanced on the sill like a signal flame.

I cupped my hands to my mouth and called up as softly as I could, "Fisher?" There was no answer and I called louder. "Fisher, are you awake?"

I waited with my head cocked, listening, more and more agitated when no one called back.

"*Fisher!*" I whispered, dropping to my hands and knees and feeling around in the dirt for something to throw.

I was prying a cherry-sized rock out of the ground under the oak trees when the dogs came pouring around the corner of the house again. I froze on my hands and knees and held as still as I could, trying not to do anything that might make them start barking. They surged around me, snuffling and whining against my face.

"Shh." I waved a hand at them, but they just wriggled and bounced at me, hanging their heads and grinning nervously. "Shh, get away!"

They didn't bay or bark, but their whimpers were sharp, and they pressed close to me, snuffling into my hair. I tried to make myself smaller, certain that at any moment, Fisher's grandma was going to hear the commotion and come out to find me crouching in the yard.

Finally, whispering all the worst words I knew, I pushed them away and got to my feet, retreating over to one of the big oaks.

I'd always been able to see in sharpened ways—hidden animals and dropped buttons and all the things that other people missed. My mother had called it second sight, but I thought now that maybe it was only first sight, but with better vision.

Since the moment I'd gotten out of the cellar, though, there was no denying that it was getting stronger. Now the second face of the world was everywhere, in the nervous wriggling of Fisher's dogs and the sap that ran like blood inside the trees. Leaves were moving in tiny shivers, rustling in the air, and for the first time, I had an inkling of what my mama must have always known. The power of the dirt was not in bewitching the world or forcing things to grow, but just in reading the truth of living things and being able to give them what they needed. Everything in the yard seemed to be calling for Fisher.

I stood against the trunk of the oak with my arms wrapped around it. The very bark seemed to hum. Then I boosted myself up and began to climb.

At the top of the tree, a branch ran along the edge of the roof and I stepped out over the rain gutter and onto the steep pitch of the shingles. I crawled across to the window and looked into a long attic room.

Fisher's bed was tucked under the slant of the ceiling. He

lay on his side, on top of the bedclothes, with his face turned toward the wall.

The state of his back was terrible in the lamplight. The yellow glow made his bruised skin look ten times worse, and for a second, I just sat on the roof in the shadow of the tree, staring at how the blood had soaked through the makeshift bandages and was dripping onto the blankets.

"Hey." I tapped the screen. "Fisher."

He didn't move.

I tried to pry the screen out of the frame but couldn't get my fingers in the gap. He was lying so still that it scared me, and I fumbled in my pocket for the screwdriver. The end of it was dirty from everything that had happened down in the hollow, and not sharp, but I stabbed it through the screen, ripping a jagged hole all the way down.

Then I peeled back the edges and slid in headfirst, hitting the floor with a thunk. My foot got caught in the ruined screen and I landed hard on the rug, taking the lamp with me. It rolled wildly, so that the light danced over the walls and the peaked ceiling.

On the bed, Fisher raised himself onto his elbows and stared dimly around the room. When he saw me sprawled on my stomach with my feet hanging out the window, his eyes cleared and he tried to stand, but only succeeded in falling out of bed. The thump he made was teeth rattling and he hit the rug with most of his weight on his elbows, rolling sideways. When his shoulder touched the floorboards, he made a short, painful noise.

With a little cry, I yanked my feet in through the window, taking half the screen with me, and scrambled across the floor, waving him to stay still. "No, no, no, stay there, stay there."

But he was already trying to get up. He pushed himself onto his knees, then lost his balance and fell against the bed frame. With a mighty effort, I dragged him up, supporting his dead weight with my arms around his chest. As soon as I touched him, I could feel the heat coming off his body, burning through my shirt. The smell of the hell dogs was all over everything.

I held my breath and wrestled him back into bed. He hit the mattress with a thump and a low, painful sound that caught in his throat. I knelt beside him and leaned over.

He was sweating, his skin shining and waxy white. The fallen lamp threw oblong rings of light and shadow on the ceiling. His hair stuck to his forehead and the pillowcase was damp.

He rolled his head to look at me and blinked like he was trying to focus. "Shit," he said thickly. "Get out."

"You are not in charge of this anymore," I said, and I meant every word. "You told me you were okay, and it's not true, so now I'm in charge, because otherwise, I'm scared you might die."

Saying it seemed worse than thinking it. I had soaked up my mother's deep abiding belief that if you said a thing, it might come true, and as soon as it was out, I wanted to take it back.

Fisher just shook his head, squinting at me in the lamplight. "I mean it. You have to leave before she hears you."

"Who?" I said, leaning closer.

"Who do you think? That harpy, Isola."

"Your grandmother? You're talking that way about your *grandmother*?"

"That doesn't stop her from being a raging bitch." He pushed himself up on his elbow and looking blearily around the room. "You wrecked my screen."

"I know—I'm sorry." I touched his shoulder, trying to push him back onto the mattress. His skin was dangerously hot. "I'll find a way to fix it later, but for right now, just lie back down."

Fisher winced and lay back, easing himself onto his good shoulder. There was a muscle in his jaw that wouldn't quit fluttering. While the rest of his face might have passed for furious, that muscle twitched and shuddered, like he was trying not to let me see how much the whole thing hurt.

I sat with my back against the side of the bed and hugged my knees, looking around his room.

From the outside, the Fisher house looked big and clean, but Fisher's bedroom was a cramped affair, all old spindle furniture and yellowing wallpaper and floorboards that needed a coat of varnish. It was a long, slope-ceilinged room, with two little gable windows and a plank floor with an old Persian rug laid out in the middle.

On the bed, he made a low groaning noise and I pushed myself up from the floor and knelt over him again. He lay staring at the wall, an empty, far-off look on his face, like he was trying to make something come clear, but I could see that his eyes had already slid out of focus.

He looked miserable, and I wondered if he didn't know that I was looking or if he was just too hurt to care anymore. The way he dug his teeth into his lip made me feel wrong for watching him and so I busied myself with undoing the ruined bandages.

"This is going to hurt," I said to him as I worked at the knots. I meant it to sound brave, but my hands were shaking. "You might want to get ready."

He jerked away, looking back over his shoulder at me. "What are you doing?"

"I'm going to look at the damage. Now hold still."

I began to pick apart the strips of torn sheet. They were stuck with blood and with the black mess from the hell dogs' teeth. The skin underneath was raw and pitted, like he'd been splashed with frying oil or water hot enough to burn, but when the poison touched my own hands—same as when it had jetted all over my arms from the hell dog's punctured neck—nothing happened. It didn't hurt at all.

Fisher sucked in his breath, but held still as I peeled back the cloth.

"Goddamn," he whispered. His voice sounded so dry and cracked I could barely hear it.

All down his back, the cuts lay open like mouths, pale at the edges and bright, burning red in the center. Around them, the tarry poison was like nothing I'd ever seen, oozing like a living thing, eating away at his skin. Every time one of the gashes tried to knit itself closed, the poison foamed up and the wounds broke open again. The tattoo of the tower looked violently black against his skin.

"Okay." I said it under my breath like I was talking to myself, and stared down at his savaged back. "Okay."

I swallowed hard and closed my eyes, and when I did, I could see what was working on him, like I was seeing the very nature of his blood. His body wanted to heal, to stitch itself back together, but the poison was in him, black as oil, chewing up everything. When I leaned close, I could hear the sound of his heart sucking it through his veins. If there was any hope of his getting better, it would have to come out.

With a fear so big I could hardly breathe, I laid my hands against his back and held them there, feeling the heat shining off him. My skull hurt, pounding behind my eyes. I pressed down harder, pressed until my whole skin seemed to hum, and when I finally sat back, the poison came bubbling up out of the cuts like water out of the ground.

I grabbed the corner of the blanket and started cleaning off his back, not caring that the stuff was soaking into the sheets, stinking like the devil, only caring that it wasn't inside him anymore.

But even being utterly sure that drawing it out was maybe the *only* thing that could save him, I felt a needle of fear at what I had done. There was a lot more to what I was than just being able to see how things worked. This was closer to defying the laws of nature. The fiend had said to keep my craft low and this was so far from low it was disgraceful, even if there was no one else around to see it. This was absolute proof, as if any was needed, that I was something powerfully not right.

Every time I wiped his back, his breath caught like he was trying not to yell out loud. The whole room seemed to flicker and pulse. It was a blessed relief when the black ooze gave way to real, untainted red and when I wiped it away, all that was left were the raw, clean edges of the cuts. He might be hurt, and hurt bad, but at least the poison was out.

There were about a hundred things I knew I should be doing—not from schooling or memory, but just from common sense. Fisher probably shouldn't be lying in this hot, hot room with no air, on a lumpy pile of blankets, and it was probably a bad thing, how his lips were turning blue.

When I touched his arm, the pure shock of it made me pull my hand back. I'd expected he'd still be feverish, but his skin was slippery and freezing.

The change had come over him so fast I could barely believe it. He tried to say something, but his teeth were knocking together. He was shivering so hard that the whole bed rattled. Finally, he quit trying and squeezed his eyes shut.

The room was devilishly hot, the way top-floor rooms always got in summer. My dress was sticking to me and it seemed impossible that his skin could have gone so cold in just a few minutes.

I got up on the bed with him and rubbed his hands

between mine, trying to get them warm, but there was noth-ing I could do. In less than ten minutes, he'd gone icy to the touch, so see-through and chalky his skin was like the skin inside an egg.

"This is bad," I said, and I was saying it half to myself. "This is really bad."

"I'm just cold," he said in a mushy whisper, running his words together. "It's fine. I'm just cold."

"Here, get under the covers." I yanked on the quilt, try-ing to drag it out from under him.

He struggled onto his elbows, clumsier than before. I helped him under the blankets, careful of the gashes that crisscrossed his back, but even as he settled onto his stom-ach, it was clear the pain was too much to take. For one trembling instant, the whole room seemed to glow a bright, singing red. His cheek thumped hard onto the pillow and he made the smallest, softest noise, barely a noise at all.

When I leaned my elbows on the mattress, he turned toward me. His expression was agonized and I remembered how he'd looked when I'd seen his face for the first time, only a day ago. It was shocking that a person could change so completely in a single day. Last night in the zoo, he'd seemed nearly electric, strong and sure and full of life, but now he was horribly bloodless. I could see his pulse beating faintly down the side of his neck.

I leaned over him and touched his cheek, which was rougher than it looked, and faintly freckled. Now the freckles stood out like marks on paper, and I sat beside him, running my fingers along his cheekbone, trying to smooth out the pain from around his eyes.

He tried to say something, but when he moved his lips, no sound came out.

"It's okay," I said.

I said it again and again, in case it worked like a prayer. In case saying it over made it truer.

Under my hand, his cheek was damp and cold. He lay very still, his breath grating out of him like every lungful was work.

I sat on the floor with my legs curled under me, and when he started to shiver so hard that the whole room seemed to be trembling with it, I put my head down close to his and sang the Clementine song. I sang "Oh Dear! What Can the Matter Be," and "Froggy Went A-Courtin'," and all the silly nonsense songs of my childhood.

My voice was raw and rusty, but the longer I sang, the easier Fisher's breathing seemed to be. I kept my hand on his forehead, and then when he got fitful, I let him close his fingers around mine instead. The way he held on, so fierce and tight it hurt, was almost enough to reassure me that between us, we could get him through the night.

ISOLA
CHAPTER THIRTEEN

I woke up at dawn, still kneeling on the floor. I'd fallen asleep against the mattress with my head cradled on my arms.

Up on the bed, Fisher lay motionless. Sometime in the night, he'd tossed the blankets away and now they were all crumpled up around his feet, bloody and poisonous. His back was an ugly mess, but he was still breathing.

When I reached over to touch his arm, he stirred and sat up. For a minute, neither of us said a word. It gave me a dazed, wobbly feeling, not knowing what to say to a boy after cutting the shirt off his back and spending the night on his floor. Then I figured that even if I'd had lessons and rule books and every advantage in the world, I'd still probably have no idea. It just wasn't the kind of thing most people came up against.

Fisher winced and leaned sideways against the headboard so his back wouldn't touch. He was squinting at me. "You kind of look like hell."

My dress wasn't as bad as it could have been—mostly just rumpled—but there was a smudge of blood down the front from dragging him back into bed the night before, and the skirt was covered with mud and grass stains.

"It's not that bad."

He raised an eyebrow, then reached over to touch my matted hair. His hand was shaky, like even that little bit of effort was too much. "It *is* that bad. You look like you just fought your way out of a bear."

His fingers skimmed my hair, catching in the ends.

I jerked away, ducking my head. "And you look like you almost died. What am I supposed to do about it?"

He let his hand drop. "Just . . . go home, get cleaned up. You don't have to walk around wearing my bad day, is all."

I nodded, pushing myself up on my knees and trying to get a look at his back. The skin around the cuts was purple with bruises, but even in the early light, I could tell that they were fading. Nothing like the way the scrapes on his arm had closed the other night, but enough to make me hope he was getting better.

The blankets were in a bad state though, nearly ruined with blood and the black ooze that had bubbled up from his skin.

"Get up so I can change the bed," I told him. "You're not sleeping on that."

When he stumbled up, I yanked the covers back and dumped them on the floor. There was a bloody splotch in the middle of the mattress, but it was nothing compared to the sheets. I stripped everything, piling it in the middle of the rug.

"Take them down and put them in the wash," he said, sinking into the rocking chair, leaning forward so it wouldn't touch his back.

I personally felt that we should probably rather burn them, but didn't say so, since they weren't my sheets. Instead, I just bundled them up and hauled them toward the door. "What do I need to do?"

"Run it cold, with lots of bleach."

I stood in the doorway, trying to work through the steps. There were plenty of things I'd learned in school or knew from watching my mother. This wasn't one of them. "I've never used a washing machine."

The look he gave me was petrifying. "Put the blankets in. Put in bleach. Turn it to cold. Do not let Isola see you."

His tone was intensely unhelpful, but I just stuck out my chin at him and carried the blankets into the hall.

Whatever the outside of the Fisher place looked like, his grandmother didn't have much patience with housekeeping. I had to wind my way through a maze of sagging cardboard boxes and dusty junk just to get to the stairs. Newspapers were stacked in wobbly piles, narrowing the hallway to a foot-wide corridor of trash and spiderwebs.

I carried the blankets down, lugging them out to the washer on the back porch. I piled them in and did just what he'd said, pouring in a slop of bleach and twisting the knob until the machine clanked and water ran into the barrel.

Then, I climbed back up to the attic, where I poked around until I found a creaky linen closet stocked with sheets and a spare quilt. I pulled them down and took them back to the other end of the house, picking my way along the hall.

My hand was on the knob of Fisher's door when a voice spoke directly behind me. "What in the name of little Lord Jesus do you think you're up to?"

I turned so fast I lost my balance and bumped one of the towers of junk, sending a whole mess of yellowed newspapers sliding to the floor.

I stood on the landing, with dusty trash all around me, hugging a stack of blankets and facing Fisher's grandmother.

She was a tiny, wrinkled woman, wearing a flowered housedress with tatty lace all over the front. She looked shriveled up and sort of crumpled, but her voice was as nasty and gleeful as a crow's.

"What are you doing in my house?" she said, shuffling her way through the scattered newspapers.

She had on ratty bedroom slippers and was scuffing them along the floor. The other day, Shiny had called her a big fancy witch, and I had to admit, she did look spooky.

I faced her, clutching the quilt against my chest. "I was just visiting Fi—Eric. I'm sorry."

"It's a bit early to come calling, wouldn't you say?"

"I'm sorry," I said again, and even to myself I sounded like a fool.

Isola shuffled closer, stepping around a broken carriage clock. She stopped directly in front of me with her arms folded, staring up with dark, narrow eyes. "You spend the night then?"

Even before I could answer, I felt a hot flush of shame. No matter the reason, it wasn't the kind of thing that nice girls did. "I—"

Isola laughed, dark and gleeful. "Course you did—going around with that one, you'd probably do just about anything. Nothing but trials and trouble since the day he was born."

The way she said it seemed to imply that I was a not-insignificant part of her trouble. It was an insinuation that was wildly unfair and I was well on my way to setting her straight when she shuffled right up to me, waving a finger under my nose.

"Oh no, don't you tell *me* he's any good. Don't tell me he hasn't been messing around where he shouldn't. He *knows* he ain't supposed to be down in that devil's hollow, running around like any kind of trashy, crooked folks, letting everyone know his business."

Her eyes were small and bright and black, fixed on me in a way that made my face hot. Suddenly, it seemed that we were looking at each other with more gravity than was normal for strangers.

"He knows how to stay low," I said. "He acts just as normal as anyone when he's in town, and maybe he's got a powerful gift, but it's not as though he advertises."

Isola watched me in a sly, cagey way that made me feel like just by defending Fisher, I was telling her too many things about myself.

Then she narrowed her eyes and leaned so close her voice

seemed to burn in the air around me. "Like anyone can keep a secret around here for long. Now, you got about a minute to gather yourself up and get out of my house."

"How you deal with your grandson is your business," I said, staring back at her. "But what grudge have you got with me? You don't even know me."

The way her face changed then was frightening.

The air in the house felt heavy suddenly, like it was pressing down on me, swallowing me up. We were the only two people in the whole world, chained together, comrades or enemies or something else. Her closeness pushed and picked at me, like she was moving around in my head, but when I tried to push back, there was nothing. Just a feeling like falling headfirst into somewhere black.

Then, without warning, Isola breathed out and backed away. Her face had gone ashy, but she still managed to give me a look that was all vexation.

"Blackwoods," she said, and nothing after that.

I thought she'd scoff, or say how she didn't have to know me to want me out from under her roof, but she just waved a hand like she was showing how done she was with the whole business and went shuffling back down the cluttered hall toward the stairs.

The sight of her leaving should have been a sweet relief, but for a minute, I only stood with my back against the door, holding the blankets and feeling trembly all over. The image of the sheet flapped huge and white in my head and I closed my eyes against it until it was still.

When I went back into the bedroom, what I found there was not inclined to improve my state of mind. Fisher had gotten up from the chair and moved to sit on the bare mattress, where he was wrestling his way into a long-sleeved shirt that buttoned up the front and was a dark burgundy color.

I stood over him. "What are you doing?"

He began to do up the buttons with his good hand. "Getting dressed so I can go out there and act normal for her."

"That's crazy. Can't you tell her you're not feeling well?"

He laughed, shaking his head but not looking at me. His mouth was pale and there were purple smears under his eyes. "I don't *get* sick. Ain't you figured that out yet? And what were you thinking, stomping through the house like that? I told you about a million times not to let her see you."

I stood over him, trying to think up an argument against going around in a sorry condition just to prove his grandmother wrong. "I don't know if you know this, but you are still *bleeding*."

Fisher laughed his short, barking laugh. "You have to admit, the shirt's a handy color."

The way he kept on in that low, even voice made me want to scream. I turned away and began to straighten up everything I'd knocked onto the floor when I came in through the window, righting the tipped lamp and taking deep breaths as I did it so that I wouldn't shout at him.

When I was finished, I turned to face him. "Why are you going to all this trouble to keep her from finding out you're hurt?"

For the first time, he looked at me with something like pain. "Because if I don't, she'll make sure I never leave the goddamn house again."

He was doing his best to look angry, but in the middle his voice broke, like he was begging for something I didn't understand.

I stared at him. His grandmother might be a little terrifying—or a lot, even—but then, so was he. Even slumped over on the edge of his bed, he looked like something to be reckoned with. "You really think she could keep you shut up here if you wanted to leave?"

He started to shrug, then winced when the shirt pressed against his back. "She's done it before."

He said it like it didn't matter much, but his mouth looked pretty grim.

I nodded. The light around him was wavering and agitated, and I didn't know what else to say, so I said, "You have to move so I can make the bed."

As soon as he was on his feet, the room suddenly seemed much too small. The ceiling was so low it almost brushed the top of his head, and I could see the way the walls seemed to press in around him, like he was trapped just as well and truly as I had been.

"You can't go down there," I said, and I said it kindly, even though his invincible act was getting a little tired. "I understand you want to, but you can't because if you try, you're going to go flat on your face again. You need to rest."

Fisher let his breath out like he was sagging under

177

something too heavy to bear. No matter how hard he tried to look all right, his bad arm kept wanting to draw up against his chest. His hands were shaking. Finally, he sank into the rocking chair and slumped forward. The way he bowed his head seemed so hopeless and so private that after a second, I looked away and busied myself remaking the bed.

"Before you do that with the blankets and everything," he said behind me, "you need to flip the mattress."

I struggled with the edge of the pillow top, but it didn't budge. "It's too heavy."

"Just pick up the corner and get your knee under it." Then he muttered something else, but he said it at the floor. It sounded like, *How do people survive?*

I turned around, fully meaning to tell him exactly how we survived and what he could do about it. But all my temper died as soon as I looked at him, the pale cast of his face, a few dark flowers of blood already seeping through his shirt. It was painfully apparent, suddenly, that all his snarling and glaring was because he didn't know how to be hurt. That faced with any of the normal dangers of the world, he didn't even have to think about it, because he could always heal. And he acted like that made him so invincible, or like he didn't need anything, when the truth was, he'd come to depend on something that wasn't always going to save him.

I wrestled the mattress onto its edge, but it gave me the devil trying to get it turned around under the sloping ceiling. It thumped on the floor and I waited, out of breath, for

Fisher to tell me not to make so much noise, but he just sat there, looking sick and half-asleep.

I made up the bed with fresh sheets, tucking in the corners without speaking to him. His way of being so stupidly cool was maddening.

When he sank onto the mattress though, his jaw was hard, like he was trying not to cry out and I relented a little.

"Can you sleep, do you think?"

He nodded and eased himself down on top of the covers, resting on his side.

"Can I leave you?"

"You can do whatever you want."

I stood over him for what felt like a very long time, arms folded, lips pressed together. "I'm not *fighting* you," I said finally. "So can you just be decent with me for two seconds?"

Fisher closed his eyes and looked away, and I knew then that he couldn't. He was always fighting everyone.

INK
CHAPTER FOURTEEN

With no place else to go, I walked back to Myloria's along the Crooked Mile. I was so tired I was nearly tripping over my own feet. It seemed impossible that after everything, it was still only the morning.

As I passed by the Heintzes', I stopped to look over the fence. Things seemed quiet, apart from the rows and rows of empty cages. Some of the bunnies and the birds were back in their coops and I guessed they just hadn't had the sense to run very far.

At the Blackwood house, I let myself in and trudged straight to the bathroom, keeping one hand on the wall. I found some rose-scented salts under the sink and took a bath, but even soaking up to my neck in the powder-pink water didn't do much to wash off the way things weren't all right. It just made the air around me smell more like flowers and less like poison.

When I'd finished, I sat on the edge of the tub, wrapped in a towel, and considered all that I'd seen and found out since yesterday. The whole predicament was so big and messy and strange, though, that I didn't know where to start.

Maybe Fisher had made the creatures of the hollow come for him, the same way he'd made the dogwood bloom. Or maybe everything that had happened was simply because I was there with him, and I was the one who had called the hell dogs out. The one who had made the whole world crazy.

And then there was the reckoning star. The creek fiend had told me to see to it, but the only star I knew of was the one in the huge, splattery painting that hung over the front of the bank building—the five-pointed symbol of the humors.

After I'd sat thinking over all the possibilities so long it felt like I was going in circles, I left it and got up. I changed into another one of Emmaline's dresses from the box in the hall. The folds of the skirt were full of dust and the print was faded, but it fit like it had been made for me, and that was a consolation at least—that something in this world seemed like it could have been made for me.

As I started back through the house, I heard a thin, electric buzzing noise. It seemed to float in the air like a song, and I followed it down into one of the dark halls. A door at the end was propped open with a metal statue of a cat, and I let myself in.

The room I stepped into wasn't a normal room at all, but a long glass-paned greenhouse, with pale sunlight shining down on all kinds of flowers.

I could feel the hum of the place, the same way the plants in my mother's garden had always hummed, full up on all her love and pride and care. Myloria's plants were different, though—the hum was wilder and thinner. It shook instead of sang.

Everything about the greenhouse seemed so much more carefully tended than her kitchen and her daughter and her black, ruined house.

The air was fresh in a way that made the fake-rose smell of my wet hair smell faker, and it was filled with another, louder kind of buzzing, this one high and electric.

At the back of the room, Myloria sat on a wooden stool with her bare feet hooked on the spindle. She wasn't alone. A blond-haired girl lay face-down on the table, shorts pulled halfway off her hip. Myloria was leaning over her with a tattoo gun, carefully marking out a trail of dogwood flowers.

When I came closer, picking my way between the rows of plants, I saw that the girl on the table was Davenport Heintz. I was surprised to find her there, but it relieved me to no end to see that she was okay after the way her father had gone crazy on her at the zoo.

On a little shelf next to Myloria's elbow were a lot of bottles and jars and a row of tiny pots that sat along the back of the workbench. In her right hand, she held the tattoo gun. In her left, she had a little plastic cup balanced between her two smallest fingers. She dipped the point of the gun into the cup and it came away covered in ink.

It made a certain kind of sense—of course Myloria would have to do something for a living. When she bent over Davenport the snakes on her back rippled as she moved, their scales almost seeming to shine like something living.

Davenport's hair was flopped over her so I couldn't see her face. All the way down her hip, the dogwood flowers fell in a fluttering spill. The ones farthest up her back faded pinker and pinker until they seemed to catch fire. Above them, something else was taking shape but was still only in outline, like a picture that was planned, but not drawn yet.

"Is it okay if I stand and watch?" I said to Myloria. "I won't touch anything."

She didn't look away from the little garden of branches and blossoms, but she nodded. The air smelled like blood and electricity, noisy with the buzzing of the gun.

When she ran the needle along Davenport's hip, tiny dots came up, round and red and slick. Delicate. Myloria wiped them off with a rag as she went. Davenport gasped each time, but didn't move. The flowers were pinker and more lovely than the real thing, with a certain ragged edge to the petals so that they almost seemed to flutter.

"Those are nice," I said, watching them unfold. "But why are they all catching on fire?"

Myloria looked up this time, shaking her head. "I don't know. I just do the tattoos like the ink tells me to, and sometimes it comes out meaning things, and sometimes it doesn't. Only time will tell."

Davenport was gripping the edge of the table, making little breathless noises, like sobbing.

I climbed onto the edge of the workbench and reached for her hand. "I didn't mean to get you into trouble with your dad," I said, letting her squeeze onto me as Myloria went over her skin with the gun.

"It's all right," Davenport whispered. "If it wasn't for that, it would have been for something."

The way she said it was so hopeless that it wasn't even like she was asking for help, only sure that help was never coming.

"Why do you stay there with him?" I said, watching Myloria fill in the delicate veins on a leaf. "If it's so bad?"

She rolled her head toward me, and her face was red and puffy with crying. "Where else am I supposed to live? Anyway, he's been like that my whole life."

"You could go somewhere else, couldn't you? What about your mama? Doesn't she have people?"

Davenport shook her head. "My dad won't say anything about her except she's dead. I mean, I think he won't talk about her family because he knows I'd go there in a heartbeat, but whatever."

Her voice wavered and I squeezed her hand harder.

I started to tell her that it would all be okay and not to cry, but Myloria was wiping away the last of the blood, covering the ink with a pad of gauze. "That will be enough for today, I think."

Davenport rolled herself off the table and yanked her shorts up. Her face was still red and puffy, streaming with tears.

After she had gone, Myloria sighed, packing away her tools. "That poor, silly little girl."

"I think she's nice," I said.

Myloria nodded. "So nice she doesn't know what to do with herself, and right now, maybe the ink is it. I suppose she's got to find *some* earthly way to drive her daddy crazy."

"He wouldn't want her to get a tattoo?"

Myloria shook her head. "That man would be happiest if she never left the house. This'll be her way of getting back at him, and he won't be able to do a thing about it, 'less he cuts it out of her skin."

She said it lightly, but her mouth was tight. My hair was dripping down my back, soaking through my dress, and I shivered.

✳   ✳   ✳

"Hey," Shiny said, glancing up as soon as I came into our room. "Where *were* you last night? I kept hoping you were going to come home."

I stood in the sad little slot of a bedroom, feeling heavy and sticky. "I don't want to talk about it."

I was so tired suddenly that my eyes hurt, and everything about the room felt strangely off-balance. Shiny was sitting in the middle of the bed, with a plastic tray of paints and a deck of big, painted fortune-telling cards spread out all over the quilt. The floor around the bed was a sea of crumpled paper.

"What's different in here?" I said, blinking in the arrows of light that filtered through the plank walls.

Shiny gave me an impish little smile. "I did it for you," she said, pointing down at the bed, which was in pretty much the same spot as before, only I saw now that it was jacked up on four cinder blocks like a dead car. "I figured if you were going to be sleeping under there, you'd want a bit more room."

I sat down on the corner of the mattress, taking care not to disturb the row of witch cards and trying to look more excited than I felt. "It was nice of you to think of that."

Shiny shrugged and looked away, and I understood that this was her try at a real apology. She chewed her thumbnail, looking shamefaced. "What I said yesterday, about the— about the thing. I didn't mean it."

I fiddled with my damp hair, trying to work my fingers through, but it was like wire. "No, you did. But it's okay. Maybe you should have."

The cards were spread out in front of us, and when I reached for one, I saw it was handmade. Witch cards were usually the kind of knickknack you saw in tourist shops or movies about Gypsies, and I hadn't known such a thing could be made by a regular person.

The picture on the card was a girl in an orange vest with a hunting knife in each hand, five others arranged in a ring around her head, their points all facing toward the center.

I held it up, feeling how heavy the cardboard was, how rough the edges were. "Did you make these?"

Shiny nodded, scraping them together in a stack. "Some. Not the ones of the old-timey people. Those belonged to Rae's great-grandma, back in like the thirties. We found them in the Daltons' Tuff shed last year, down in the bottom of some

186

crate and wrapped in a wedding dress. A bunch were missing, though, and what was left was half-ruined with mildew. I told Rae I could probably fill out the missing ones."

The cards were lovelier than they had any right to be, considering they were mostly scenes of the most everyday things, but they'd been made magical by Shiny's way of seeing, and by the light, perplexing lines of her paintbrush.

"They're pretty," I said as she stacked them carefully and tucked them in the top of the dresser. "They're really pretty."

She smiled and cupped her hands over her shoulders so that her fingertips covered the places where Myloria had inked the wings. The gesture made her look uncommonly shy and not like normal, flashy Shiny at all.

"Did you want those?" I said suddenly. "Those tattoos. Did you ask Myloria to draw them?'

Shiny didn't look up. "No one *asks* Myloria for any kind of tattoo. She just gives it to them. She does a picture of what she thinks they're supposed to be."

"She thinks you're supposed to be an angel?"

Shiny smirked and shook her head. "She was just trying to make me not so fiery and figured I needed some air to soften me up."

"Did it work?"

She raised her eyebrows but didn't answer.

"So, Fisher didn't ask for her to draw that tower then?"

Shiny threw back her head and let out a long, howling laugh. "Are you kidding? No one in their right mind would just walk out into the Willows and ask for a full-back tattoo of the tower of ruin. That's practically the worst card in the witch deck. It's like making some special request to be branded with bad luck and destruction."

I thought about that. "Well, he does like to break stuff."

She laughed again, but this time it was more of a giggle, and I felt glad to be able to say something about Fisher without her getting mad about it.

"Does that mean he needs destruction, or that he is destruction?"

"You're stuck on him," Shiny said, shaking her head. "Destruction is destruction, and either way, you've got that boy on your brain every minute."

There was a stubborn streak in me that wanted to argue. I had a lot of other things filling up my head too. But since the moment he'd carried me out of the canning closet, they all came back to him in their various ways.

"I can't help it," I said finally.

Shiny rolled her eyes.

"What I mean is, I didn't just *decide* to think about him. I've been thinking about him as long as I can remember. Sometimes it feels like I've been thinking about him forever." I kicked my way through the drifts of crumpled paper that lay spread over the floor. "All those years I was down there, I was dreaming. And some of the dreams—or memories, even—were about a boy with muddy eyes and a light around him, and when he came to get me, it was sort of like I already knew him."

Shiny leaned closer, watching me with her fingers twined together. "You dreamed about him before you knew him?"

"It wasn't just him," I said. "By the time I got out, I'd had so many dreams, it was like I already knew *lots* of things."

She studied me with a worried line at the corner of her mouth. "Where did you go last night, really?"

"I went to his house, but it's not like you think."

Shiny raised her eyebrows. She didn't say anything, but her expression was so doubtful she didn't need to.

"He was hurt," I said. "We were down in the hollow yesterday, and something bad happened. Like you said—like the world was coming apart. Like everything grew teeth."

Shiny's eyes were big and unblinking. "He took you with him, down in that place, with all the craft and the fiends and everything?"

I nodded, feeling wrung out and like I needed to curl up and sleep for a year. "And then got ruined for it when the hell dogs came out."

"Well what does he *expect*, messing around down there?"

Her tone was brassy, like she was saying he'd gotten exactly what he deserved, but her eyes were scared, and I knew she was thinking about the fish, with its dripping spines and its teeth.

I shook my head, not knowing how to make her see. "It got so wild and awful all at once. It was like it came at him, like it had a personal grudge. Is that how things started at the reckoning?"

Shiny gazed back at me. She was sitting very still, like she could hardly dare to breathe. "I don't know. I don't know what goes on down in Wixby Hollow, or how it works. For all I know, they've got craft lighting up everywhere and monstrous things down there all the time, but that's just one more reason you should *not* go around messing with it!"

"If that's true, though—if the craft is just lighting up every which way—maybe it was just being how it always is. I mean, if it doesn't have to follow any kind of natural laws, how can anyone really say what's normal?"

Even to myself, though, I sounded like I was trying too hard to convince someone.

"I don't know much about the hollow," Shiny said again, and she closed her eyes when she said it. "But the kind of thing you're talking about sounds pretty far from normal. I'm pretty sure what you're talking about can't come to any good."

FIREFLIES
CHAPTER FIFTEEN

The farther along it got into evening, the clearer it was that there would be no supper, and neither Shiny nor Myloria seemed very motivated to do anything about that.

I'd just gotten out a box of Bisquick and was reading the directions to fix myself some pancakes when I heard the roar of a familiar engine. I stepped onto the porch just in time to see Fisher's Trans Am come skimming onto Weeping Road and scream up to the house in a long rooster tail of dust. Then it cut off, and the yard was so quiet that the silence seemed to be a solid thing, like it was clapping in on my ears.

I sat down on the sagging front steps and watched him get out of the car, trying to look however I would if I hadn't seen him make dogwood flowers grow from nothing or watched him pass out in the road or seen him without his shirt on, bleeding all over the bed.

He came up the steps to me, moving stiffly, but looking better than he had. The way he held his arm close against his chest, though, made me think he was not yet fully recovered. He stood beside me where I sat, but didn't say anything, even though I waited what felt like a year.

Finally, I sighed and looked up at him. His back was broad, lumpy along one shoulder, like maybe he'd bandaged himself up, but the bandages didn't fit too well under his clothes.

Now that I knew the shape of the tower, I could picture the line of it. I sat with my arms around my knees, tracing it in my head, the way it narrowed to a jaggy point at the back of his neck.

He glanced down at me, like he could feel my eyes on him. "You studying me like that because you've got something on your mind?"

"Yeah, I do." The steps creaked under his boots and I shaded my eyes. "You're supposed to be home in bed, working on not getting yourself killed."

"Well, I don't do so great with sitting around the house. I just needed to get out."

I pointed to his arm, the way he held it awkwardly against his chest. "Are you sure you're okay?"

"I'm fine," he said, dropping down onto the steps next to me. The nearness of him was delicious, and I wanted to reach over and touch the edge of his T-shirt because it looked like it might be soft and I wanted to find out, and because he was close enough to touch.

"You look like you got some rest, at least," I said finally, when I'd been staring at his T-shirt long enough that I had to say something.

He nodded. His face was tired, but his color was better and the dark circles around his eyes were gone. "I would have got more, except Isola can't stay put. Kept me up, wandering around the house all day. Swear she must've gone up and down that hall a hundred times."

I remembered Isola that morning, her eyes bright and hungry like she was trying to study the truth right out of my face.

"You *were* in pretty bad shape. Maybe she was worried."

He shook his head. "You got all my sheets and stuff in the wash. And she didn't say anything, except to get after me just now when I was leaving, for having a girl over past nine. Sometimes I think I'm about to lose my damn mind, living with her."

I thought of Myloria, with her vague ways and her empty eyes, like she was always looking past me.

"It might not be so bad," I said. "To have someone pay attention or try and take care of you. She's mean, maybe, but I don't think she's stupid."

He glanced at me, and his eyes were exhausted. "Maybe, but that sure doesn't make her any more fun to deal with." Then he jerked his head toward the back of the house and pulled himself to his feet. "Come on, let's go for a walk."

I almost asked him again if he was feeling all right, but let it go. We climbed down off the porch and headed out past the barn. Behind the house, the ground sloped away to a little fenced-in garden and a wooden shed with a wire run full of chickens. Farther down, a rickety pump house leaned awkwardly, and beyond that, a tire swing hung from one of the willows that stood along a bend of the creek. Old pieces of broken farm equipment were scattered here and there, sinking slowly into the ground. A hay rake sat in the shade near the swing, looking like a giant mouth of bent, rusted teeth. It was strange to be reminded that this land used to be good for something besides rot and sadness and ruin.

We'd only gone down past the edge of the yard when Fisher stopped and took a deep breath. He was still trying to act fine, but I could see the first strands of bright, electric red pulsing out of him, shining ugly into the dusk.

"Just stop working so hard to seem like it doesn't hurt," I said when I'd got tired of pretending I didn't see the way he clenched his jaw. "It's not like I can't tell."

He didn't answer or argue, just closed his eyes, cradling his arm against his chest.

"How bad is it?"

He laughed. "I think I can feel every damn muscle and nerve stitching itself back together."

I picked a broken stick from out of the weeds and swung it, knocking the seeds off an early milkweed. "You shouldn't have come out here, then. You should have stayed home to heal up."

He gave me a tired, rueful smile. "I don't know much about how that works. I've never really had to worry about it before. Last night, though. Last night was *bad*. It hurt so much it was hard even to breathe."

"I know," I said.

He made a little gesture with his good hand, like he was

drawing someplace that only he could see, and wouldn't look at me. "Every second, it was me deciding to take the next breath, and knowing if I let myself, I could pass out and then nothing would hurt anymore."

I dug around in the weeds with the end of the stick. "Why didn't you then?"

"It wouldn't have been passing out." He stared out into the field, full of tall grass and morning glories. "It would have been dying. So I just breathed, and worked really hard at not dying."

Suddenly, I could almost feel the weight of the songs I'd sung him, the way his hand felt in mine.

"What happened to us yesterday?" I said.

The question seemed too small to conjure up what it had been like to see the world come undone, ready to chew up him and me and anything else it came across.

"I don't know," he said. "The hollow kind of lost its mind, I guess. I mean, it always sort of changes moods along with me, but not like that. The dirt there works in ways it never does out in the regular world, but that's the first time I've seen it do anything like that."

I took a deep breath and tossed away the stick. "I don't know, but I'm pretty sure *I've* seen something like it."

Fisher glanced at me sharply. "What are you talking about? Something here, out in the regular world?"

"Not any kind of fiend or hell dog," I said. "But Shiny and I found something in the creek the other day. This monster-fish with a whole bunch of wrong, scary teeth. She cut it apart and we buried it, but I don't think that will really make a difference if there are more of them."

"I don't know what's happening," Fisher said. "I don't know what this is."

"Dangerous," I said.

He laughed low and dry in his throat. "Yeah, that." Then his face went stony again. "I keep trying to figure out what that was yesterday, and I can't even start to make sense of it. All I can think is, what if that's just what the hollow's like now? It's the only place I ever really feel okay, and what if this means I can't even go there anymore?"

The edge in his voice was something like pain.

"It isn't safe there," I said.

"I know—I know it's not, but maybe that's *why* I like it. Or part, anyway. Town is safe. For me, everything is safe."

I nodded. I didn't like to point it out, but there were some things about town that seemed pretty far from safe.

Fisher was walking faster, kicking at a pokeweed bush as we passed, and now the words were spilling out. "When Isola's mad at me, sometimes she tells me I shouldn't even be here. That the only place for me is down in the hollow. She says it to be mean, but the thing is, it's true. It's the only place I really . . . belong. It's kind of amazing there."

I looked out at the empty pastures, at every tree and flower and blade of grass, at the muddy patches by the cow-stream, the crickets and frogs rustling around in the ditch. "But that's not so rare or—or so special. *Every*thing's amazing!"

Fisher didn't answer, but he looked like he was thinking

196

about that, or thinking about something. Whatever was on his mind did not look particularly comfortable.

We crossed the little dirt bridge that ran over the ditch, and opened the gate into the back pasture. We walked out through the hay and sat on the trunk of a fallen tree. We were close enough that I could feel the warmth of him in the air against my skin, but not quite so close that we were touching. Around us, the fireflies were coming out, lighting up around us in the grass, tiny and bright.

"It's hard to be around you," he said, and his voice sounded so strange.

I let out a crowing sound, almost like a laugh, but not. "Then tell me to go away, if I'm so awful. Or at least, don't come over to go walking."

"It's hard to be around you," he said again, and he said it with his face turned away and his shoulders hunched. "But you're not awful. I just—I always want to tell you everything."

"Then why don't you tell me?"

He shook his head. "It's not . . . it's not easy."

"Things don't have to be easy," I said.

Fisher was a silhouette against the sky. He was leaning forward, looking out over the pasture with his hands clasped between his knees. His profile was wistful in the dark, and suddenly, he didn't look fierce or stoic or defiant. He looked tired.

His hair was dark and shaggy, hanging his face, but his skin seemed to shine up out of the dusk, brightening the line of his nose and mouth and chin. He looked forlorn against the sky and I watched him, waiting for something to change.

For him to stop looking so unbearably lonely. It seemed like maybe if you had crooked blood and a secret world and an iron skin, you were always lonely.

"Fisher?"

"What?"

"Are we friends yet?"

He laughed softly. "Yeah. Yeah, I guess we are."

"Fisher?"

He turned toward me and I kissed him. Not the way the magazines or movies talked about, but awkward and too fast. His mouth was warm and soft against mine and then when he made a little hurt sound, I pulled back.

For awhile, we just sat like that, side by side, quiet and still in the middle of the field. My cheeks were getting hot, so I stared off someplace that wasn't him. The other day, I'd made up my mind in ten seconds that I was going to kiss him, in some far-off make-believe way that didn't feel real or mean anything. Doing it though, actually doing it, was so much more scary than anything I'd wished for or imagined or bragged about to Shiny.

When I glanced over at him, he was just looking out across the empty pasture at some far-off spot in the grass.

"What's wrong?" I said.

He squinted at me and his voice was hoarse. "How did you know I wanted you to?"

"Wanted me to kiss you? I didn't."

He swallowed like he was having a hard time catching his breath. "And you just decided to do it anyway?"

"Well, yeah. It was what I wanted, and you looked like you needed it."

He reached for me, grabbing me around my waist and pulling me toward him. His hurt arm was shaking and he rested his hand against my hip. His other hand was flat on my back, pressing me hard against his chest. I could feel his heartbeat through his shirt and he was kissing me like it was the only real thing, and there was no field, no fireflies, no dusk. Like he could breathe me in and there wouldn't be him and me at all anymore, just one solid thing. I put my arms around his neck, pulling him closer.

His teeth knocked against mine, pinching my lip and I gasped. "*Ow*."

"Sorry." He pulled back, shaking his head. "Sorry, I don't have a lot of practice at this kind of thing."

The way he looked at me was almost shy, like he was worried what I would think.

"No, it was fine." I took a deep breath and couldn't stop the spinning feeling, like everything was full of a pale, quiet light and the world was about to fall away. "It was good."

He reached for me with his good hand, touching the side of my face. "I could do it again."

"I wouldn't mind."

LILIES
CHAPTER SIXTEEN

The thrill of kissing Fisher was still zinging around in my head the next morning. He'd kissed me in the field, and walking home, and then again on Myloria's porch, and one last time as I was letting myself into the house.

I caught myself going over it again and again, till I had to stop for fear of wearing out the memory before I was done with it.

The day was long and aimless, like all the other days at the Blackwood house, and with no chores or errands or appointments, time seemed stuck in a way it never had when I was little.

By the time the sun started to get low, I'd had about enough.

"Hey," I said to Shiny, who was sprawled out on the bed, working on her witch cards again. "I'm going into town to see the fair. You should come if you want."

She rolled her eyes like that was about the most worthless thing she'd ever heard, but as soon as I left the bedroom, she followed me out.

We were in the front hall, getting our shoes, when Myloria came wandering in after us.

"I hate to be a bother," she said, "But I have to just ask. You are not intending to be selling any kind of craft with that Dalton girl, are you?"

Shiny straightened up, holding a boot in each hand. "Rae is not 'that Dalton girl.' She's my friend, and she does honest *work* for honest money. Don't pretend like you know anything about that."

Myloria's mouth got very thin. "This is an upright family, and we don't need to resort to charms and snake oil to make our living."

"*We* need to be able to afford dish soap or milk! We need to be able to *buy groceries*."

Myloria blinked and looked away. "Well, I can't help it if you want to lower yourself to tricks, but don't you go giving people the wrong idea about us."

Shiny snorted. "Like that we survive on possums and live in a decrepit old ruin like a couple of crazy people? No, we certainly wouldn't want to give them *that* idea!"

With a huff, she rammed her feet into her boots and stalked out onto the porch.

I stood in the hall across from Myloria, waiting for her to turn away or else to scold me too, but she didn't move or say a word. When we looked at each other, I could see a broken heart inside her but not any way to do a thing about it, and after a second, I followed Shiny out.

On the porch, I was greeted by Shiny's back. She was leaning on the railing, under the long row of wind chimes, glaring out into the yard.

"Do you think we could stop and invite Davenport to come with us?" I said after what felt like forever. I had a feeling I knew what she'd say, but it was worth asking, and I was tired of waiting for her to turn around.

Shiny pushed herself away from the railing and reached for a mangy broom that was leaning by the door. "Are you serious? The girl's a straight-up weirdo."

I put my hands on my hips. "Shiny, you have to start being friendly to people sometime. You can't just hang out with me and Rae."

She pushed her hair back from her face and hooked it behind her ears, shaking her head. "I can't even believe you sometimes. Here you come, sassing around like some ridiculous little Pollyanna, like you can help everyone sort out all their problems."

"What are you talking about?"

Shiny affected a high, babyish voice. "Oh, let's invite Davenport—never mind that she's nearly a goddamn mute! Let's run around with that Fisher boy and teach him how to be civilized, even though he's the devil on wheels!"

"That's not what this is. Don't be stupid."

"Yes, it *is*. You're just going around giving your time and your goodwill to people who don't deserve it. No one around here wants our help!"

"How do you know they don't? And anyway, what have you got against Davenport? That she's got a crazy daddy? That's not even fair. That's like blaming you for Myloria."

The look Shiny gave me was terrible. "He is *nothing* like

202

Myloria. People in the Willows are supposed to stick together, but at the reckoning, it was her dad right there in front, tying rags and lighting bottles."

This new piece of knowledge just made me deeply sad for all of us. I didn't know how to feel vengeful or angry the way that Shiny did. I could only grasp the aftereffect—that she was hurt and I was hurt. Maybe everyone was.

Shiny scowled, shaking her head. "He was hateful back then and he's hateful now." She turned away and began sweeping the porch with a vengeance.

I sat on the steps and leaned my elbows on my knees while Shiny muddled around with the broom, pushing the dust over the edge and into the flowerbed.

"Fine," I said, looking down into the yard. For just a second, I could see that clear, perfect picture in my head again—the neat, well-tended flowerbeds and the candy-pink peonies. It hurt the spot between my eyes. "Fine, we don't have to ask her. But you have got to quit acting like she's some kind of horror. She's not the one who made you get stuck out here in the Willows, with everyone acting like you're the devil."

Shiny stared out at the weedy yard. "No, I know that. When I stop and think, I do know that. It's just easier, some-times, pointing it at her, or at anyone. Because when it's the reckoning, then it's something too big to point fingers toward at all. Then it's no one's fault."

But the words made something tighten in my chest— a tangled knot of guilt—telling me that it might be mine.

The blank sheet seemed to flap and ripple in my head, waiting for a picture to come clear. I nodded, but I was remembering the day I found the stone tomato, there on the vine like a secret, tucked in with all the regular ones. That one round, perfect stone suddenly seemed like the center of my whole life, powerful enough to ruin everything.

* * *

In town, all of Main Street was alight, blazing with colored streamers and carnival lights. It seemed like pretty much everyone in Hoax County was wandering through the tents and the arcade games, talking and laughing. Down at the end of the street, the rides were all lit up, turning like giant steel pinwheels. Lights raced and flashed. The metal cages rocked, and the screams tumbled down to us from a long way off.

Rae was sitting up on one of the sawhorses by the curb, nearly finished with a corndog on a wooden stick. When she saw us coming, she jumped down and slipped her arm through Shiny's.

"You ready to make a dollar?" she said, pointing across the street to where a little group of girls was lounging on a picnic bench, looking bored and glossy. "I see some chickens waiting to pay good money for love charms."

I squinted at them, trying to see what Rae saw. "But they look so clean and normal. Are you sure they're the kind of folks who want what you're selling?"

"Clementine," Rae said, dropping her empty corndog stick into one of the metal trash barrels. "I'm going to let you in on a secret. Around here, you don't have to look too far to find someone willing to pay for something crooked. Everybody you meet is talking out both sides of their mouths."

Shiny studied the girls and shook her head. "You go if you want, but I have no desire to make small talk with Laurie Tuttle and her friends. And don't you *even* tell me to be nice."

Rae dug primly in her bag and pulled out a grape sucker. "Don't take that tone with me, Shiny Blackwood. I wasn't thinking any such."

"Well, *sorry*—I just figured this was the part where you explain to me how everyone in this shitty little town is not so bad, how if I give her a chance, Laurie is just a sad girl with a big nose and an overbearing mother, and how Mike Faraday has some kind of crush on me!"

Rae surveyed Shiny with her eyebrows up and the sucker sticking out of the corner of her mouth. "Well, he does. But so what? Him liking you's got nothing to do with whether or not he's a bag of bullshit."

Shiny just gave Rae a long, sulky look, but when she turned away, I saw that she was smiling.

Rae took Shiny's arm again and tugged her toward Main Street. "Fine, we'll peddle sin some other time. But when you finish up those cards for me and we get a real moneymaking scheme going, that's the day you start being nice to people. A person cannot run a business if they're chasing off every second customer because they don't like someone's face."

"It's not the faces," Shiny said, "so much as just the *generalized* ugliness."

The three of us made our way along the sidewalk. People were gathering all along the street, and Rae said it was because they were waiting for the parade to start.

We stood on the corner, watching the floats as they came through, each one preceded by a pair of little kids carrying vinyl banners printed with the name of the association or club responsible, the Campfire Girls following along behind the Junior Farmers and the baton twirlers and the 4-H float.

"Oh, no," said Rae mildly, peering over her shoulder through the crowd. "Here comes trouble."

Fisher was cutting his way through the crowd, followed by Mike Faraday and the Maddox brothers and a handful of other boys. He looked taller and more wonderful than I'd ever seen him, his hair curling against his neck, his eyes fixed on mine. His T-shirt showed a jagged row of thin pink lines on his bare arm where only two days ago, the skin had been laid open, and I could tell by the way the shirt pulled across his shoulders that the bandages were gone.

He cut straight through the crowd, coming up to me like it was nothing, reaching for my hand.

"Hi," was all he said, and I said it back, trying not to smile too hard.

When I leaned my arm against his, his skin was slippery and smelled like salt. The easy way we leaned into each other made my heart skip. His hand was very warm, rough on the palm and the pads of his fingers.

The other boys all watched us from the safety of the curb, and I couldn't tell if it was me they were eyeing, or if they were just making sure to stay well back from Shiny.

Fisher twined his fingers with mine and when he did, the feeling was the best thing in the world, like it was always better to be this tangled up, to always have a piece of each other.

"Do you mind if they come with us?" I said, glancing at Shiny.

She rolled her eyes grandly. "What do *you* think? Anyway, I'd be more concerned about whether or not *they* mind it, because if a single one of them calls me any kind of craft-this or crooked-that, I cannot guarantee their safety."

It didn't matter, though. The boys were already falling back, wandering away from us into the crowd, but Fisher stayed right where he was. He didn't let go of my hand.

The carnival was in full swing, lit up all over the east side of town. We wandered through the booths and tents, looking at the chickens and the pigs. After we'd seen the fair, we went down to the midway and pitched pennies into rows of plastic cups to win cheap wire-handled sparklers and silk roses, which Shiny thought were the most hilarious things in the world, but she kept pitching for them anyway. She and Fisher were doing a good job of pretending not to notice each other.

He pitched at a velvet rabbit with a plastic hat sewed on until he won it, and I laughed. The idea that he should want anything with a stuffed bunny was ridiculous, but when the man from the carnival took it down from the hook under the awning, he handed it to me.

I tried to pass the bunny back to Fisher, but he shook his head. "It's yours."

"I don't have anything for you, though."

Fisher shrugged and looked away. "You're not supposed to. It's like a . . . thing."

"Well, that seems kind of unfair."

"Sexist, you mean," Shiny said, slinging another penny into the cup, holding her bunch of roses like a beauty queen.

Rae didn't pitch for anything, just stood by and sucked her sucker, watching the rest of us and reaching up from time to time to twist the ends of her hair.

The carnival was like a dream from being little, and I was happy to stay there forever, smelling fryer oil and sugar and farm animals, watching the crowds and the colored lights.

I would have spent another hour just standing next to Shiny while she pitched for roses, but Fisher took my hand, pulling me over to the midway rides, where he led me through a rusty little gate and paid the fare to ride the swings. The seats hung on thin, jingling chains, and the speakers played Neil Diamond songs with a crackling hiss that made me think of my mama and how she'd danced around the living room in the evening.

As the ride began and the swings rose up, Fisher leaned sideways in his seat, reaching through the forest of chains for me until I reached back and let my fingers get twisted up with his. The swings rose higher, so that my feet hung out over nothing. Every time the ride dipped, I wanted to tuck my legs up so they wouldn't drag over the roofs of the tents, even though I knew we were much too high.

I leaned back in the seat, laughing at the way the wind caught in my hair, and nothing in the world was wrong, and everything was beautiful. It didn't matter that the town was small or that Shiny was angry or Fisher sometimes acted like he wanted to destroy himself and couldn't tell me why. Up here in the swings, there was only warm, heavy air and "Sweet Caroline" on the speakers and Fisher's hand holding onto mine.

From off in the hills, a whole mess of black clouds was rolling in. The sky overhead was still clear, but if the wind didn't change direction, we were in for a storm.

When the ride stopped, we climbed off and filed down the metal ramp with everyone else. I was all set to get back in line and do it again, but Fisher leaned toward me, smiling, kissing my cheek, my ear, the corner of my mouth.

His lips moved to mine and I smiled against his smile, because in the warmth of his kiss, I understood that this was my life. This was my home, and the years I'd missed were gone but not lost, because I knew the taste of the dough from the fryer cart, and my mama used to dance around the house with Neil Diamond on the radio, and nothing was ever really forgotten.

I put my arms around his neck and leaned into him, his body warm and solid. Since last night in the meadow, he seemed less guarded, more sure. He kissed me harder, lifting me off my feet, and wrapped his arms around my waist so tight our whole bodies pressed together, and we sank back into the shadows, against the empty raffle booth.

He put his mouth against my ear. "You know how I said the hollow was the only place I ever felt okay?"

I nodded into the curve of his neck, holding on so tight the tips of my fingers left pucker-marks in his shirt.

"This is better."

And I laughed at that, even though nothing at all was funny. He smelled like all the things I had missed and wished for and wanted, and I turned my face and looked down because looking at him was almost too much to bear at once.

On the ground around us, there was a strange thing, like someone had dropped a box of glass Christmas ornaments at our feet, so that even the dirt seemed to flash and glitter.

I grabbed his hand and pointed. "Look."

Lilies grew in huge bursts, pushing their way up through the weeds by the empty raffle booth, blooming in clusters around Fisher's boots. They were white. And red. And gold-and-yellow striped and pink and orange. It was like watching a garden grow in fast-forward, leaves sprouting out and uncurling, turning darker as they grew, and flowers opened in huge splashes of color.

The sight was so strangely beautiful that at first, I didn't understand. Then he spoke and my blood got cold.

"Oh God," he said, and his voice was dark and awful, like opening a door and finding something rotten. Like the moment in the hollow just before the hell dogs came out of the trees.

I dropped his hand. The air was suddenly electric.

Fisher stood under the awning, shaking his head. "No."

He said it hoarsely, again and again until the words all ran together in one noise, low in his throat. Around our feet, the lilies bloomed, bursting with huge clusters of flowers.

"Holy *shit*," said a voice behind us, and I nearly jumped out of my skin.

But it was only Shiny, coming up behind me with a paper cone of cotton candy, her arm through Rae's. Shiny, who stood in the dirt at the edge of the midway, was gaping at me.

Fisher was still staring at the ground with a look of pure horror. Then he plunged away from me, stepping down hard on the flowers. The petals all shriveled and turned black, but they didn't stop growing. Now they were transforming, turning to thorns and brambles and all kinds of poisonous blooming plants. They lay on the ground like disease, monkshood and foxgloves and nightshade. Strange, hungry kinds of plants I didn't know, but they all looked sharp and toothy, more like animals than plants at all.

On the other side of the midway, people passed in bunches, laughing, eating fried dough and candy apples, holding rainbow paper hats. The fair moved in peaceful currents around us, so many people it seemed impossible they didn't look over. All I could think was that in a second they'd look and see the toxic flowers, and then it wouldn't matter whose name was Blackwood, Dalton, Fisher, or DeVore—we'd all burn.

Suddenly, I was cold. I knew that in a minute, someone would look, someone would glance over and see that

211

the ground was sick with craft straight out of the hollow. They'd see what we were, and then we'd find out how kind the town was to the old families *really*. We would see exactly how much things had changed.

I was nearly frantic for something to save us, some way to hide, when the string of lights hanging over the midway burst and glass went raining down into the crowd. The four of us stood frozen in the shadows. I could feel the tight hum of some sort of craft that had nothing to do with Fisher, and I looked over in time to see Rae snap the wicker bag shut. On the ground at her feet a little speckled egg lay broken open. Something powdery and black had spilled out from the cracked shell and was smoking in the dirt. She looked back at me with wide, worried eyes, but didn't say a thing.

Out in the midway, everyone had stopped and was staring around in the new darkness. People were muttering, stepping out of the way and looking up at the dangling wires, and I yanked the tarp off the raffle table and threw it down on the dying flowers.

They were still moving, squirming under the canvas. In a minute, they'd crawl out where everyone would see, only by then, they might not even look like plants at all anymore.

"Fisher," I said. "*Stop*."

He stood frozen with his shoulders squared, breathing hard as vines crept from under the edge of the tarp and crawled over his boots.

I stepped into the middle of the canvas, feeling it ripple and squirm under my feet. "Stop right now."

212

His throat worked, like he was swallowing down the strange, unholy power that seeped out of him, clenching his hands and breathing in huge gasps, but it didn't seem to make any difference. "I can't. It's too far gone."

Shiny stared at the rumpled tarp. Her stick of cotton candy hung limp in her hand, pink sugar sticking like fur to the side of her leg. "Is he doing that? My God, Clementine. Make him *stop*!"

Rae was the one who moved, though. She darted across to Fisher like she was about to slap him. "Hey!" Her voice was so sharp and unlike her, it made the hair on my neck stand up.

He spun around to face her, but his eyes were flat and out of focus.

She stood between us, looking up at him. She was tiny and fierce and her hair stuck out in delicate twists around her head. "If you can't get control of whatever bullshit is going on right now, then you climb in your redneck trash machine and get yourself down in the hollow where you *belong*!"

"*No*," I said, pushing in front of her. "You can't do that. You're in no state to go down there now—it'd kill you. Look at me."

When Fisher didn't answer, I reached up and grabbed his chin. I could feel the power of his craft running right there under his skin. "*Look* at me. Yes, it's bad, but you can fix it."

He took a deep, shuddering breath. Then he took another. At the edges of the tarp, the flowers were dying back, turning into a little heap of soggy black rot. Into nothing.

They sank back into the ground, while he stood shivering and gasping.

After what felt like ages, Shiny let her shoulders slump and breathed out. "Holy shit."

Fisher didn't look at her. His voice when he spoke was hoarse. "How can that happen?"

But no one said anything. I wondered if the word on everyone's tongue was *reckoning*, if we just didn't even have to say it because it was what we all were thinking.

Then, from the midway behind us, there was an uneasy muttering, a scuffling of feet, and I looked around. The Maddox brothers and Tony Watts were all standing in the shadow of the raffle sign, staring like they'd been stricken dumb.

I started toward them with the little velvet rabbit held against my chest, already coaxing them not to say anything, not to make a scene, but all three of them stepped back from me like I was something diabolical.

Cody Maddox spit in the dirt at my feet. "Get yourself straight to hell," he said, and the words sounded raw, like they were caught in his throat. "You and your devil cousin— get right back out to the Willows and *stay* there."

The way he said it was so nasty I couldn't think of anything to say back. I could barely breathe.

Shiny drew herself up and stepped in front of me. Her shoulders were hard, and I could already feel her skin going hot and crackly. "Don't you *even* talk to her like that."

"No, Shiny," I said in a small, shaky voice. "It's okay. I mean, it's not a big deal. He's just scared."

"*Okay*? I saw what you just did. You were the one trying to clean up the mess, and this one here—" She jerked her head at Fisher. "Well, I saw where it came from, too."

Luke Maddox shook his head, slow and heavy. He never took his eyes off Fisher. "Listen to her, trying to blame it on you. Have you learnt your lesson now, running around with your Blackwood girlfriend? Maybe they're good for a tumble, but this is what happens when you mess with fiends."

I turned to Fisher, waiting for him to explain—to *tell* them—that it hadn't been me, but he just stared back, not moving, not blinking. He didn't say anything.

"Fisher," I said, but his face was blank. It already told me everything.

He turned and crossed the lot to them, not saying a word, not looking back.

I stood over the place where the vines had grown. My heart was a hammer under my bones, beating hard enough that I felt it in my back teeth. It had begun to rain a little, the sky spitting fat, chilly drops on the packed dirt.

Fisher's back was to me, getting farther, farther.

Shiny grabbed the velvet rabbit from me and threw it. "Leave, then!" But her voice was cracked, like something was caught in her throat.

"He isn't close to good enough," she said without looking at me. Without really looking anywhere.

The ground around the tarp was empty, like nothing had ever been there.

PART IV
CREEK

THE DOGWOOD BRANCH
CHAPTER SEVENTEEN

In the morning, Shiny lay in bed with her head burrowed into the pillow. Outside, rain still spatted unevenly against the window.

I stood over her in the little room, trying to figure out how she could sleep so soundly. Every time I thought of last night, my throat hurt so much that I had to stop.

During the night, the clouds had broken open and the fitful sprinkling had turned into downpour. I'd woken up in the dark, listening to the storm on the roof and feeling sorry for myself in a muddled way that just got worse each time a clap of thunder rolled across the sky.

Now the rain had mostly stopped, but behind the house, the creek had grown to an ungovernable size. It had overflowed its banks and now it was creeping up toward the yard. I wondered if we were in danger of its flooding the house, but the swell seemed content where it was, leaving muddy puddles under Shiny's tire swing.

The gray day made the inside of me feel grayer, and it was a feeling I didn't want. I needed to find something useful to do. I left the house, wearing a battered raincoat and a pair of rubber galoshes that didn't fit, and headed up the road.

Although the Blackwood place was the closest piece of land to the creek, it was the rest of the Willows that seemed to be underwater. At the Heintzes, the whole yard was knee-deep, and I was mildly comforted that at least it was one piece of destruction I was not responsible for.

Up at the edge of Harlan's north pasture, I climbed the fence, being careful not to slip on the wet boards, then marched over to where my suitcase still lay, half-buried in the weeds, one plaid sleeve sticking out and looking draggly and wet. I picked it up and hauled it onto the road.

I felt satisfied with myself, virtuous for remembering to come back for it and relieved that it was still where I had left it. After a second, though, the virtuous feeling faded and I was right back to having nothing else to do.

The problem was that without things to keep you busy, your chest could hurt. You could think about what it meant to live somewhere that hated you, or remember that a boy you thought was kind or loyal or brave wasn't actually any of those things when you got right down to it.

From the pasture, I could see the bluff that led down into the hollow. I was half-tempted to go down and look for the white-haired fiend with the blurry eyes and ask her what to do. The place was full of craft and hell dogs, but that wasn't the reason I decided not to go. It was that I couldn't help thinking how Fisher might be down there. The idea made it hard to even think straight. I just couldn't tell if the fog in my head was because I didn't want to see him, or if it was because I secretly wanted to see him so bad it made me dizzy.

Instead, I walked along the shoulder of Foxhill Road, wandering back out toward my burned-down house without really knowing why. On the hollow side of the blacktop, the ground was wet and muddy where the flood had come up and then receded, but on the Willows side, the entire birchwood that backed up against the Heintzes' property was underwater. The trunks of the trees stuck up like fingers, going on for acres.

I was looking out at them when I felt a thin little tug like the niggling whisper of craft. Something was there in the woods. It called with the same insistent hum that I got sometimes when I looked at Fisher, but the tone was different, high and wavering with a whine underneath that made my ears ache.

I set the suitcase down and went straight off the side of the road and into the trees, slopping over the muddy ground and into the floodwater.

I waded along, careful of the roots that bucked up from the ground. I'd gone just a little too far into the trees to see the road when something snagged at my raincoat and I turned.

A fishhook was stuck barb-deep in the yellow rubber at my shoulder, tied to a piece of fishing line so thin and see-through it was almost invisible. I tried to follow it with my eye, but the line disappeared up into the branches. I jerked the hook out of my raincoat and ripped the line down, winding it carefully in my hand.

I turned in a circle, looking up into the trees, but could see nothing around to make the dangling hook seem less bizarre.

By the time I'd gone another hundred feet, though, I'd come across three more, pocketing each one and ripping down the lines as I went, and every time I found I another, it only served to prove they'd been put there on purpose.

I waded on, following the hum that rang in my ears.

I was deep into the woods, up to my knees in water, when I suddenly got a very clear kind of double vision telling me that something was wrong in the ground, something was there that wasn't supposed to be, buried just under the dirt.

I found a stick and poked it into the water, muddling around until the end hit something hard and slick. Then I got down and scooped away the mud, getting my fingers under the edges and prying it up.

The thing in my hands was made of glass and wires and looked like something from outer space, but when I turned it over, I saw on the back that it was stamped with the word *Magnavox*. It was a television tube. I'd seen them when I was little down at the dump, and Marvin Coil, who worked there, had shown me and Shiny how if you put a rock through one, it would explode with a terrific pop.

I stood perfectly still, holding the tube in both hands. It seemed to me that if you stepped on one buried in the ground, it might explode then, too. It seemed very clear that I was someplace I wasn't supposed to be.

I set the television tube carefully on a fallen log and then, with the sleeve of my raincoat pulled over my hand, I put a piece of shale through it. The sound it made was very loud. I tucked the pieces under the log and covered them with mud, then slopped my way deeper into the trees.

I passed a waterlogged duck blind and a little flooded dock with a johnboat tied at one of the posts, which was barely poking out of the creek. And the whole time, I walked like I was being called, following the high, whining hum of craft.

Then I broke through a stand of birches into a little clearing occupied by a tin-roofed shed. It was gray with weather and open on one side, full of shelves, lined with rows and rows of mismatched jars. They all had paper labels, marked with nothing but dates. The glass on some of them was smoky, but something crackled and glowed inside like dark, ugly lanterns. The air around them seemed to buzz.

It reminded me of how the air had buzzed and crackled in the hollow, but now it looked wrong. I had a bad feeling that whatever was sitting in the jars was gone-over. Rotten.

The stuff was aged past all benefit or reason, and I understood with a sinking feeling that I had stumbled upon Greg Heintz's craftshack. Here was where he kept every bit of dirt and stone that he carted off from the hollow to sell.

I was about to back away when something in the muddy water caught my eye, something small and pale pink.

A broken dogwood branch floated by the shed, and I picked it up. Long strands of hair were caught in the bark, white as corn silk, snarled around the places where the blossoms had been knocked loose and a few pink petals still clung, raggedy and broken. There were no dogwood trees anywhere in the birchwood.

The end of the stick was dark with something that looked like blood. The hair was the same color as Davenport's.

※　※　※

When I climbed the porch and knocked on Greg Heintz's door, he yanked it open almost as soon as my hand touched wood. The front door opened straight into the living room, and behind him, I could see a low ceiling looming over a pair of plaid chairs and a blue velvet couch covered in plastic.

Up close, he was even taller than I'd remembered, with eyes that looked too shrewd and too pale in his sunburnt face. I stood in front of him, holding the dogwood branch and trying not to look shaken up inside.

"I'd like to see Davenport, please," I said, suddenly very aware that I was carrying around a tree branch and a suitcase.

He gave me a long, ugly look, head to toe and back again. "She isn't here."

Suddenly, more than ever, I needed to know where she was—to know that she wasn't somewhere she needed to be saved from. I was gripped by a horrible fear that something had happened out in the birchwood.

In the doorway, Greg Heintz was looking at me in a way I did not like. His eyes were deep-set and silvery, shining out from a sunburned face. "What are you doing out here with a suitcase? Fixing to run away?"

The strange, coppery note in his voice made me hold the

dogwood branch tighter. "I want to talk to Davenport right now. Where is she?"

"That is none of your goddamn business. Now, you are kindly welcome to get off my porch."

"Did you *hurt* her?"

He looked at me like I was out of my mind. "Hurt her? She's up to Reedy's selling ice cream in a stupid paper hat. Why would I hurt my own kid?"

I had all kinds of things I wanted to say to him—that every time he so much as looked her way, he hurt her. That being near him was not good for any sort of living thing.

But I just tilted my chin up and said, "Because my cousin says you've got a temper, and because I don't think you treat her right." I held up the soggy branch. "And because I found this out in the woods, bloody and tangled with her hair."

Another man might have been worried at that, or started asking a hundred questions, or at least gotten short with me for telling him how to raise his girl, but Greg Heintz did the strangest thing. He laughed. "You'd be hard put to hurt a creature like that. Davenport's fine."

I stared up at him, not liking his fixed gaze or his tight-lipped smile. The branch was damp and I held it tighter.

Greg Heintz loomed over me, hands in his pockets. "Now, if that's all you came for, it's time for you to be leaving."

❊ ❊ ❊

In town, the excitement of the fair had died down a little. Main Street wasn't as crowded as the night before, but there were still plenty of people milling around the booths and

225

tents, looking at which pies and which pigs had been special enough to get ribbons.

I wandered through, trying not to think of how good it had been last night before everything went to hell. The smell of the carnival made something ache in my throat, but it was a dumb, pointless ache. I walked right past the arcade games and the giant swings without looking at the place where Fisher and I had pitched at prizes. Where we'd held hands and kissed and where he'd walked away as soon as it got bad. He'd chosen the easy side, just like Shiny'd said he would, and now the truth was out and at least I knew. I didn't need him.

Inside Reedy's, the air smelled like fake strawberries and glass cleaner.

Davenport was behind the counter, and as soon as I saw her, something in my chest let go and I felt like I could breathe again. She was scooping pink ice cream into a Styrofoam dish, sprinkling it with rainbow candies and handing it across the glass to one of the sleek, glossy girls Rae had been planning to sell charms to the night before.

Over by the Coke machine, a bunch of other girls in swimsuit tops and denim shorts perched on the edge of one of the tables. They were watching Davenport with bored eyes, licking on their ice cream, and at first I thought they were waiting for her to finish so they all could leave together, but after a second, I knew that wasn't the case. The way they looked at her was sly and smirking.

She glanced up when I came in, then turned away fast.

Her eyes were a pale January-blue, milder and softer than her father's.

"Hey," I said, coming up to the counter, careful not to lean on the glass, which was slick and smudgeless, like she might have just Windexed it. "Have you been doing okay?"

At the question, Davenport's eyes got wider, but she nodded. "Why wouldn't I be?"

I stood awkwardly with the branch in my hand. "No reason, I just got worried, is all."

"Well, I'm fine." Her expression was strange though, flat and far away. She stood limply against the counter with the scoop in her hand. "What are you carrying around that piece of nothing for?" she said finally, studying the stick with slow, watchful eyes.

Her tone was barely even curious, and suddenly I wasn't so sure about what I'd found out in the woods, or my fear for her, or anything that had happened all morning. "No reason. Just found it and liked the flowers."

In the corner by the Coke machine, the girls all were laughing, whispering back and forth until it was about to drive me crazy.

Davenport set down her scoop and looked at me like she wanted to be anywhere but here. "You going to buy anything or what?"

"I haven't got money," I said. "I just came by to see how you were."

"Then you can't stay in here," Davenport said. "There's a policy. You have to buy something or leave."

The tallest, pinkest girl crunched into her cone and said, talking past me to Davenport like I wasn't even there, "What's the matter, Davenport? Don't want people to see you hanging around with your own kind?"

Davenport only mumbled something and hunched her shoulders, but I gave the girl a long, measuring look. "There should really just be a policy where people can't stay in here if they can't watch their mouths."

The girls were looking at me like I had every kind of disease. One by one, they slid down from the table, knocking into me as they passed, my shoulder here, my elbow there.

"Your roots are showing," one said, eyes roaming over me in a slow crawl.

The way she said it, I could tell she wasn't just talking about where the cherry-red faded into dark. She meant my everything, my entire past, all right there in the state of my hair. My hand wanted to rake through the tangles, but I wasn't about to give her the satisfaction.

"Your bad manners are showing," I said as they all swished past me. As retorts went, it wasn't very snappy, but I was well past caring.

Davenport just flicked the rag and looked down through the glass countertop at the half-scooped tubs of ice cream. I wanted to tell her it would all be okay, but as the girls clopped out of the shop in their platform sandals, I knew it wouldn't be, and it wasn't.

"You should go," she said again. Her voice was low and toneless.

"Don't you get lonely around here? I'll stay and keep you company awhile if you want."

"I'm not supposed to go around with any Blackwoods," she said to the countertop. "My dad thinks it doesn't set the right tone for the family."

It seemed like quite a rude thing to say, especially considering that she had been down to see Myloria and get her dogwood tattoo just the other day, which in itself went a long way toward showing that she did not always do what her father said.

"You were just at our place," I pointed out. "Getting work from Myloria."

"That was for business," she said. "It's different if you go to someone crooked for a fortune. I wanted to know mine, and now I do."

"Myloria doesn't tell fortunes. She does tattoos."

Davenport shrugged. "Not every fortune comes from a crystal ball or a deck of cards. Your aunt's supposed to have a good hand with ink, is all."

The dogwood branch hung limply in my hand. It was still wet, even though I'd been carrying it around for most of the afternoon. I held it up. "I found this stick, and it's got blood on it, and I was worried. You really don't know anything about it, even though it's like what's drawn on your back?"

"No. I don't. Maybe someone bagged a deer." The way she said it was flat, and her eyes flicked to the door again, making it very clear she was done with me.

I wondered what her father would say—what he'd *do*—if

he knew about the dogwood tattoo, but all I said was, "I'll go if you want, but if something happens, you know where to find me."

Davenport looked up, cutting her eyes to the ceiling. "I don't have a single idea what you're talking about. Ain't nothing going to happen around here."

Her voice was trembly, though, sad and lost, like she was a balloon tied to a railing and waiting for someone to come back for her.

Out on the street, I stood under the striped awning of Reedy's, feeling stupid and confused, like maybe I'd just invented myself some trouble because Fisher wasn't around to make the real thing.

I was about to call it a day and start back home when someone said my name, and I knew it was him before I even turned around.

He was standing in front of the Shop Mart, carrying two sacks of groceries and looking unreadable.

"What?" I said. It was strange to say a word and have it fly through the air at someone like a slap. I thought how if I were Shiny, I would be heating up, getting ready to burn down everything. Instead, my throat hurt like I'd been sucking on an ice cube, and all I wanted was to look away.

"I need to talk to you," Fisher said, stepping down from the curb and crossing the street to me. "About what happened at the fair. About last night."

"Well, then you'll be disappointed that I have nothing to say to you."

"What happened last night," he said again. "That wasn't what you think."

I turned on him, holding the branch like a weapon. "You don't know *what* I think."

He bowed his head and looked away. "Well, I know what I'd think, then. I'd think if someone acted how I did last night that they were ashamed of who they were and didn't want to people to see them having anything to do with anything like craft."

"And you're saying if you thought that about a person, you'd be wrong?"

"No, that part's true. But why I walked away rather than just sit there being ashamed and honest is something else. Mike and them don't have a cool head about craft, and not about the Blackwoods. If the Maddox boys told Mike or anyone what they'd seen, it would get pretty ugly pretty fast, so I took them out there and talked them down. They listen to me, but only as long as they don't have to think too hard about what I really am."

"You're telling me Mike Faraday and them are so scared of craft that if you didn't talk them out of it, they'd come after *me* over something *you* did?"

I thought Fisher would laugh at the ridiculousness of that, but instead, he just nodded. "People around here are happiest when they can blame everything on the Willows. Your being there would mean you getting blamed. Who knows, maybe they'd feel that way about me if it wasn't for Isola, but how can I say? She's around and she's in charge."

"She must be scarier than she looks."

Fisher leveled me with a long, steady stare. "You have *no* idea. Look, I can't explain it right, but she's something else." He glanced up the street and hoisted the groceries higher. "Okay, here's what. I know Myloria, and she isn't going to feed you anything worth eating, so you might as well come over and get a real meal. If you come for supper, I'll show you something so you understand."

"Are you sure? I mean, about me going over there to visit with Isola?"

He nodded. "As long as you can stand her being like she is."

We stood on the sidewalk, facing each other. The canvas banners were hanging over the empty stores, making the whole block into an out of order comic strip. They gave the street a still, eerie feeling, like it was dressed up for Halloween.

"Fisher?" I said when we'd stood so long it seemed indecent, the dogwood branch dripping to eternity in my hand. "How's your craft?"

"How do you mean?"

I looked up at him. "How do you think I mean? Has your craft been acting up all over the damn town lately?"

He hung his head so his hair covered his eyes. "No," he said finally. "I think last night was nothing but a fluke. I just need to make sure to keep it low, is all."

I nodded, pretending an ease I did not feel, more certain than ever that this was all another part of the mess we couldn't see, all the histories and secrets that lay buried under the years.

He raised his eyebrows. "Now, you want to tell me what you're doing walking around town with a broken stick?"

"I found it in the creek below the hollow, and it was all snarled with blond hair and I got scared something had happened to Davenport."

"And had it?"

I shook my head and then glanced back toward Reedy's.

In the window, Davenport stood in her white paper hat, ice cream scoop clutched in a pale hand. I raised my own hand to wave, because it was what polite people did, then caught sight of her face. The way she looked at me—at us— was this strange, sad, wanting look, like her heart was somewhere off in the distance. I let my hand fall back down.

THE SECRET ROOM
CHAPTER EIGHTEEN

At his house, I followed Fisher through the long front hall and into the kitchen.

He thumped the groceries down on the table and Isola looked up from the stove. She'd been poking at something with a wicked-looking two-pronged fork, but as soon as she straightened and saw us, she gave Fisher a look like someone had set her hair on fire.

She dialed it back fast, though, and said to him, "Well *there* you are. Thought I was going to have to send out the search party. Now run and get me the big dish off the top of the china dresser."

As soon as he was out of the room, she turned on me with the meat fork in her hand. "Did I not tell you to stay good and far away from this place?"

I stood with the table between us. "Fisher invited me for dinner."

"And does this face look like I got a welcome mat laying out for Blackwoods? You keep away from my house, and keep *far* away from that boy."

"If you're so worried who Fisher goes around with, maybe you should tell him to stay away from *me*."

Isola raised her eyebrows. "Do not sass me. Do you think I'm stupid? I know what you've brought home to us just by being loose in the world."

The way she said it made a shiver run through me and I hugged my arms around myself. "And what is that, exactly?"

Isola turned to the sink and began trimming a pile of string beans. "Craft and craft and *more* craft. I know who you are," she said, pinching the ends off the beans like they'd done something to offend her. "Clementine DeVore."

The words were fierce and full of blame. I stared at the back of her head, trying to work out how she was the only person in the whole town, apart from a couple of girls I'd played with when I was little, who had any very clear idea of who I was.

When she glanced over her shoulder at me, her face was like stone. "When I tell you to stay away from that boy, do you think I'm joking?"

"No, ma'am," I said.

"Then do you mind telling me why it doesn't seem to stick?"

"Fisher dug me out of the cellar of my house because he heard me breathing," I said, and my voice was husky. "I know he's got a powerful kind of craft and the more we're together, the more it seems to get away from him, but we can't seem to stay apart. I don't *want* to stay apart."

Isola nodded, but it was heavy. She started scooping the beans into a pot by handfuls, like she needed something to do with herself. "Well, I can't say I'm surprised, I guess—craft calls to craft, and trouble will always find trouble. And your cousin and that little Dalton, well of course you'll be thick as thieves with them. Things is getting bad around here, same as last time. All I got to say is, five is a terrible number."

"How do you know about that?" I said, coming around the table.

Isola put the lid on the pot and turned to face me. "Because I know a thing or two about the past, and a thing or two about what they call sympathetic magic. Only really works when you get together, don't it? And more is better, although how you all could have got to that Heintz girl is a mystery to me."

"Heintz?" I repeated it dumbly, flat and empty like a word I didn't know.

Isola nodded. "It seems to me her daddy would do everything in his power to keep her from going around folks like you, and don't you deny it."

"He doesn't just try," I said, thinking of how nervous she'd been of me at Reedy's. "She minds him, too."

At that, Isola threw back her head and laughed a nasty little laugh.

"Well, she *does*."

Isola turned away and shook her head. "Minds him! As though any one of you sorry young creatures ever minded anyone." She was still laughing when Fisher brought the plate back in.

The dinner was better than anything I'd had in a long

236

time—maybe better than anything I'd had in my whole life—even though Isola and Fisher were making rather a performance of being hateful to each other.

"Why don't you ask your little friend whether she runs around with you 'cause she's playing daredevil or 'cause she just don't know any better?" Isola said, stabbing at the roast with a fork.

Beside me, Fisher closed his eyes. "Could you not? Please."

Isola clucked at him and started spooning up mashed potatoes and dishing it out onto the plates. She slammed one down in front of me with an icy sniff that seemed mostly for show. I put butter on my biscuit and ate it.

Isola watched me devour my supper with the bright attention of a sparrow. "Well, I'd like to say I'm surprised to find a Blackwood in my house, but I guess it's what I could expect. Wouldn't any halfway *decent* girl run around with trash like that one."

I was sorting my peas out from the carrots, which I knew was bad manners, but my hands wanted something to do. "Eric's been nice. He took me to Greg Heintz's animal zoo the other day."

Fisher snorted and shook his head, reaching across me to take the gravy boat.

"I kind of thought you took *me* to the zoo," he muttered in my ear.

I cut my meat into pieces, trying not to smile at the warmth of his breath on my cheek.

"Nothing funny about any of this," Isola said, watching

237

us both. "So you can just quit smirking, missy. I heard from Betty Lind at the laundromat that her Nathan seen a cougar in the Willows on his way back in from the city. Now, what do you say about that?"

I suspected she knew I had several things to say to that, but I elected not to say anything at all.

Fisher dropped his head into his hands. "Isola, what are you doing? Why can't you just act decent and have some kind of civil conversation?"

Isola narrowed her eyes at me like I was a piece of machinery and she was studying out the best way to take me apart. "What have I got to say to a stranger?"

"*Isola*," Fisher said, staring hard at her.

"If you're hurting for a subject, you could mention the weather," I said in my sunniest voice, mixing up my peas and gravy with the back of my fork.

Isola gave me a vexed look, but her eyes were flashing like she might laugh. As soon as the beginnings of a smile crossed her mouth, though, she reined it in and scowled instead. "You have got the table manners of a starving cat. Don't that Blackwood woman ever feed you?"

"Shut up," Fisher said, and his voice hung in the hot, humid air of the kitchen.

Isola pressed her lips together and shook her head. "Mister, you want to get your mouth straight. What do *you* care what anyone says about any of that trash out in the Willows?"

He gripped the edges of his plate with both hands. "Isola, if you don't shut up, I'm going turn over this whole table, swear to God."

Isola threw her head back and laughed a dry, crackly laugh. "I'm only telling the plain truth, mister. If you don't like it, keep it to yourself."

Fisher scraped his chair back. "Come on," he said, jerking his head toward the door.

I got up to follow him, folding my napkin and laying it next to my plate. "Thank you for dinner, Mrs. Fisher. It was good."

Isola just stuck her chin out and gave me a mean, ornery look that I suspected was an inch away from a smile.

Fisher was out in the front hall by the stairs. When I came up next to him, he took a deep, shuddering breath and let it out, but didn't say anything. Then he reached for my hand and pulled me into the sitting room.

It was stale and dusty, the way rooms get when no one ever uses them for actual sitting, and taken up by a couch and two matching chairs, patterned in the most unfunny sort of plaid so that the whole place looked like a tablecloth. The lamps were colored glass, and the bookcases were full of china figures with oversized heads and big soppy eyes. Most of them seemed to be tending some kind of tiny sheep.

There weren't many other knickknacks around—just the sad children and the sheep—but there was a photograph of Fisher on the back of the piano. He looked younger, thirteen or fourteen. He was holding a caught fish and looking very unhappy to be there.

"That in there," I said finally. "She does it a lot, right?"

He shrugged but didn't answer, so I knew the answer was yes.

"She's a good cook, though."

"Yeah. She is."

"Well, that's not nothing. I mean, I'm about to starve to death over at Myloria's."

He looked at me with his head ducked down so his hair hung in his face. "You know, it's no problem for you to come by. If you want."

"*Oh*, I think it's a problem for Isola."

"Then she can deal with it. Look, come over whenever you want—as long as you don't mind her picking on you over every stupid thing and taking some kind of shot at you whenever she gets a chance."

"I don't mind."

The look he gave me was sidelong and strange. "Everybody minds Isola, but not you. Why is that?"

I shrugged. I didn't know how to explain how the hard, unguarded edge in her could seem so true and so familiar. It seemed honest. "Maybe somebody who cares enough to scrap with you—cares enough to notice you're actually in the room—is not all that bad."

At that though, Fisher looked away. "That thing I was going to show you," he said, and he jerked his head toward the upstairs. "You might as well see."

He led me up to the top of the house. The attic was just as dusty and cluttered as it had been the morning after I'd brought him home from the hollow, piled high with broken spindle chairs and stacks of newspaper.

As we passed, Fisher stopped halfway along the hall and put his hand against the bare wall directly across from his bedroom. He left it there a second before leading me back into the tiny sewing room.

"You're showing me the Singer machine?"

"Nope," he said, crossing the room and shoving up the window.

"So, showing me the roof."

He looked back at me, swinging one leg out over the sill. "Kind of."

We clambered out across the shingles. The roof was warm, leaving bits of tar and grit stuck all over my hands. We crawled around to the other side of the house from Fisher's room, where he stopped at a gable window and pressed his hand against the glass. For a second, it looked like it wasn't going to open. Then he gave it a shove and it went, the wood screeching where the frame had swelled tight.

The room was the same size and shape as Fisher's bedroom, with the same sloped ceiling. There wasn't much furniture in it, just a stained card table and a dusty mattress lying on the floor.

The built-in bookshelf across from the window was mostly empty, but there were a few stray pens and dead spiders here and there, and on the middle shelf, a stack of photo albums—matched memory books in different colors and a wedding book made of white and gold leatherette like a bible.

Fisher stood in the middle of the little room, looking around himself.

I kept waiting for him to say something, explain what it was he was showing me, and when he didn't, I wandered over to the shelf and picked up one of the albums.

I was kind of hoping to see pictures of Fisher when he was little, but the first page was all black and whites, printed on slick, heavy paper and mostly square. The girls in them were young, barely teenagers maybe, with short, curled hair that made frames around their faces. In the photos, their lips were so full and dark they looked black, but I knew that in the light of the flash, they would have been wearing starlet-red lipstick.

The next page showed a couple standing in front of a flowered archway. The woman was one of the girls from the early pages, older now, and wearing a ruffled formal dress with a corsage of lilies pinned to the shoulder. The man wore a white shirt and a pair of black dress pants held up by suspenders, but that was about all you could tell about him, because someone had taken scissors and cut his face out of the picture.

"Not too forgiving, then," I said, staring at the faceless man.

Fisher snorted. "If there's one thing Isola knows about, it's holding a grudge."

As I flipped through the book, a picture began to come clear, a strange, mysterious version of New South Bend, filled with secrets and hard, knowing stares.

I turned to the last page, where the only picture was a

photo of a bunch of girls sitting together up on the bed of a pickup, glamorous in black and white, even though their knees were scraped and the one balanced up on the curve of the wheel well wasn't wearing shoes.

Fisher frowned, bending over the album. "That one's Isola," he said, pointing to the girl with the floppy hat and the sailor dress. Her arms were bare and she was smiling a sly, hell-raising smile, cocking one eyebrow up into the low-slung curl of her hair.

"And that's Emmaline Blackwood," I said, pointing to the dark-haired girl who was sitting next to her, perched on the edge of the turned-down tailgate, her face hard and proud, her chin up. The way she caught the sun, it lit her bones, showing off Spanish and Irish and Choctaw, and under that, something else. The dark of her eyes glowed hungrily, already taken up with the power of the hollow. She was fiercer than Myloria and my mother. The kind of girl who might grow up to run wild through the hollow and keep company with things best left alone.

It was a shock to see her there, my own grandmother sitting so comfortably with Fisher's, arm slung around Isola's waist. The two of them leaned into each other like sisters, and I remembered the look on Isola's face when she studied me in the hall that first morning and then backed away. Like someone had just walked over her grave.

Behind me, Fisher had started to pace, crossing the floorboards in long strides like the room was making him restless. His boots thudded hollowly, and every now and then I heard a little jingle. There was something under the mangy rug, but when I went to turn back the corner with my foot, he went still, his hands closed into fists.

"Don't," he said, and his voice was so choked that I could hardly make out the word.

I pushed the rug back anyway. Under it, the floor was marked by a rectangular trapdoor with a metal ring for a handle. I sat on my knees next to the wadded-up rug, looking down at the door.

Fisher only turned away and didn't say anything, but I could see the restless agitation coming off him like heat lightning.

"Where does this go to?"

He looked down and touched the edge of the door with his toe. "There's a pull-down ladder in the bedroom downstairs, but if Isola catches us messing around in here, she'll go nuts. It's safer to use the roof."

I remembered the odd stretch of bare wall on this side of the hallway. "Why is the door to this room papered over? What *is* this place?"

Fisher looked away. "I wasn't supposed to be here," he said. "But I showed up, she didn't know what to do with me, and so she made it that anyone who came into her house couldn't go snooping around and find anything."

I looked at the bunched-up rug and the trapdoor. "That's kind of crazy."

Fisher nodded. "It's Isola."

"How long were you in here?"

He shook his head. "A long time. My mom brought me back here one night. I was seven, and Isola put me in this room. It seemed like forever before she decided it was safe to let me out. Then she acted like I just got here, started telling everyone I'd come up from Shreveport or somewhere."

I looked around the empty room, which was missing every kind of thing that made a bedroom—no dresser, no toys or curtains, just the mattress and the card table and a broken chair. "For how *long,* though?"

Fisher let out the dry, barking laugh he did when something hurt almost too much to stand. "Two years, maybe? I can't remember. I can't even remember nights and days— just one long blank, like staring at a wall. After a while, I was so ready to lose my mind, I wrecked everything I could get my hands on."

In my canning closet, time passed in big smears, with the speed of dreaming. For Fisher, the time had gouged its way into his skin. He had felt every second of it.

I stepped over the rug, kicking it back into place. The trapdoor echoed a little under my shoes. Being near him was the closest thing to knowing what to say, and I leaned my forehead against his chest, listening to the beat of his heart.

"I have to tell you something," he whispered, and just from the catch in voice, I knew it would be bad.

"It's okay," I whispered back, because it seemed wrong to talk too loud.

"Isola said she did it to keep me safe, but that's a lie. It was to keep the town safe. She did it because I'm dangerous."

I squinted up at him. "Well, I know *that*, but it's no reason to lock you up."

"No," he said, and his voice was raw, lower than I'd ever heard it. "Listen. I came to town when I was seven—the week before the whole damn world went crazy and your house burned and everything in Hoax County went to hell. Isola lies about it, though. She tells everyone I wasn't here. That way, they'd be stupid to think I had anything to do with it."

"Well, maybe she's still nervous for you—she wants you to be safe."

Fisher let out a long, shaky breath. "I'm not *talking* about Isola. What I'm trying to tell you is, I know the truth." He closed his eyes before he finished. "I'm the reason the reckoning happened."

I stared at him.

"That can't be," I said finally, with my arms around the wedding album.

I'd been so sure that it was me. That I was at the heart of it. I was the one buried down in the cellar, and now, almost the minute I was out, everything seemed to be starting over.

Then I thought of what Isola had said—that one craft called to another.

Fisher was standing with his head bowed, not looking at me. When I touched his arm, he flinched and stepped back.

"Don't you get it?" he said. "I'm the reason for everything that's happened. I'm the reason you have nothing."

I stood holding the wedding album full of pictures of

my grandmother. In a dusty room full of dead bugs and broken furniture, with a boy who had saved me from darkness, and who sometimes looked at me like he could see into my thoughts. Who could make me feel like I was seeing the world through his eyes.

I didn't know how to make him see that it wasn't his fault. Or, if it had to be someone's, that it was both of us. All of us. The fiend had tried to tell me that day in the hollow, but I'd been too scared for Fisher and too scared of myself to really see it. The reckoning was bigger than a single person. There were five points on the star.

"You should hate me," he said.

I set down the book and put my arms around him. When my arms tightened, he swallowed hard, a long, painful swallow that made his chest jerk. He stood against me, not moving, not speaking. After a second, he hugged me back.

The things I had were mine and some of them were broken, but they were real. They were so very far from nothing.

THE DYING BIRD
CHAPTER NINETEEN

Later, Fisher drove me home. He walked me up onto the porch and we stood looking at each other under the light. In front of me, he was warm and solid, but now that the sun was down and the air was humming with crickets, I was starting to lose my sense of things again. Suddenly, I found myself nearly swallowed by the feeling that had gripped me on the day he'd carried me out of the cellar, like the world was too much, too full—like it was spinning away from me.

I had a sudden, desperate feeling that if he touched me, it might prove that I was real. I wanted him to grab me and shake me, or press me hard against his chest, and then I might be sure that I was solid too, and not a trick of my own imagination.

It was with a start that I came to a disquieting realization. Solid or not, it didn't matter. I had to go on anyway. I was standing on a rotting porch at night, in a place that was either outside or inside my own head. I had no sense of time or distance or territory, and no way of knowing which world was the real one. Just being here at all would have to be enough.

Then Fisher put his hand on the side of my face and all doubt and uneasiness vanished. There had never been anything but this moment and this porch and the two of us.

He smiled down at me. "I'll see you tomorrow, okay?"

I nodded. The way he said it made it so he wasn't asking to see me again, just telling me about something that would happen in the future. Tomorrow.

We stood in the halo of the porch light, white moths beating their wings around us, leaving powdery streaks on his shirt. He leaned down and kissed me so fast it was like a race. His mouth was soft and warm. I went inside without looking back or saying anything else.

Outside the cellar, time moved in ways that made it impossible to catch hold of. It was always slipping. Silence seemed the only trick I knew to keep the moment in one perfect piece, like a scene inside a snow globe. Exactly how it was.

✳   ✳   ✳

Shiny was already asleep, curled in a ball with the covers pulled over her head. She'd left the lamp on for me.

Under the sheets, I lay staring up at the sagging bedsprings, following the shape of the wires in the dark, tracing how they crossed under the mattress. I smiled to myself at the memory of Fisher's mouth, near and surprising and hungry.

I was just beginning to drift off when a sound close by pulled me back to wakefulness. All through the room, chimes were jingling. When I rolled over, though, no one was there.

Then, I caught sight of the mirror.

A woman was in the room with us, standing at the foot of the bed. Her face was pale in the dark. Where her eyes should be, there were only two hot circles of white, glaring light.

I lay perfectly still, staring at her reflection. As I watched, she met my gaze in the mirror and raised a finger to her lips. I was looking at one of the Blackwood fiends, and she was looking right back at me.

Then, from outside the open window, there was a huge commotion of screeching and squawking, so loud it seemed to be coming from directly by my ear.

In an instant, the fiend was gone and Shiny was out of bed, groping around in the dark for her boots. I rolled out after her, stumbling along behind the sound of her footsteps.

In the kitchen, she didn't even slow down, just kicked open the door to the sideboard as she passed it and grabbed an old walnut-handled shotgun from inside, all in one movement. Then she flung open the back door with the gun in her hands and her hair flying everywhere, and went storming across the yard toward the chicken coop.

I ran out after her through the yellow circle of the porch light, grass sticking to the soles of my feet, wet against my bare ankles.

From the hen house, there was the soft, irregular sound of the door bumping against the frame in the breeze, but it wasn't loud enough to cover the screeching that came from inside.

Shiny went stalking up the path to the coop with the shotgun. In the dark, she was almost glowing.

"Shiny!" I shouted it, not to stop her exactly, or to call her back, but because her skin was gleaming like a piece of hot iron and I knew I would never catch her. "What are you doing?"

"Saving my goddamn chickens!"

She came up to the shed and stopped with her feet planted wide on either side of the little dirt path, then flung back the door. Inside, the noise cut off. Then a huge, dark shape came bolting out past her.

She swung the gun up and I heard the short, mechanical pull of her finger on the trigger, but nothing happened. I stood in the yard with my hands held near my ears, waiting for a boom that never came.

The creature went thundering across the grass and Shiny moved with it, tracking the shadow along the barrel of the gun and swearing like fire, but under the words, she sounded scared.

The thing bolted past me, ugly as sin, all hooves and tusks and a huge, humped back. In the light from the porch, I saw blood across its muzzle and tufts of feathers around its mouth. Then it was gone, lumbering away into the shadow of the trees.

Shiny let the gun fall to her side. "What the hell was that?" she whispered. "Was that a razorback?"

But both of us knew it hadn't been any razorback. The thing was monstrous, too big, too mean and hungry. Too bloody.

"Should we go after it?" I said, staring into the woods. "Maybe we can still catch up to it, kill it, and bury it before anyone else sees?"

Shiny let out a long, shaky breath. Then she tucked the gun in the crook of her arm and squinted at me. "You are not seriously telling me you want a piece of that thing."

Wordlessly, I shook my head.

Neither of us felt much better when we got inside the coop. Most of the chickens were okay, but two were dead, a few had their feathers ruffled like they'd been stuffed in a sack and shaken, and one was barely even twitching anymore.

Shiny brought it out into the light by the back steps and laid it down, getting ready to cut its head off with her buck knife. She had a flat, grim look, the same as when she'd cut up the catfish, but I couldn't tell if her set face meant she was tired or sad or just pissed off at the way of the world.

I got down next to her to watch how she did it, but the chicken was still struggling and twitching. I didn't want it to be afraid. When she raised the knife, I reached out and touched the bird's feathers, running my fingers over the torn place in its neck.

There was a mess of broken bones in its back, and I put my hands on its warm, shivering side. I could see the shape of its body better with my eyes closed, better than I had ever seen anything in my life. The vision was like the night I had touched Fisher's back. I pressed my hands over the curve of the bird's chest and squeezed very gently, letting the bones slide together and knit there, letting the blood move in and out of its small, perfect heart.

After a second, the chicken struggled over and tried to get up.

Shiny put down the knife and looked at me with her mouth open. "Clementine, what did you do?"

The chicken lay flapping and kicking on the back steps.

"You made that come back from the dead."

"No," I said, still crouched with my heart beating hard, my hands out in front of me. "It wasn't yet. I mean, maybe it was about to be, but the heart was still going. It wanted to stay alive."

We stood looking at it as it picked itself up, rumpled and wobbling from side to side.

Shiny watched it straggle back to the coop, then turned and stared at me. Her eyes were burning with their strange, unpredictable heat, flickering under the porch light so she seemed to be lit from inside.

"*What?*" I said finally when she just knelt there, not saying a word.

"You," she said. "I always thought that any Blackwood would be drawn to the dirt, just like Myloria and Aunt Magda and everyone else in the family, the same way brown eyes beat blue. I thought I was the special one and here you walk around every day, brimming over with fool's light."

I shook my head at her, not knowing how to make sense of what she was saying.

She let out a shaky laugh. "You're like a little piece of the

253

hollow, just walking around. I mean, craft like mine is pretty uncommon, but light is *rare*. Forget blue or brown, that's like being born with *mismatched* eyes or something. It's supposed to be the hardest one to work, but it's got more power than all the others put together. It's the one that winds them up and sets them going."

"You're saying I'm like an engine for the reckoning."

"Not an engine," Shiny said. "Maybe more like fuel."

Her voice was reassuring, like she was explaining to me how everything was all okay, but nothing could make the truth any better. I was still the force that had started the destruction.

There was a part of me that had known—*known* my craft wasn't anything like Shiny's or Fisher's, or even really like my mama's, for all that I had memorized the names and the uses of plants. Since Fisher had taken me out of the cellar, every aspect of what I could do had been mysterious, hard to understand or anticipate. It should have been a relief to know the nature of it, to have it named, but I couldn't think of anything but the horrible truth of what it meant.

When I'd rested my hand on the dying chicken, I'd felt the beat of its heart, and then the light had come, not like it was coming from inside me, but just running through me like a pulse of electricity through a wire. It was huge and it was powerful, and it didn't feel like mine at all.

❊　❊　❊

In the kitchen, Shiny broke the shotgun and peered inside. "Goddamn it, Myloria—do you want us all to die of home invasion? She keeps taking the shells out."

She dragged a shoebox out from underneath the china cabinet and slammed it down on the table. Then she laid the gun across her lap, loading both barrels and snapping the action shut.

I watched her, thinking maybe this was just how a person survived out in the Willows. But I couldn't help thinking that Shiny's life was littered with dead things.

I picked up one of the shells, mystified at the way it floated in my hand. "It's light."

Shiny nodded. "For general defense only. I get a bunch of spent shells from Roy Wallace at Spangler's. He buys tricks off of me and Rae sometimes for favors, and one of the favors is, he saves all his cases for me and I load them up with rock salt. Not like it would do much damage, but it'll scare off anything smaller than a bull and it's cheaper than buckshot."

She was talking fast and sociable, like she was trying to distract me from everything I'd just learned. I was grateful to her for her trying, but it wasn't much help, considering I wasn't even sure how I felt.

All evening, I'd been thinking I'd made my peace with the reckoning star. Maybe I still had.

It was just a little harder now that I knew some points were built to take more blame than others.

I ran my fingers over four shotgun shells that didn't match the rest. They were tucked in the corner of the box and the plastic part was green instead of red. I took one and hefted it. It felt like a regular shotgun shell. "These ones aren't packed with salt, though."

255

Shiny reached over and snatched it back from me. "For emergencies," she said, dropping it in the box. "Now, don't touch them."

"Shiny," I said, watching her load the gun with rock salt and put it back in the cupboard. "What happens when the bad stuff from the hollow gets all the way up to town? When that monster hog gets seen on some nice, quiet street, what then?"

She didn't answer right away.

Then she looked up with wide, sober eyes. "They come for us."

The way she said it was like someone digging in for a war. Someone ready to fight any creature that came near her. Even in her own kitchen, out in the Willows, ten years and a crooked mile away from men with guns and gasoline, her skin seemed to glow hot.

"How come your house didn't burn to the ground like mine did?"

I already had an idea. I just wanted to hear her say it, like hearing how powerful she was might make me feel less dangerous.

She shrugged, but wouldn't look at me. "I don't know. I guess I stopped it."

"You were just little, though. How does a kid stop a house from burning?"

She shook her head. "It was scary. When the reckoning hit, everything changed so fast. One second, I was just regular Shiny, hot-tempered and hot-blooded. The next, it was like I was made of white, powdery ash or something. That's what I mean about the hollow. The light from the hollow touches stuff, and when it does, there's no stopping it."

"It lit something in you?"

She nodded. "It was all through my veins and in my skin, and I just knew that with the fire in me, I could walk through a flame and not be hurt."

"But you couldn't save the house?"

She shook her head. "I was barely strong enough to keep it out of the kitchen. And then the fire went down, and *that* was worse, because in a minute they were going to come in and when they saw we hadn't burned, they were going to take care of it themselves."

"What did you do?"

Shiny gave a dry little laugh. "I prayed. All I could think was if I really had fiends in my blood, if we really had a spirit or a demon in this house, then someone would come and fix it, but no one did. Do you believe it? Ten or twelve different fiends on the Blackwood tree, and not a single one of them came."

Her face was hard and it was no real mystery, I thought, how she had started to hate everything.

"But neither did the men from the coalition," I said. "What happened?"

"Someone else came instead. Someone out in the yard, talking to them like they were dogs, and they all just shut up. The wind stopped blowing. I could feel the power getting sucked away, like something running down the drain, and the fire went out altogether. Then everything was just . . . ruined."

"But who was it?"

Shiny shook her head. "It's like I think I should know. I think I should remember, but when I try, it's blank. I know what happened, and that someone came and said something, but I can't remember what or why."

The thing she described was like the empty memory of who shut me in the cellar. The work of someone more powerful than anything I could imagine. "How can a person be made to forget something like that?"

"It wouldn't be hard with craft," she said. "Especially not during the reckoning, with all that light blowing things up."

"What do you mean?"

"I told you, fool's light works like an electrical charge or a battery. It makes any other craft way stronger than it would be otherwise. People who know how to gather it up from the hollow and distill it down can use it to do crazy things."

I thought of the shack in the birchwood behind Greg Heintz's house, stacked with jars of strange billowing smoke, hissing and crackling, going to rot.

"You're saying I'm like a poison that makes everyone else's craft go crazy."

"Not like that, just something that makes us . . . more. I mean, I feel like just being near you makes me stronger. Not wild or out of control—my temper's a little worse, maybe— but mostly I just feel brighter."

I nodded. "But it doesn't even seem to be that big of a deal. I mean, you're never so unwound that you're going to start burning things up on accident, and Rae doesn't seem bothered by me at all."

Shiny smiled. "Well, with Rae, it's hard to tell if *anything* bothers her. I think maybe you make her more distracted— or farther away. That's the thing about air, though—it's all ideas, and ideas can mess up the world big-time, but they don't go ruining the animals or making the creek rise. Anyway, I wouldn't worry about Rae. I think the worst you can do to her is just making a smart person smarter."

"So, you think the real problem is Fisher, then," I said, and even saying it made my heart sink.

Shiny took a deep breath, and then another, like she was trying out all the words she wanted to say before she said them.

"We have to stay away from him," she said finally, and none of the breathing or the reconsidering of her words had made any difference. It still hurt to hear.

"You mean, *I* have to."

"Listen to me. His humor is dirt, and dirt is the realest, rawest thing in the world. Around you, he doesn't get vague, and he doesn't get mean. He *changes* things. Real, living things that can tear down houses or hurt people. And maybe he's kept his craft pretty low so far, but last night was out of control. What if it gets worse?"

I shook my head. "You don't know that it will. I think it's the first time anything like that's ever happened around him unless he was down in the hollow. Maybe that, what happened at the fair, maybe it wasn't even him. What about the fish? He didn't do *that*!"

And I remembered, too, what Isola had said about five being a terrible number. Even if Shiny and Rae and I had a better hold on our craft than Fisher did, he might not be the only place to lay blame. There were five points on the star, and that meant there was still the power of creek.

But Shiny's eyes were fixed far off out the window, past the barn, past the dark hay fields. "Clementine, craft gets wild in the hollow because there's all the fool's light down there." Then she reached across the table and touched my collarbone. "Fisher gets like that with you, because of all the fool's light in here. And you want to run around with him like it's no big deal?"

The thing I didn't know how to make her see, though, was that it *was* a big deal. He and I were tied together by something I didn't understand, but it hummed at me like a radio signal. I couldn't untangle myself.

"I didn't choose him," I said. "But I'm not going to abandon him, either. There has to be a way to keep it low. Maybe he can find a way to rein it in. Maybe he can figure out how to control it."

Shiny sighed, covering her face with her hands. "Maybe. Maybe he can control it, or maybe he'll try and fail and everything will go to hell, and you'll be there to suffer for it, because you couldn't stay away."

"I'm sorry. I just—I like him."

"I know," she said, but when she looked up, her face was tired. "Too bad he's probably going to be the death of us."

THE BRIDGE
CHAPTER TWENTY

In the morning, we didn't talk about it.

The ground around the Willows was still muddy and waterlogged, but things were already starting to dry out. The chicken seemed no worse for wear, and Shiny and I watched it peck around in the wire run along with the rest. I wondered how long we were going to keep not talking about it.

The fiend by the creek had said that the hollow was leaking out, finding a hold in the natural world, but the incident of the lilies at the fair had seemed a lot more like the natural world was working through Fisher, and if that was true, then he had gotten the fuel for it from me.

The idea made sense up to a point, but no matter how I turned the particulars over in my mind, there was more to it, because when it was just the two of us, he was fine. If the other night was any indication, it was when the others were around—Shiny and Rae—that things spun out of kilter. Two of us together weren't enough, but three or four, and it was a different situation. I didn't like to think what would happen with five.

Five kinds of wrong blood. Five kinds of full-scale craft

that added up to the reckoning. The only humor missing was creek, but Isola had seemed to have her own ideas on that account. The more I thought about it, the more I wondered if she wasn't right.

At first glance, Davenport was not the clearest candidate for someone born crooked, but after what I'd seen out in the birchwood, nothing I could learn about Greg Heintz was likely to surprise me much.

It was just after ten when Fisher's Trans Am came screaming into the driveway. The sky overhead was a watery blue, and I had already made up my mind what we had to do.

"Are you here to take me back down to the hollow?" I said when he came to the door, sitting down on the floor in front of him and pulling on my secondhand galoshes.

His eyebrows went up and his mouth opened like I had asked if he would take me to the moon. "*No.* Why the hell would I want to do that? You saw what happened last time. You know—that day it nearly killed me? For what earthly purpose would I want to take you back there?"

I pulled a ratty sweater out of the orange crate and put it on over my dress. "Because what you've got, you're going to learn to control it. And it seems like it would probably be better to practice down there where no one can see."

"What are you talking about?"

"You were dangerous at the fair," I said. "But then you came to your senses and got it low. If you did it once, you can do it again."

❊   ❊   ❊

We were quiet on the drive up to Harlan's pasture. Fisher seemed lost in thought, but I could tell just from the way he clenched his hands on the steering wheel that he didn't like where we were headed.

"This is a really bad idea," he said finally, when we'd slid down the side of the bluff into the boggy stream bed that led through the hollow.

"It's only bad if you can't figure out how to control it. And you have to, because losing hold of it in town again is going to . . ." I didn't like to say the rest, though, so all I said was, "You just *have* to."

Fisher led me through the moss and cattails and out into the meadow. It had bloomed since the last time we'd been there, full of cherry-red poppies bending gently in the breeze. The flooding hadn't touched a thing down here. All over the dogwood tree, flowers opened like butterflies as we came up the tiny hill. They started out pink and then bloomed other colors, slowly and completely, seeping red, blue, purple in the soft, hazy light.

"Are you okay, still?" I asked, keeping a close eye on him for any sign of mayhem.

"Yeah," he said, toneless and stone faced. "Yeah, I'm good."

The way he squared his shoulders told a different story, though. It was the same way he'd looked that night at the fair, standing horror-struck over the tarp, like he was barely hanging on. I didn't like the way he kept himself so still, like he was breathing too carefully, or was a bomb that could go off at any minute.

We settled ourselves in the meadow, and I looked up at him. "Okay, so when you change the color of the tree or make something grow, how do you do it?"

"Down here, it's easy," he said. "I just think something, and then it kind of happens. On its own, almost. Like it always wanted to do exactly that, and I'm just there to . . . let it."

I nodded. I was beginning to believe that my own kind of craft was the same. Last night, the chicken had wanted to be alive, and once I was seeing the heart of it, I could just move the parts to give it that, because everything in it had wanted to be better.

"Do it then," I said. "Make something happen."

"Okay," Fisher said, but he kept glancing around the meadow, looking nervous. "Once it gets started though, it doesn't want to stop."

"Well, how did you stop it at the fair the other night?" I tried to sound offhand and only succeeded partway.

Even though I understood his reasons for it, I could still feel the slap of how he had turned his back, like *I* was the one who'd conjured up the monstrous flowers and let them out into the world.

He laughed softly, even though the question wasn't funny. "I didn't really think it through. You were telling me to get it together. I thought about you. I thought how you'd been walled up so long, and that if you could keep cool and figure out how to get rescued after that many years, I could do it for thirty seconds."

"Okay, so make something happen and remember that I was in a cellar for a really long time, and if I can do that, then you can keep your craft low. Whatever wants out, let it come."

"That's going to be pretty dangerous."

Even as he said it, he was already up and restless, pacing circles around the trunk of the tree, his boots leaving a fairy ring of mushrooms as he walked. They started as harmless morels and went straight to spindly white destroying angels in about two seconds.

"Your mushrooms are turning poisonous."

Fisher nodded, keeping his lips pressed together. The grass was going brown around his boots now and he paced faster, raking his fingers through his hair.

"I think you should go," he said under his breath. "I can feel the hell dogs coming. They'll be here in a second if you don't get moving."

"Don't think about it. That's as good as you calling them."

"I can't *help* it." He was breathing fast and shallow, clenching and unclenching his hands.

"Stop!"

As soon as I said it, he went very still. He was shivering, looking past me to the edge of the trees. My eyes darted to the shadows there, following his gaze.

The whole wood seemed to be moving, alight with tiny glowing embers—the itchy red eyes of the hell dogs.

"Fisher," I whispered. "You have to stop *now*, before they come out here."

But it was too late.

The dark, low-slung shadows of the hell dogs were creeping around the edges of the clearing. The clouds were coming in.

"It's time for you to run," he said in a low, hopeless voice.

The pack moved around us, flitting between the trees, making a wide net. They had us completely surrounded.

Then something caught my eye behind them and I froze. A fiend was standing in the tall grass at the edge of the meadow, looking straight at me. Her face was long and birdlike, and she didn't speak or move, just stood with her hands clasped against the front of her dress, watching as the dogs circled. Every time their course drew near her, they snarled and shied away like she was poison.

Even as they skirted her, though, their eyes were still fixed on us, and I half-expected them to bolt from the woods.

Fisher stood with his shoulders squared and his hands in fists, like every muscle in his body was devoted to holding them back, keeping them at bay.

Then he glanced at me, just once, just for a second, and it broke.

One of the hell dogs came darting out across the grass, all claws and jaws and dripping teeth. Then it lunged, careening up at me through the sea of poppies.

I kicked it. The impact when my foot connected with its side was heavy and solid, knocking the dog away.

"You better get this situation under control *right* now,"

I yelled, scrambling back through the crumbling flowers, away from where the dog crouched, black and oily. *"Now*, Fisher—there are more of them!"

But as he turned to face the woods, I saw the strangest thing.

A row of pale shapes was appearing out of the trees. A whole crowd of fiends were gathering around us, watching like ghosts as the scene unfolded. Their eyes were bright and curious.

There was no time to wonder at their sudden appearance, though. Already, the hell dog had shaken itself off and was back on its feet. It crouched to spring again and I turned to run.

Even as I did, the grass was growing longer, going to bindweed and brambles all around me, catching at my legs. The dog hit me in the shoulder, knocking me into the sea of blackening poppies.

There was the swampy reek of its breath, its weight on my chest, and I swung my arms up and caught it around the neck. As soon as I touched it, it seemed to go insane, slashing at my face as I tried to hold it back.

Fisher ran across to me, turning his back on the woods, and I was so terribly sure that in a minute, the dogs would swarm us the way they had on the day they'd almost killed him.

On top of me, the hell dog thrashed and twisted. Its fur felt matted, greasy between my fingers, and I was sure I might scream. The hot cloud of its breath was in my face, and its eyes were red and oozing and mad.

Then, the toe of Fisher's boot came flashing down, catching it in the side of the head and sending it tumbling away from me.

For a second, I lay on my back and the dog lay next to me, writhing on the grass, trying to right itself. Before it could get to its feet, though, Fisher slammed the heel of his boot down on its throat. There was an awful crunching sound and then it stopped moving. I sat up, already bracing myself for the onslaught of the hell dogs, but it didn't come.

The fiends stood all through the meadow now, arranged around us like sentries.

I'd been so sure that down here in the hollow, this was Fisher's place—his world—but he wasn't the one calling them.

The day I'd first come down, the creek fiend with the blurry eyes had told me that it was my wise, old blood drawing all the fiends out of the trees. Then, the whole state of affairs had seemed like just another feature of being where I shouldn't, but now I knew that what she'd really been talking about was the fool's light. I could feel the warm, electric tug that drew them, pulling like a magnet, humming in my bones.

They had come to see me.

I searched their faces, each one strange and wild and distinct. Some looked like people, and some more like animals, but all of them were lovely and terrible. The white-haired fiend from the creek was not among them.

The one closest was broad, heavy through the shoulders with a thick jaw and flared nostrils, almost like a bull, and as I raised my head to meet its gaze, I understood why the dogs still hadn't reached us.

Every time one of them tried to slink past, the fiend caught it by its scuff, turning and flinging it back into the woods. On the other side of us, the woman on fire stood wrapped in her bed sheet, burning so bright that the pack all retreated, cringing in the shadows. Farther back, under the dense canopy of leaves, another fiend glowed faintly in the dimness, standing so still the air around her seemed to crackle. It was the same one I'd seen in the bedroom mirror the night before, with her face stark and empty and her eyes full of light.

By the head of the path that led back up the bluff, a man in a white church shirt and black trousers stood in the shade of a sycamore. He was wearing a blindfold and a flat-brimmed preacher's hat, and his face was thin and sallow, with no hair or eyebrows as far as I could tell.

He grinned at me, showing row upon row of jagged teeth. Every hell dog for an acre seemed to be slinking over to him to crouch at his feet like pets. His smile was full of a manic light, and I thought that I had never seen anyone so hungry.

"Fisher," I whispered, "I know it doesn't really look like it, but I think it's all right now."

He was standing over me with his fists clenched and his feet planted, waiting for the pack of dogs to lunge at us.

But when they didn't come, and he understood that they wouldn't, he let himself breathe and sank down next to me.

I rolled onto my hands and knees. There was a scrape on my chin that was settling to a low throb. The skin felt hot and raw, but I wasn't really bleeding.

Fisher crouched over me, examining my face. His hands were shaking and I was scared that in a minute he would try to touch the black ooze smeared across my chin, stinking and stinging where the dog had scratched me.

Around us the air crackled with a dry, frantic electricity, like at any second the lightning would start, but the hell dogs were slinking away.

"It's okay," I said, catching him by the wrists. "Calm down. I got it all over my hands the other day and it wiped right off. It's not poison. At least, probably not to anyone but you. It's like you practically wished yourself a place that could *hurt* you."

Fisher didn't answer, but after a second, he nodded. He bowed his head and then the panic seemed to run out of him. The air lightened. He pressed his hands against his face.

Over in the trees, the fiends had faded back into the shadows. In the clearing, everything was impossibly still.

✻　✻　✻

When I'd held my hand against my chin long enough that the little bit of bleeding had stopped altogether, we started back toward the Willows, cutting down through the bottom of the hollow and out onto Foxhill Road.

The flooding had receded everywhere except over at the

north side of the Heintzes' property line, where the Blue Jack Creek wound through the birch woods. There, the standing water was just as a bad as it had been yesterday, with no signs of going down.

As we headed for the car, both of us were quiet, though I suspected for different reasons.

I was considering the way the fiends had all gathered in the meadow, like they were coming out of the darkest corners of the hollow to find me. I guessed that Fisher was probably thinking about how he'd been able to get some measure of control over his craft, but not enough.

From the road, we could see a fallen oak tree that had washed up onto a little slab bridge that spanned the creek at the back of the Heintzes' property. The bridge was two inches underwater and the tree's branches made a kind of net where little heaps of trash had floated by and gotten caught. Beside a tangle of wire and a mayonnaise jar with the label half off, a pale shape lay in the water.

My heart leapt, slamming in my chest. I was so afraid that it was something strange and wrong and awful. Something with teeth.

I dropped Fisher's hand and took off toward the creek, already thinking how to kill it, to hide it like Shiny had done to the fish. I was halfway to the bank before I saw that the thing in the water was no monster. A woman lay facedown in the tangle of branches beside the bridge. From where I stood, her skin was bluish. Her hair looked white.

I splashed out onto the bridge and dropped to my

knees, leaning out into the water to catch hold of her. Long strands of willow root and waterweed had wrapped around the woman's wrists and ankles, sticking to her bare legs. She had a length of rope tied tight around her neck like a snare.

I knelt there on the slab, drying my hands on the front of my shirt again and again. She lay with her head to one side, hair fanning out like a web in the current. It was the fiend who'd come to us in the hollow the day I'd followed Fisher. She'd licked his blood off the screwdriver and warned me about the reckoning star. Now she floated in front of me, cold like twilight. Like creek water.

Fisher moved behind me, splashing closer. After a second, he touched my shoulder.

"Is she drowned?" I said, but even before I said it, I knew it was a stupid question. The rope around her neck was horrible. She'd been dead before she ever went in the water.

Fisher didn't answer. He pulled her out, laying her tenderly on the bridge, where the bottom end of the splintered oak trunk had fetched up onto the slab. Her head rested against the tree, so still she almost looked like she was sleeping. Her hands were long and gnarled as claws.

I stood over her. Before, she had seemed cold and alien and monstrous. Now she looked like a fairy or a mermaid. She looked magical. Not like something that could ever die.

"What are we supposed to do?" I said, shivering in the water.

Fisher didn't answer. After pulling her out and laying her

down, he'd turned away. He sat on the edge of the slab with his arms crossed over his chest.

"Close her eyes." His voice was hoarse and ferocious, breaking.

I got down on my knees and rested my hand on her face. Her skin was cold. I touched her eyelids, pressing them closed with my thumb and finger, but they just fell open again, sorrowful and cloudy.

"Do you have any money?" I said. "Any coins?"

Fisher dug in his pocket and tossed a handful of change at me without turning around. I crawled across the bridge, picking quarters out of the water. I set them carefully over the fiend's staring eyes. They glinted silver in the daylight, bright like falling stars.

I brushed the hair back from her face and tried to undo the rope, but the knots were wet, too solid to move, and I left it.

"What do we do now?" I whispered.

Fisher didn't answer. He was sitting on the flooded bridge with his head in his hands. Water ran and lapped around him, washing over his boots, tugging at his jeans.

I reached out to the fiend, holding her hand in mine. It was limp and cold. Her claws were smooth, digging into my skin.

"We have to bury her," I said. "It's the only way to keep the hollow from spreading."

Fisher nodded, but didn't open his eyes or look at me.

"I'll go and get help. Will you stay with her?"

"What do you think's going to happen to her *now*? Nothing can get at her, nothing can hurt her."

I held the fiend's hand tighter, trying to keep my voice from breaking. "Please. *Please* stay. I don't want to leave her like this."

Fisher looked up at me, but he didn't answer as I got up from the muddy water and started back toward the flooded bank. He didn't move from the bridge.

THE FUNERAL
CHAPTER TWENTY-ONE

Shiny was out behind the house, sitting on the tire swing and shoving herself back and forth with one foot. Rae was perched on the rusty seat of the hay rake, with her ankles crossed and a giant cardigan sweater tucked around her like wings. A red bicycle with rainbow streamers on the handlebars and a wicker basket was lying next to her, tipped over in the grass.

I ran up to them, rumpled and muddy, my damp dress sticking to my legs. "Shiny, we have some bad trouble."

She looked up with her hair in her eyes. "What are you talking about?"

"There's a fiend lying dead at the back of Greg Heintz's property. She's out there in the creek with a rope around her neck, and it's pretty clear that someone killed her."

Shiny brought the swing to a stop and stood with her knees locked, holding onto the ropes, looking off toward the high, muddy creek. She stared so long, I wasn't sure she'd understood.

Then she turned back to me. "What's it doing to the creek water? Is it doing anything? Is the water going bad?"

"I don't think so—at least, not yet. But I don't know how long that's going to last."

"Okay," she said. "Here's what we'll do. There's a little cemetery down at the south end of the hollow—just an acre maybe, and just for the old families. The ground's rocky enough down there that we should take a pickax, and there's some shovels in the barn."

"Fisher would help," I said, although I wasn't so sure. He'd looked pretty discomposed when he dragged the body from the water. "He's waiting at the bridge."

Shiny climbed off the swing and stalked across to the barn, grabbing the garden shovel down from the wall and shaking her head. "We don't need him."

"Shiny, we have to do this fast and I don't know if we'll manage without him. You think that two of us and Rae are going to be able to dig a grave and get a body across the creek before dark? We need all the help we can get."

Shiny scowled, but Rae got to her feet, brushing the grass off her dress. "We should get Davenport first," she said. "She's going to need to hear this."

Shiny and I both looked to Rae with our eyebrows up and our mouths open.

"What? You say somebody killed one of those things on her daddy's property, and I'm saying that her daddy is a maniac and likes to kill things."

"You really think we should just knock on the door and tell her?" Shiny said.

Rae's face was stony. "She lives out there in that house

276

all by herself with a man who hates fiends louder than any-one I've ever met and who might now have killed one. I'm not saying he's going to hurt her. All I'm saying is, for the love of God, do you really trust him *not* to?"

Shiny was still looking doubtful, but I knew Rae was right. If there was one thing that worried me more than the thought of what Greg Heintz had done out in the birch-wood, it was what he might still be inclined to do. Isola had as much as said that Davenport was tied to the star just like the rest of us, and if the pronouncement was right, it could mean she was in a whole lot of danger.

"Okay," I said finally, tipping my head back and raking my hands through my hair. "But we have to hurry. Let's get the tools together and go get her."

✳ ✳ ✳

When we got to the zoo, I was surprised to see how bad the property still was. Even with the creek down and the roads clear, the ground around the Heintz place was wet and muddy.

As we crossed the stretch of soggy yard, I glanced around me, keeping my eye out for Mr. Heintz, but I didn't see any sign of him, and his truck wasn't parked in the driveway. I could only hope that he hadn't had an itch to go roaming around out in the woods to check how his craft shed had weathered the flood.

The little house looked faded and lonely, sitting tucked back under the cedars. I stepped up onto the porch and called in through the open door. "Davenport? Hey, you in there?"

She came out in a cotton print dress that looked home-made and about a million years old. She was tangle-haired and barefoot, looking like a completely different person than the girl who paid money for Myloria's needle or scooped ice cream in a stupid paper hat.

"What's going on?" she said, sounding dim and sleepy.

I was more than a little nervous about how we were all standing there in the middle of the yard, worried that her dad would come back at any second.

"Get shoes," I said. "I'll tell you when we're away from the house."

She gave me a long, bottomless look, then disappeared into the house, coming back with a pair of cracked rubber boots with the tops cut short.

I waited till we were out in the road before I stopped and turned to her. "Davenport, how much do you know about what your dad does out in the birchwood?"

She stood looking at me like I'd asked if her daddy owned an airplane. "They're woods," she said simply. "He fishes and hunts, puts out trip wires, and finds things. You can do a lot of stuff with woods."

"Well, you know about the fiends, right?" I said. "You know they're like demons or little gods, and they've got a kind of craft that can stir up the whole world?"

She nodded, watching me with her face half-turned away. "I know your family is supposed to be in with them some kind of neck-deep."

Beside me, Shiny let her breath out between her teeth,

but I just nodded. "Yes, that's about the shape of it. But listen—"

I was meaning to explain about the body in the creek, but Shiny got there first, talking over me. "Look, there's a situation in the woods, and it's really important to get it under control before someone finds out and comes raging down into the Willows again with a gas can. Whatever happens, you can*not* tell your dad."

Davenport's eyes flicked down and away, then back to Shiny before she nodded. The glance made her look small and scared, but by now, I knew she was no stranger to keeping secrets from her dad.

I moved closer, trying to sound low and reasonable. "We found something out on the slab bridge."

Davenport backed away, shaking her head. Her eyes were suddenly big and unfocused. "What do you think you were doing, coming on our property?"

"Davenport, listen to me. We found one of the fiends from Wixby Hollow, murdered in the creek behind your house. She's out on the bridge, and someone needs to get her in the ground before all the craft seeps out of her and starts spreading."

Assuming it hadn't already, but I didn't see how it would do anyone any good to mention that.

Davenport shook her head. "No, no way. I'm not having anything to do with any bodies, and certainly not with any kind of fiends."

Rae turned on her, and for the first time since I'd known her, she looked mad. "Are you soft in your head? You think

279

any one of us *wants* to do this? But we're in it now, just the same as you are, and if you have even a scrap of love for this town, or the Willows, or your own skin, then you are going to help us put this thing to bed."

Davenport flinched, hugging her shoulders, shaking her head again and again, like she could never stop shaking it. "I can't. Rae, I *can't*."

The way she said it was shaky, though, like a wall of tears was welling up inside her, and I couldn't tell if she was just that scared to be punished for even being out in the road with us, or if she was truly that sorry she couldn't help us.

Beside me, the air around Shiny was going white-hot, how it did when she started to lose her temper. "Look, I just think it's pretty low, how you can't be bothered to keep all of us down in the Willows safe from crazies like your own father! He killed that fiend, as sure as shit, and now the body is lying out there messing up the creek by the second, and you won't even help?"

Davenport looked nearly anguished. "What are you *talking* about? He never—" Her voice broke and she tried again, nearly choking on the words. "He's—"

Then she stumbled back from us and took off running back to the house, tripping over her old boots, down the road and away from us.

Shiny turned back to me with an aggrieved look, shaking her head. "Well, shit. That went well."

"Come on," Rae said heavily. "These things don't bury themselves."

We left the road at the edge of the Beekman property and waded out through the flooded birches in single file, more or less headed for the slab bridge. I kept my eye sharp for hooks or traps or buried TV tubes, but we made it through the woods with no incident

Fisher was sitting where I'd left him, with his elbows on his knees and his head down. He'd been good as his word and hadn't left her alone, but he was at the far end of the bridge from her, as far away as he could get, and had his back to her.

When I splashed out to him, he looked up. I stood over him in the water, trying to see the shape of what he was feeling but I couldn't. If it had a color, it was muddled, like he was lost in his own head. Maybe it wasn't a clear feeling at all.

"Can you help dig a grave?" I said, waving to the bundle of tools that Shiny carried. "We'll get her there, if you can dig."

Shiny started over to us with the shovels, but stopped short, ankle-deep in the creek.

As soon as she'd stepped up onto the slab, the muddled feeling coming off Fisher was not just a feeling anymore, but a solid thing. It churned around us, spreading through the water. Below the surface, willow roots were rippling and twisting their way onto the bridge, crawling over the cement like snakes, and out to where the fiend lay, pale and still.

"Shiny, get back," I said in a tight whisper. "But just

leave one of those shovels."

When she'd retreated back into the trees, the water settled and went calm around us. Fisher was holding very still, the way he had in the hollow when he was trying to keep the dogs from coming out.

"We need you to go down into the bottom of the hollow and dig a place," I told him. "Shiny says there's an old graveyard there." I glanced over into the water, where the roots had sunk below the surface again and were waving gently in the current. "When you're done, you shouldn't wait for us."

Fisher didn't answer, just took the shovel, then splashed out across the slab to the other side of the creek.

After he was gone, Shiny took off back the way we'd come, splashing noisily along the creek. I followed her, being careful not slip off the edge of the bank and into deep water.

It took a ways, but Shiny found what she was looking for. At the place where the creek curved south, she waded out onto the little wooden dock. The dock was lower than the slab bridge, so that only the tops of the posts showed above the water. Shiny wrestled with the rope tied to the rickety flat-bottomed boat I'd seen the other day. The boat was riding high on the current, knocking into the corner of the dock.

We untied it and floated it down to the bridge, where we let it fetch up against the slab. Rae was standing ankle-deep in the middle of the bridge, looking up at the sky so she didn't have to look anyplace else.

The fiend still lay against the fallen tree. I wondered if

maybe Fisher and I should have tried to pull her farther up out of the creek, but we wouldn't have known where to leave her. The water went on forever.

She had little cuts all over her hands, and her legs were scraped and bruised, but she'd been in the water so long there wasn't much blood to run out of the wounds. Or else, she'd never had much in the first place.

Between the three of us, we laid her in the bottom of the boat, me and Shiny doing most of the lifting and Rae standing in the bow with her feet braced against the sides to steady it. The fiend's body was heavy and her hair stuck to my arms and tangled between my fingers. Her skin was cold, slippery with a film of plant scum.

We got her arranged, then took turns pulling the john-boat along by its rope while the others pushed. The whole production was the strangest thing, the three of us wading through the trees, leading the boat between us, and the creek fiend lay in the bottom, still and peaceful and sad.

When we reached the back edge of the birches, where the woods opened out into the bottom of the hollow, we dragged the boat up the hill. The ground was still muddy there, but out of reach of the water.

Once we'd got the boat above the creek, Shiny straightened and popped her neck. "We should get her ready," she said softly, looking down at the boat. "For her funeral."

Shiny and I sat with the johnboat between us, picking twigs and leaves from the fiend's hair. In the knotted tangle behind one of her ears, I found a beetle, black and squirming. I pulled it loose and threw it into the weeds.

Rae held the fiend's head in her lap, working at the tangles with Shiny's comb.

"I feel like we should maybe have a prayer," Shiny said. "Or sing, or something."

I looked down at the body between us. Her face was strange and delicate. "What song?"

"I don't know. A hymn maybe?"

But I didn't know the words to any hymns. The only song I could think of was Clementine, and since the words were all about drowning, it didn't seem right.

Before either of us could pick something, though, Rae began to sing softly, almost to herself. The song was "Shall We Gather at the River." The sound of her voice was clear and sweet, ringing through the trees.

Shiny was bent over the boat, fishing around in the pockets of her shorts. She pulled out a spool of ribbon and began to unwind it.

The ribbon was printed in a faded cabbage rose pattern, and she cut a length off with her folding knife. Then she got down on her knees and set about braiding the ribbon into the fiend's wet hair. Then Rae and I did the same.

I didn't ask what we were doing it for, but Shiny answered anyway. "For safe passage," she said. "So on the other side, they know that she had people."

Afterward, we dragged her up to the top of the little hill, leaving a wide gouge where the bottom of the boat cut through the muddy ground.

The graveyard was barely even a yard at all, just a tiny clearing in the trees, dotted with leaning headstones and full of weeds. The graves were untended, some so old that the ground had started to sink, reminding you that there were bodies buried there.

We stepped inside, dragging the boat behind us, the bottom scraping against stones.

The ground was damp and rocky, and witchgrass grew in coarse tufts. I wound my way through the rows of graves until I came to one that was newer than the rest, sunken and weathered but without a crust of lichen and moss. The stone said:

MAGDA MARIE DEVORE

SISTER, MOTHER, FRIEND

I stood in the weeds, looking at it—the last evidence of my mama.

The sight was like a slap in the face and suddenly, I remembered. I remembered everything.

The night and the men and the voices, but more than that, I remembered hands grabbing me from my bed, leading me down into the cellar, and the tight, painful grip of fingernails digging into my wrist.

Hold still, the voice had said, and now it had a face. Bright black eyes shining in the dark of the cellar—Isola standing over me, pinning the trickbag in my collar and then taking out a needle. My mother behind her, crumpled and sad.

After that, though, the memory stayed white. No sting

as the needle went through, no pain. Just a blank sheet that spread all the way to the corners of the world, eating up time in huge, hungry bites.

I wanted so much to sink down in the dirt and cry. To be heartbroken, standing over my mother's grave. I knew it was what I was supposed to do, but it had been so long. The wound was a deep one, but old and knotted. Full of scar tissue.

"Hey," called Shiny behind me. "Hey, he's got the hole dug over by the—oh." She said it softly, coming up to stand beside me.

I only nodded, raking my hands through my hair and turning my back on the headstone.

Fisher was already gone, farther into the hollow or else home, or just somewhere the three of us couldn't wind up his craft anymore. He'd left a long, narrow hole in the corner of the graveyard, flanked by a mound of weedy dirt, shallower than I liked, but it would have to do. It seemed awful to just dump her into the ground like that, without a service or a coffin, but we bent and dragged her out of the boat. The ground left smears of dirt on her wet legs, and caked on her bare feet.

I stood at the edge of the pair of graves, looking down at her. "Is this how they buried my mother?"

Shiny turned on me, wild and fierce as ever. "*We* buried your mother. And we did it in the evening, with songs and flowers, and we said a prayer. There wasn't a preacher, but goddamn it, Clementine, it was a real funeral, and it was a good one."

I nodded, looking down at the fiend. "This one should be a good one too."

We covered her, taking turns with the shovel. Shiny was the fastest, working like a demon, and I was pretty sure she would have done it all, but it seemed better to split the work between the three of us, so that we each had a hand in it.

When the grave was filled, we stood over it, not speaking. After a time, Shiny reached out and took my hand, twining her fingers through mine.

We stood in a huddle over the grave of a stranger, in the back of a small, secret graveyard, surrounded by all the old families—crooked families, fiend families. My family.

BLACK WATER
CHAPTER TWENTY-TWO

By the time we started home, the clouds were coming in. All three of us were exhausted, covered in dirt, and none of us were talking. I was lost, stuck deep in the knowing that Isola had done this to me. She had taken me down into the cellar and left me there to disappear, to rot and shrivel and be forgotten. The idea was black and hateful, even for Isola, but the thing that made it so much worse was that my mama had let her. My mama had stood by and watched as Isola put me away. Her pale, frightened face had been the last thing I'd seen, and I went over the memory again and again, turning it in my head, trying pry it open. No matter how closely I examined it though, nothing would come clearer. My mother and Isola had put me in the cellar, and the memory was only what it was.

Out on the Crooked Mile, Shiny strode past the driveway that led up to the Heintz place, swinging her shovel and heading for home, but Rae pulled her sweater tight around herself and said, "I don't know, but I think we should see about stopping by to check on Davenport."

The way she said it was light, overly casual, like we were

just stopping by to be neighborly. It was not like the way a person would stop by to make sure someone was doing all right since we'd last seen her. To make sure her father hadn't done something violent to her in the few hours since we'd left her.

We came up the driveway, dragging our tools. Greg Heintz's red truck was pulled up crookedly by the porch, with the driver's side hanging open and the engine running, and for a minute, that was the only thing I could get my head around, it was so eerie and strange.

Then we saw something so much stranger and so much worse that we all just stopped, watching the scene unfold with a cold, unearthly horror.

Davenport was standing in the dooryard, slump-shouldered and windswept.

Her father lay in the dirt at her feet, and everything about him was and would be and *could* be nothing else but terrible.

"Oh, God," said Shiny, grabbing my arm and squeezing hard. "You think he's having a heart attack?"

But whatever had afflicted Greg Heintz was no heart attack. He lay on his back, water gushing from his mouth, pooling around his head while Davenport stood over him, her arms limp at her sides and tears streaming down her face.

The water was everywhere. It seemed to seep straight from his hair and his clothes, washing across the ground in a pool.

I tore loose from Shiny and ran across the yard. The water was coming too fast and unforgiving to stop it, but I got down next to him anyway, trying to roll him over on his side to keep him from choking on the flood that was filling up his mouth. He only gasped like a stranded fish. I could hear a deep rattle in his chest and knew that he was already dying.

Davenport stood over us, slack and wordless.

The sky was nearly black behind her as she watched—me in my soaked dress and her father on the ground. She looked into his empty, blue-lipped face. His eyes were open, but the light behind them was gone. His chest stopped moving and he only stared at the gathering clouds.

"Davenport," I whispered, still cradling the back of Mr. Heintz's neck and knowing, knowing with a slow, dumb hopelessness, that there was nothing I could do to help him. "What happened?"

But I understood that this was the creek. The craft was in her blood, and now it was working through her, filling up her daddy's lungs even as she stood over me, tears dripping off her chin.

"Don't you look at me like that." Her hand was against her mouth. "He was ready to kill me, and I did what I had to."

The note in her voice was like steel, and cold to the bone.

As soon as I reached out to her, though, her face crumpled. She flung my hand away, then turned and bolted for the house. The door slammed, and then came the sound of Davenport shooting the bolt. I wanted, more than anything, to run after her, try to find out just what had happened, but I couldn't see how the answer mattered in the end. Mr. Heintz was already gone.

I laid his head gently on the ground and stood up, trying to wipe my hands dry on my dress. It felt wrong to leave him lying in the dirt with the pool spreading around him, but there was nothing else to do for him.

Shiny and Rae were standing back by the gate looking shaky and stunned, so I folded his hands on his chest and left him.

❉   ❉   ❉

At home, we went around back to where Rae had left her bike, but she didn't make any move to leave. None of us knew what do next.

Shiny sat down on the back steps, staring out at the pasture. "I didn't think a person could be down-hollow, in secret," she said, after a minute. "I didn't think it was possible to be *anything* without everybody and their brother knowing."

And it was true that no one ever let her forget it. And even when Fisher pretended a story that his grandmother had been telling the whole town since he was kid, everybody still knew, even if they didn't like to admit it. It was the kind of secret that about a hundred people were all busy keeping.

Rae was looking thoughtful though, shaking her head. "That's only 'cause you don't listen to any sort of trashy stories," she said. "But people still tell them."

"Stories about what?" I said.

"About Greg Heintz. Like that he had a real taste for the hollow and liked to get at the fiends down there. That his family was an old creek-born family and so he liked the

291

creek fiends best of all." Rae's voice was icy. "And when Davenport was born and he was living alone out here with a new baby and couldn't say exactly who her mama was, well everybody assumed things. Stories like that. Like nice people don't listen to."

"So she's been living low this whole time," I said. "She's been covering for herself, and he's been covering for her too."

Rae nodded. "And now look at her. Just as wild as anything they got down in the hollow. The creek is a big kind of craft, and goddamn but it's getting away from her."

"Because of me," I said, seeing Greg Heintz and his blue, swollen face every time I closed my eyes. "I'm the one who did it to her. Just by being here, I made her into something dangerous. She's too powerful to hold it in, and it's all because of me."

Rae didn't answer right away. Her eyes were narrowed and she was biting her lip, shaking her head in a slow, considering way. "Maybe, yeah—maybe it came from you at first, but not anymore."

"What do you mean?"

"Maybe your being here is why Shiny's been so ornery lately and Eric Fisher can't get a handle on his urge to overgrow the county, but you are not why Greg Heintz is dead, okay?"

"How do you know?"

Rae pursed her lips. "He killed a fiend and left her *lying* out in the creek, seeping craft everyplace! He treated his own daughter like shit for her whole life, and now that she's come into some power, you think bygones are bygones? Creek is all feelings, Clementine, and he didn't drown up there because of how much she wanted to give him a *hug*. So yeah, maybe you're the pointiest point on the star—maybe that's true. But he didn't die because of you. He's been messing around with all the wrong things, pulling craft out of the hollow for ages and look what it finally—"

She broke off though, looking behind me, watching something that made her voice die and her eyes go wide.

I turned with an ache in my chest, knowing that whatever I was about to see, it could be nothing good.

At the edge of the field, the creek ran high and dark, slopping over its banks, too black to be normal. Too black to be water. It had changed in a matter of minutes.

As we watched, a huge shape rose toward the surface. When it broke through, we all gasped. The fin broke first, then the tail with spines that stood a foot above the water. The thing was bigger than the biggest catfish, bigger than a rowboat or a bull, bigger even than Shiny's truck. It seemed to fill the creek, rising up from nothing, and then the head broke, and I saw the gleaming horror of its face.

It was slimy and flat-nosed, its skin gray-green and its mouth a huge, hungry gash evil with teeth, its eyes like lanterns, glowing yellow-green in the afternoon light.

Shiny screamed, a sharp, short little scream that echoed across the yard and then cut off, but I just stood with a hand against my mouth, afraid to breathe or look away. Rae was huddled against me with her hands clasped under her chin and her whole body shaking.

"What was that?" she whispered, her voice sounding thin and high-pitched.

Shiny answered in a flat, faraway voice. "Does it matter?"

Off in the distance, the sky had started to turn colors, and they were all the wrong kind—blacks and greens and poison.

"What are we going to do?" I whispered.

Shiny was standing perfectly still, the way she got when the feeling inside her was so powerful she might explode if she dared to move. "I don't think we have a lot of time. If it's the same upstream, the coalition is going to be coming down here, and I think this time, they'll burn the whole Willows to the ground."

I looked up. The clouds overhead were dark as thunder and there was only one person who might have any idea what to do.

PART V
LIGHT

BAD MAGIC
CHAPTER TWENTY-THREE

I ran.

All around me, things were moving in the tall grass, and the sky overhead was darkening. I didn't want to leave the road, but it was faster to cut straight through the fields and so I did, plowing through the empty pastures and the trees.

I ran full out, crashing through the weeds, jumping the ditch that butted up against Foxhill Road. From the top of the hill, I could see lines of trucks, pulling out of the long farm driveways and onto the blacktop.

The sun was still shining in places, yellow and watery through the clouds, but they all had their headlights on. The lights looked like giant pairs of pale, staring eyes.

The sight of them all together nearly made my heart stop, but then I saw they were all headed into town, full of men with toolboxes and stacks of boards. I still had time.

In town, I walked tense and fast, not daring to look around in case any of them saw me, saw my face and decided I was someone worth dealing with. But they were all deep in their own tasks and no one said a word to me. The wind was ripping through the streets and everyone I passed was busy with the shops, taping over the windows and tying down the awnings.

By the time I got to the Fisher house, I was shaking and out of breath, covered in scrapes and fallen leaves.

"Isola!" I shouted, slamming into the kitchen. My voice sounded rageful and raw, like someone else screaming.

She was at the table, rolling out a pie crust like the world wasn't falling apart in one big smear outside her window.

She looked up, hands covered in flour. "And there's a fine way to invite yourself in."

I stood at the head of the table, looking at her across the spread of flour and pastry and all the little homey things. "The reckoning is here," I said. "You know what that means for us out in the Willows—I know you do. I *know* it was you that buried me alive."

There was a minute where I thought her blank eyes meant she didn't understand a word I'd said.

She gazed at me with her cool stare and her thin, ruinous mouth. "And kept you alive, too. For all the good it did. And here you are again like a bad penny, out in the world to wreck everything."

The way she looked at me was black with blame, and I understood it, but in my heart, I knew she was wrong. I was not a person who broke things. I was the one who found ways to fix things, the one who wanted to see things mended.

"I didn't *do* this, Isola. But in another minute, it won't matter. Shiny says they'll come for us, because at the reckoning, it's what they do. They'll drive us out or kill us if you don't tell me how to stop it!"

Outside, the wind was buffeting the house, making harsh, hungry noises that I'd never heard a wind make. Someone's freshly washed day dress flew against the window, one clothespin still clinging to the shoulder. The dress stayed for a second before peeling off again and flapping away across the yard. I could hear the steady rumble of the storm, and under that, another sound. A low, foreboding sound, like something waking up.

Isola only sat at the end of the table, the cut-glass window behind her. Her hair looked terribly thin with the light shining through it, brittle and crunchy like spun sugar. Finally, she looked up.

"You and your cousin were born too late for this place," she said. "Back in the day, the old kind were welcome in the town as any normal folks. Oh, but we had a wild time when we were coming up."

"You and Emmaline Blackwood. You and my grandmother."

Isola nodded. "This town wasn't always the sick little armpit you see now, and not so hateful when it came to having dealings with the old kind."

"Fiends, you mean."

Isola's smile was thin and hard. "Sure, but folks don't usually go around naming themselves an ugly name. That's for other people to do for them."

"But the town—you're talking about a time when the . . . old kind lived here like regular people?"

"No," she said. "But they came and went as they pleased,

and they took care of it like it was their own. And back then, maybe it was."

The idea was too incredible to think of though. It seemed impossible that a place could change so much and so badly. That people like me and Shiny could be hated for things our grandparents and great-grandparents had done by people who didn't even seem so much better.

"What can you tell me about Greg Heintz?"

Isola snorted. "The things I know about Greg Heintz would make your hair curl."

Her eyes flashed dark and wicked, leaving a shimmery feeling in my head. I understood that I was seeing just a glimpse of her power, seeing into her store of secrets. She was the one who knew all the dirtiest games in town, knew every scandal and lie and whisper.

"Greg was a mean creature," Isola said. "Even as a boy. And when he was grown, he got to going around with some sort of creek fiend. I think he thought he was going to start himself a powerful crooked family, just like in the old days, but she was what she was—too wicked and too wild—and he got his heart broke."

The way she said it was self-satisfied and I nodded, but I was picturing wicked and wild. I was picturing the pure opposite of Davenport and her pale, see-through skin. Her woeful, shining eyes.

"Any other, they would have just gone on by, but not Greg. When his girl out-the-creek was through with him, well, he let it be known that he was not through with her. No one had heard a peep from the coalition in thirty years, but next thing anybody knows, he's handing out tracts and calling meetings. Going around grilling people about their family trees, and what do you know but there are some around here just young enough and dumb enough to join up."

"There were enough people to start a whole coalition, just because one man said so?"

Isola laughed, a dry, ugly sound. "There always are."

"Underneath that, he was so *crooked*, though. Fisher told me Greg's been taking stuff out of the hollow for years and selling it. I saw a craft shack back in the woods on his property. It was all full of fool's light, all going to rot."

Isola nodded. "There's nothing like someone that's angry and afraid for being a hypocrite."

It seemed to me, though, that Hoax County was a whole place of hypocrites, full to the top with hate and fear and loss.

"And what can you tell me about Davenport?"

Isola scowled and pressed her lips together. Then she set down her rolling pin and looked me square in the face. "Why do you want to know it?"

I stood at the head of the table, trying not to come undone, but my hands kept shaking. They kept wanting to go into fists. "Because an hour ago, I saw her murder Greg Heintz by some kind of magic."

Out in the road, a gun went off with a sound like the very sky was breaking in two, and someone screamed, but I was scared to go to the window and look. I was sure that if I did, I would see every savagery and horror from the hollow come to life out in the world.

Isola stared back at me with her mouth mean and her eyebrows raised. "Then it looks to me like he made his bed. What do you say about that?"

"I say I need to know exactly what bed this was."

She laughed, but it wasn't a good one. "The kind of bed that's a long time coming."

"When the creek fiend left him, that was a good thing, right? It should have been the end?"

Isola nodded heavily. "Imagine how my jaw fell when I heard that that little shitweasel had got himself a baby, left on the steps like a bag of flour. Who knows—it's possible that his creek-girl brought him that child willingly, thinking it would persuade him to leave her be. More likely, he just went down in the hollow and took it from her as his way of making her sorry."

"But Davenport—why didn't you *save* her, Isola?"

Isola looked back at me, and her eyes were dark and dry and furious. "Because it wasn't my *business* what that man did in his own house, raising his own child!"

Outside, the sky was dark and livid as a bruise.

I threw my head back, belting out a huge, shrieking laugh at the absolute cruelty of it all. "*Everything* is your business!"

Isola stared at me like I'd slapped her across the face. "You *can't*," she said finally. "Try all you want, but you can't save everyone, and even the times you get it right, they'll hate you for it."

The way she said it was mean and sad, bitter as horehound.

"Fisher doesn't hate you," I said, because her eyes were bright with trouble, and it was the truth. The truth in his thundering rages was that he loved her every minute of every day, even when he was deep at war with her. Even standing in the room where he'd been trapped.

"Well, he should," she said. "I tried to do right by him, but his mama brought him back here when she didn't want him weighing her down no more—after I had said and said how he couldn't be raised here as long as all you girls were around, and what was I supposed to do with him then? But I couldn't turn him away." She looked away, shaking her head. "Not even after the reckoning began and the whole world began to slide, I couldn't put him out. He was my flesh and blood."

"Is that how come you locked him up in the attic?"

Isola drummed her fingers on the table and looked away. "They would have taken and left him for dead in the hollow. Or else, more likely just dragged him out in the yard and ended him right there."

I wanted to reach for her hand and cover it in mine, but something in her face stopped me. "Was that really the *only* way to stop them? Fisher's so strong, and you're a regular . . . witch."

Isola shook her head. "I might have a drop or two of the old blood in me, but it's breath—weakest and most wanting of all the humors—and I was an old woman even then. And he was just a little thing, most of his powers still laying quiet, and not the big troublesome creature he is now."

The catch in her voice made me think of the photo albums put away upstairs in a secret room, stories of a secret life. The truth was clear in her stooped shoulders. She had never once considered him a troublesome creature.

"That was Fisher's hair in my trickbag, though, wasn't it?"

She nodded. "I had to bind you to someone free in the world so the trick would take. He was the clear choice. Dirt's powerful kindling for a trick. It can give and give and give. But Lord knows I didn't think it would mean him getting an itch to dig you out!"

"You didn't feel guilty, using your own grandson for fuel?"

"Someone had to be put away, and if your mama hadn't offered you up, it would have been him. As long as one of you five was put by, the light from the hollow would sleep."

I shook my head, horrified at how she could talk about a person like some heirloom dish or china figure. "Why, though? Why save me? You could have just let them burn me and it would have been over. Why *not* me? You let my mother die." The last part came out raw and shaky, but I looked at her straight on.

"The deal I made with your mama was one that eats me up to this day." The way she said it sounded too brisk and careless to mean much, but her face was dark and I believed her.

"Then why? You didn't have to. You could have said no."

"I could have, but the upshot would have been no better, and there's still some of us that believe it's a regular sin to let a child die. The choice was no choice at all. She loved you, God bless her. She knew what she was asking."

The way Isola said it made something go tight in my throat. It was painful to be sitting there in the kitchen with someone who remembered that once, I had belonged to someone, belonged to love and home and family, and could say so with absolute certainty.

"Couldn't you do anything to save her, though?"

Isola shook her head. "I did everything I knew. I helped her hide you and did every trick I had to keep you safe. They burned her out, though, and then when that was done, they went on down to your aunt's. I did *everything* to stop it. The reason you got your life is that I know how to make a trick, and the reason they stopped is 'cause after you were put away, the reckoning went quiet, and I went down there and told them to go home. But the reason your aunt's house is still standing is thanks to a lot more than me. Your cousin has a powerful way with fire when she feels like it."

I nodded. "And we're more powerful than ever now— that's something, isn't it? The reckoning star might be what's tearing up the town, but it works both ways, I think. We're stronger than we've ever been, and so I need you to tell me how to stop it now."

"They way I see it, you got two choices." The brittle crack of Isola's voice made something in me go cold. "Either you work between you to fix the trouble filling up this town, or one of you has got to die."

The way she said it was heavy, full of resignation, and the breath all went out of me. The five of us were young. We were wild and uncertain and just kids. I wasn't ready to go back in the ground.

Isola was looking at her hands. The way her skin crinkled around her mouth was mean and bitter. She didn't say anything else.

We were still sitting in silence when the kitchen door banged open. Fisher stood in the doorway, looking windblown. There was blood on his shirt and fallen leaves in his hair.

"What are you doing here?" he said, and his voice was tight.

I stared back at him. "I had to see Isola. What happened? Is everything all right?"

He shook his head. "I was just down at Carter's Garage, and no one there is listening to any sort of reason. They're getting ready to go down to the Willows—Mike and them. I tried talking to them, but they didn't hear it. They've got a lot of gasoline."

UNEARTHLY
CHAPTER TWENTY-FOUR

We left the house at a run, Isola shuffling out onto the porch after us. Her arms were folded and her face was troubled but she didn't try to stop us.

As we crossed the yard to Fisher's car, something white drifted in front of my face. It fell like snow, but the air was warm, swirling with a hot updraft.

"It's ash," I whispered, holding out my hands to the awful dust falling all around me. "The sky is burning."

I understood suddenly that for as long as Shiny had been trying to explain, I'd been wrong about the reckoning. In my head, it was ugly fish and plants that grew too wild and too fast. Now that Davenport had woken up her craft, now that it was the five of us, all those things were so small—just the little daily vagaries of the hollow—and there was a world of difference between the hollow and the reckoning.

We drove through town, holding hands across the gear-box the whole way. It was like something sweethearts did, but I couldn't help thinking that how I was holding on to him was not like a sweetheart, but like a drowner. Like I was scared someone was going to try and rip him away from me.

The clouds were huge and almost green. The wind was up, making the trees along Broom Street toss and thrash. The whole place had taken on a strange, eerie light.

The streets were mostly empty, people barricaded in their houses, the black muzzles of rifles and shotguns the only thing that showed between the blinds. Now and then, we passed signs that something terrible was happening. A bloody square of sidewalk. A house that had gone completely to brambles and kudzu vines in less than an hour. The reckoning was lunatic and it was everywhere.

We drove too fast for town, passing handfuls of trucks and off-roaders and every one of them headed out toward the Crooked Mile.

"They're going down to the Willows," I said. "We have to get there before they do—otherwise they'll . . ."

Fisher nodded once, without looking at me. Then he whipped the Trans Am around in the middle of the road.

"What are you doing?"

"We'll go out on Main and then cut down through Beekman's back acreage, just as long as the farm road isn't still underwater."

The south end of town was completely empty, quiet as a grave.

As we watched, the sky turned black in a long plume all the way down toward the hollow. The wind picked up, tearing the banners off the buildings, sending them flapping across the empty street like huge, ungainly bats. The storefronts were left naked, their windows dark like jagged, empty sockets.

At the edge of town, the fair stood eerie and deserted. One of the midway booths was standing empty in the street, bloody and covered in handprints. The windows of Spangler's were broken out, and some black bat-winged creature lay slumped over one of the frames, half in and half out. Glass lay in a glittery spill all over the sidewalk.

We rolled through the fair, everything still and empty as the end of the world.

The swings turned gently by themselves. The lights on the carousel had all gone dark. Over the roofs of the abandoned buildings, the sky was an oily black, swirling slick and ominous.

Only a few days before, Fisher and I had ridden these same swings while the speakers played old country songs and the only thing on my mind had been how he might kiss me before the night was through. Now everything was ruined.

We left Main at a dirt turn that was marked by nothing but a fencepost and cut down through the pastureland on a little tractor road that was barely a road at all, just dirt and gravel and deep wheel ruts. Fisher drove it like a maniac, plowing along through the hay and out onto the Crooked Mile.

Out the back window of the Trans Am, I could see the line of trucks as it wound down into the Willows—a long way off, but getting closer. They were taking the road slower than Fisher, and for good reason.

The town had been bad enough, but the Willows was turning monstrous. The creek wound black all through the lowlands now. Tree roots crept up from the ground like clutching fingers, snaking across the road.

At the Heintzes' place, the gate was torn half off its hinges and far off, behind the house, I could see flames out in the birch wood. The whole countryside seemed to flash and flicker like the very air was burning. I didn't see Davenport anywhere.

We drove on, toward Myloria's, and as soon as we pulled up to the house, I was out of the car, running up the front steps.

I tore through to the back of the house, looking for my family, for anyone. Shiny and Rae were in the kitchen, scraping together all the sharpest things from the drawers, and locking all the windows.

"The coalition's coming," I said. "We saw them on the road, and Shiny, there are a lot of them."

The words gave me a tight, choking feeling in my throat, but Shiny just nodded. Her face was terrible and beautiful. She yanked open the side door of the china cabinet, reaching for the shotgun and the shoebox, fingers sliding past the rock salt loads to the real shells.

She had the gun laid across the table and was loading it when the silence was broken by the rumble of an engine. The only person who'd driven up that driveway—maybe in years— was Fisher, and now a whole chorus of engines sounded, rusty and uneven, metallic clangs and doors slamming.

"Myloria Blackwood," someone called from the yard. It was a man's voice, twangy and nasal.

We went to the window and peered between the curtains. A bunch of men stood in the yard, holding shotguns and rifles and wooden bats. They had their hats pulled low over their eyes, but when I looked closer, I saw they were mostly young, and some were still only boys.

Mike Faraday was there, along with the rest of the in-town crowd who ran around with Fisher. The Maddox brothers stood side by side near the back, hair standing up like they'd walked out of a blast furnace. Luke was holding a pickax, and Cody had a kaiser blade in each hand. Behind them on the road, I could see a parade of headlights, getting closer.

Fisher moved behind me, shaking his head. "Shit," he muttered, peering out the window into the yard. "*Shit.*"

"What is it? What's happening?" Myloria had come up behind us, her flannel shirt slipping off her shoulder and her hands stained purple with some kind of ink. She looked wild.

Shiny didn't glance around. "That asshole Faraday and his hick friends are here."

"Then this is the end," Myloria whispered, sinking down onto the floor with a thin little gasp, clutching at the curtains and nearly bringing the rod down with her. "They've come for us."

The yard got very still. There was no answer but the grim metallic sound of someone hauling something heavy out of the bed of a truck. Shiny stood in the kitchen with her shotgun, a butcher knife held in her other hand like a sword. Myloria was making a thin, moaning sound.

"Myloria," Shiny said sharply, standing over her. "Maybe you're ready to roll over. Maybe you are fine and good to just sit there and wail about the world ending and wring your hands. Maybe you're all set to do exactly what you did the last time this shit got stirred up and these assholes came out here. But not me."

Myloria sat on the floor, hugging her shoulders, looking up at her daughter. "What are you going to do?"

Shiny glared at her, breathing hard. "I'm going to save this busted joke of a house and everything that goes along with it. And you're going to get up off this floor and help me. Otherwise, you need to shut up and stay out of my way."

Out in the yard, the men were shuffling closer. Any minute, one would step onto the porch, just to prove to the others that he was brave. They'd hauled all sorts of gas cans out of the flatbeds of their trucks.

Shiny stormed into the front hall, her shoulders back, her hair loose and tangled, and I followed her. For one instant, I had a strange vision of Myloria herself—Myloria young and glamorous and wild. The moment passed, though, and it was Shiny striding up the hall, ready to rip a strip off anybody who came near her.

From out in the yard, one of the men yelled, "We're not here to make trouble, Miz Blackwood."

"What are you here for then?" Shiny called back through the door.

"Just need to talk to you for a minute. We got someone out here who's got something to say."

312

Shiny shook her head at me fiercely, but I opened the door anyway, peering out through the screen. The yard was full of boys and men arranged in a semicircle, staring up at us.

Then Mike Faraday stepped into the dirt at the bottom of the steps, shoving Davenport in front of him. Her dress was rumpled and she was crying. He had his hand tight around her arm.

I pushed open the screen door and stepped out onto the porch. Shiny grabbed at me, but I pulled away and strode out to the top of the steps.

"Let her go," I said. "If you're afraid of her, then let her come up here with us. But you don't need to hurt her."

Mike Faraday only spit and shook his head. "No way I'm handing Greg's own daughter over to you, to a bunch of fiends and murderers."

I stood looking down at Davenport, trying to think how to save her.

"There!" she said, pointing with a pale, long-fingered hand, her eyes wide and hurt. "They killed my father!"

THE RECKONING

Davenport's face was frantic, her eyes as panicked as any wild animal's.

"What are you talking about?" I said, and it came out as a whisper.

Mike was the one who looked up at me, the one who answered, like he didn't even know I hadn't been saying it to him. "Greg Heintz is dead and she tells us you all are the ones that killed him."

"That's crazy, though," I said. "Davenport, tell them it isn't true!"

Davenport only stood silent, and the crowd in the yard stood silent with her. They were all looking past me.

Fisher had come out onto the porch behind me. He was holding an ax, and all the boys in the yard stepped back. Beside him, Rae was prim and tiny, with a mild look on her face and Shiny's buck knife in her hand.

Shiny stood on Fisher's other side, easy and long-boned. "Hey, y'all." She was holding the walnut-handled Remington.

A huge wind was blowing through the trees, and for a second, I thought I smelled the sharp, poison stink of the hell dogs, like they might be creeping up from the hollow along with everything else, and I knew I didn't have long before the world and the hollow would collide in some kind of all-out war.

Davenport was still standing in front of the house like she had only got there by mistake. Her homemade dress hung loose and doll-like on her, and her face was very pale.

Beside me, Shiny was staring down the boys in the yard. She had the shotgun propped against her hip. It looked dangerous in her hands, like it might be just another part of her.

She was considering Mike Faraday, not in fear or trepidation but like she wanted a piece of him and no one else would do. "I always knew I would burn you down one day."

Mike nodded slowly. He was carrying a gas can. "Funny how that works."

The can hung loose and heavy in his hand. The air in the yard was crackling like it might catch fire.

Shiny smiled a strange, ugly smile. "Funny." Her tone was sweet and sticky. Then, the way it always did when she got scary, right after the last word, rage came snarling out of her like smoke. "Now get your nasty-ass self and your nasty friends out of my yard, you redneck piece of trash."

For the longest time, none of them moved or said a word. Then, like they'd all agreed ahead of time, they began to climb up into the backs of their trucks, stuffing rags in bottles and lighting them.

I was still watching in dumb horror when the first bottle

315

flew past my head and onto the porch, a twist of rag blazing in the top, and Shiny shoved me hard enough to send me staggering out of the way, my arm throbbing where her hands had scorched me through my clothes.

"Shiny!" Rae cried as two more smashed against the boards in twin flowers of burning oil, smoking black as bad dreams and sending flames licking up the side of the house.

Without a word, Shiny knelt and scraped up the spilled oil like it was nothing more than a handful of leaves, then chucked it down into the bed of Mike's truck. The paint exploded into flames, not like a normal fire at all, but a great bonfire, burning in the yard. It towered in the air so the whole place was lit by a pillar of flame.

Everyone was staring at the burning truck, but Davenport only stood limply off to the side, looking out toward the creek.

I jumped down from the porch and darted across the yard.

"Davenport," I said in a tight, breathless whisper, grabbing her by the hand and trying to pull her toward the house. "They're going to rip this place apart in a minute. Just tell them we didn't kill your dad and we can sort this out. Or come with me and we'll leave. We'll run away to Wixby Hollow—you and me, or all of us—and stay there until we figure out how to stop this."

For a second, I thought that she would. I thought she'd make a break back toward the house with me and we could run away and this awful, awful day could all be over.

Then she pulled her hand away. "You did kill my daddy,"

316

she said. "We all did. We all hated him, every last one of us. I just took that hate and finally it made it worth something."

I moved toward her again, hugging my elbows. "That's not true. It was an accident. You didn't mean it!"

Her face went cold, awful in the light from the burning truck. "Don't tell me what I mean. You don't know a thing about me."

"I know you're as scared as the rest of us," I said. "But you're not alone. None of us really know how to work our craft and it's ruining us. We have to figure out some way to stop it, before it goes any further."

All around us, the members of the coalition were stepping down from trucks, bottles burning in their hands. I could hear Shiny shouting at them not to move, but that didn't stop the clang of their boots as they jumped down from the flatbeds.

Davenport didn't pay them any mind. "Sometimes that's just the way of the world. You can't make it better, so you might as well do the worst."

The way she said it was so chilly that at first I could only stare at her. "What are you talking about?"

The question was not much more than a dry little rasp in my throat, and she smiled.

"You know I'm no good, Clementine. Deep down, you know. You just don't want to admit it."

"That's not true." But the way she was looking at me made me falter. In the firelight, she looked more like her father than ever.

"I was down in Wixby the night you tore up his zoo," she said. "Gathering up the light for my daddy, when she came crawling up out of the creek and said she needed to talk to me. Said she was my *mother*." The last word sounded thick, like she was spitting it between her teeth, nearly sick, it was so disgusting to her.

I nodded slowly. "She was."

Davenport stared back at me, eyes pale as ice. "Well, I don't suppose I need to tell *you*, but I had no use for any sort of mother like her. No use for any sort of fiend. She was an abomination to my blood, and I don't need anything to make me more hated than I already am."

The way her face didn't change sat in my heart like a stone. "Davenport, what did you *do*?"

"Made sure she never came near me again. The next time I went down, I looked for her. I tricked her out from the creek into the trees and caught her in a trigger snare, the same way my dad caught half his zoo. All the stories talk about how strong they are, but they kill pretty easy, just like anything else."

Suddenly, I couldn't hear the commotion behind us any-more. It was like I couldn't hear anything. The clouds of ash fell softly and constantly. There was a lump in my throat that I couldn't swallow down.

Davenport had murdered her mother, and whether she hated fiends or just herself, it didn't really matter. It was done.

"This is the way the world ends." Her voice was singsong and I went cold all the way to the tips of my fingers. The hell dogs were getting close now. I could smell the chemical stink of them, feel their dark shapes creeping around in the shadows, getting closer.

From over by the porch, someone shouted, and then there was a snarl and a scream.

I whipped around in time to see one of the oily black shapes go vaulting over the hood of a truck, biting and tearing at one of the men from Carter's Garage, knocking him into the dirt, ripping at him so the blood flew in bright drops.

I stared with my hands cupped over my mouth, but Davenport only smiled. I was struck by how she never seemed to blink.

"Can't you feel it?" she said, exalted and breathless. "Can't you feel how *big* it is?"

And the worst thing was that I could. The light inside me was reaching for the craft in the rest of them, pulling me in all directions like a magnet. I felt that in a second, it would burst out of me in a huge storm and flatten everything.

I wrestled with it, breathing in little gasps. "What is it you *want*?"

Davenport laughed dryly, shaking her head. "I want the same thing I've always wanted, ever since the day I was old enough to know it was a choice. I want to get the hell out of my father's house."

"You are," I said, brushing the ashes from my cheeks. "You *killed* him. There's no one left to keep you there."

I reached out to touch her arm. Ash was raining down in powdery flakes, swirling in the air. The smoke was thick around us, making it hard to see, and everything was so hot that I could hardly breathe. Her skin was cold, though, unnaturally cold, so that it seemed to sizzle under my hand. Her eyes were wide and unearthly, the blue bleeding ragged against the white like torn paper.

"You shouldn't come so near me," she said, taking a step back. "You make it so hard to keep the creek low."

I raised my chin, blinking against the smoke. I had the strangest feeling that I was seeing the end now. That this was what it had been coming to all along. We were all lost in our own terrible powers. All deep in the grips of the reckoning.

From the porch behind me, there was a riot of shouting, but I was scared to look away from Davenport, who stood in front of me under the tupelo tree, staring so long I wasn't sure she even saw me anymore.

Then one of the boys yelled, "Don't you have any kind of loyalty?" and I knew they were talking to Fisher.

Davenport and I both turned. The boys had all climbed down from their trucks. Some of them were holding hunting rifles, crowbars, or bats, looking up at Fisher on the porch like they meant to tear him to pieces.

"Don't act so hurt," he said, turning the ax in his hand. "Like you want me down there with you. You might have been dumb enough to ignore my blood once. I might have been dumb enough to pretend, but it's getting old."

"You got to pick where you want to stand, is all," said Cody, not saying Fisher was right, but not denying it either. "This is your last chance."

Fisher nodded, slow and heavy like he was thinking about that. He stepped down into the yard, and now he was smiling.

For just a moment, none of us moved. The whole world seemed to pulse and flicker. Then Fisher turned and put the ax through the windshield of Mike Faraday's burning truck.

The sound it made was colossal.

This was the ugly business, the taking of sides. If any of them had thought before that he might join them, all question was gone the minute he swung the ax.

Mike Faraday was inching closer to the porch, still holding the gas can, but less and less like he had a plan for it.

"Stop where you are, Mike." Shiny's eyes were full of flames, and her voice crackled. "You and me, we've had some times, but this is dirty even for you, and so help me God but I will put you down."

The Remington seemed to have shrunk to nothing but two black barrels, and I watched them with the awful feeling that they were watching back. The air around her seemed to shimmer, and smoke swirled out of her mouth.

With a slow, hungry smile, she came down the steps, crossing the three feet of dirt between them in one stride, and held the barrel under Mike's chin.

And in that moment, I had never been so ungodly scared. I was certain none of them was kind or reasonable or right. They were without decency, but in a minute, Shiny was going to do something terrible.

She stood perfectly still, and her breath blew out a bright

321

cloud of sparks, hissing in the air. Her finger was on the trigger, and then, she gasped.

At first, I didn't understand what was happening—only that a cold, prickling sensation was gathering around my feet, soaking my shoes and creeping up my legs.

Davenport made a breathless noise beside me. Her mouth was so pale it seemed bloodless, and she was breathing in little gasps, so short and shaky it sounded like she was laughing.

She said in a small, shuddering voice, "Here comes the creek."

And as I turned, I saw that she was right. The water was coming up fast and muddy, pouring into the yard from nowhere and everywhere, slow at first, then all at once, rising in a wave, washing over our knees.

I grabbed the porch rail to steady myself as the whole Blue Jack seemed to leave its banks and come rushing into the yard at us.

With sharp, yelping cries, the boys went scrambling for their vehicles. Mike swung himself up onto the running board of one of the trucks, but Shiny wasn't so lucky. She screamed as the water hit her legs, sprawling in the mud as the wave broke over her.

I clung to the house, trying to keep my feet, but the water kept coming, and Shiny had disappeared. Rae gave a sharp little cry and went splashing down off the porch, flailing across the yard to her, trying to get her head up out of the water.

The creek around them was full of wicked-looking fish with spines on their backs and mouths full of teeth. Snakes

that wound through the water like thick, black cables—
rubbery looking, almost mechanical—with hell-green eyes
and horns sticking out of their heads.

Rae put the buck knife through one with barely a glance,
dragging Shiny up out of the water and hauling her back
onto the porch.

Shiny was breathing in painful gasps. Her skin had
cracked in a network of jagged hairlines. They didn't bleed,
only covered her like a spiderweb, raw and oozing. Her
whole body was shaking and Rae sat on the porch with her,
holding onto the hem of her shirt instead of her hand so as
not to touch her skin.

All down the flooded driveway, the trucks were parked at
crazy angles and as I watched, the headlights began to shatter, exploding in showers of glass as Fisher waded through
the yard, the craft humming off him in a fury, making the
water slop up in crazy waves.

Mike and the other boys huddled in the backs of the
trucks, but they were still stuffing bottles, getting ready to
light them. The rags were smoking blackly, and without
Shiny to turn the fire back, there would be no stopping them
from burning the house.

"Just get *out* of here," Mike said, and he sounded nearly
desperate. "I know you, man. I don't want to hurt you."

Fisher only laughed a hard, ugly laugh. "What can you
do to me now that I haven't already done to myself?"

His face was terrible, and I understood that the power
working in him might just be enough to crack the world.

FIENDS
CHAPTER TWENTY-SIX

The water was rising, slopping over the edges of the porch. Fisher had turned on the coalition, his gaze like stone. He glowed with the force of the reckoning, and it was hard to tell how much was his own savage craft, how much was on account of being near me, and how much was just the power of the hollow, burning its way right down the middle of us like a grassfire.

He waded through the creek toward the trucks, grinning so wide I hardly recognized him. I shivered, seeing in his eyes that this was what he had been waiting for his whole life. All his years spent fighting the power of the hollow, keeping it in check. Now it coursed through him. It had all been leading up to this one tremendous, awful moment.

The boys were watching like they didn't even know him anymore. He had lived in their town, right alongside them for so long, and now they were seeing the truth of his secret heart.

Mike swung himself into the back of one of the trucks, reaching around in the bed, and came up with a shotgun. "Fisher, stop right where you are, or I will cut you in two."

Davenport was watching me with her eyes wide. "See?" she whispered. "See, they don't want us here, they don't want us to control our craft, or be *better*. They just want us dead, and maybe we deserve it."

I stood beside her, clinging to the porch. I couldn't think of anything to say.

Up in the truck, Luke Maddox wasn't waiting for any sort of word or sign. He lit the bottle in his hand and threw it. The glass broke in a wave of orange, lighting the porch. Rae ran across to it, kicking at the flames, but they only climbed merrily, burning their way up the wall. Cody stood beside his brother in the flatbed, arm cocked back to throw another one, and in the next minute, Fisher plowed across the yard to them. He grabbed Cody by the back of his shirt and pulled him down out of the truck, sending up a huge spray of water.

The bottle left Cody's hand as he fell, arcing high. Then it exploded in a burst of liquid fire down the side of Fisher's face and neck and shoulder.

At once, the whole Willows seemed to come wildly alive. The creek churned violently, full of monstrous fish snapping and thrashing, chewing at everything they could reach. The hell dogs were on us now, pouring out of the shadows and launching themselves into the yard.

Fisher ducked himself under the muddy water and straightened.

The fire all down his right side had gone out, but chips of glass shone bright as prayers, buried in his cheek. His skin was healing around them and they sparkled in the light from the burning truck, flashing crazily as he turned on the coalition.

Luke yelled something I couldn't understand as he dragged Cody back up into the truck. I turned where he was pointing, just in time to see something big and bristling that looked like the beast that had savaged Shiny's chickens come barreling out of the trees.

It thundered through the flooded yard, scattering the hell dogs and careening every which way. It slammed into trucks, bouncing off wheels and bumpers, and toward Mike, who still stood pinning Fisher with the gun. His finger was hard on the trigger as the water churned and the dogs surged around them, and when the chicken-killing hog lowered its head into his side, the gun went off in a huge, unholy burst of buckshot and powder.

For a moment, everything seemed to shatter around me. The sound was so loud I screamed, but I couldn't hear myself. Fisher stood, the front of his shirt torn open, blood spattering out in perfect rays like someone had drawn the sun on his chest. The whole yard stopped moving. The hog ricocheted off the fender of someone's truck, dashing away again, like it only ever moved at that one breakneck speed.

I stood with my arms held out, like I could somehow stop a thing that had already happened, and even Mike looked shocked, sick at the blood that spread under Fisher's hands. Then he let the gun drop into the water and backed away. He coughed as he did it, not a hawking or a throat-clearing, but strange and thick and wet.

Two of the hell dogs had caught the scatter of the blast and were torn apart everywhere, sinking messily below the surface.

Fisher touched the front of his bloody shirt. The hollow was running in every inch of his veins, all fury and buckshot and pure, unguarded rage, but the blood was leaking out of him, leaving in bright gushes, making him stumble.

I tried to say his name, but the word was stuck. I cleared my throat, tasting murky water, tasting scum and dead leaves. I gasped, but couldn't seem to get my breath as Fisher fell back, blood billowing up in huge, dark blossoms, swirling in the muddy water as it closed over him.

I stumbled to him, half-falling, trying to drag him away from the mangled bodies of the dogs, hardly caring that I was crying a little, choking hard on a taste like creek in my mouth.

Davenport stood in the yard with the water rising around her. Everything seemed to be coming apart at the seams, but even now, she only looked small and sad and milk-white in the face of the storm. It moved across the sky in a black plume, set to wash away the whole rickety little town. Nothing to hold it back.

"Stop," I said, but it was barely a whisper. The water kept filling up my mouth. It was running from my nose now. "Davenport, you're going to kill us."

She looked at me and her eyes had gone pale, unearthly blue all the way to the edges.

"Then put me in the ground," she said.

And the way she said it, I knew the ground was not a place. Not the tiny room I'd been buried in. What Davenport was asking was still and deep and forever.

Her voice was vicious. "I've got no love for any of you, but God help me, Clementine. You are the *worst*, always messing around in everyone's business. Well, you know my business now, and I hope you understand that knowing it is not going to do a thing to help you."

Water was rushing into my mouth, and every breath was less like a breath and more like drowning. Fisher lay heavy in my arms, his blood swirling up in clouds, mixing with the blood of the mangled hell dogs, and even after I got his head up, the water didn't stop running from his nose and mouth.

Davenport was wading toward us. "You know what I've got in me—what I can do. You know just as well as I do that I can end every last one of you right now!"

Her eyes were blurry, full of rage, and I knew that she was right. If someone didn't do something, she'd drown us all, old blood or not.

Over by the burning truck, Luke Maddox was leaning on the tailgate, hacking like he'd just been pulled from a raging sea. The whole coalition had stopped packing their bottles. The oily rags lay forgotten. Shiny and Rae were huddled on the porch, choking into their hands.

Davenport only watched it all with a strange, eager look, and I understood that none of us could even begin to fix this. Maybe we couldn't fix anything. We were all built for destruction.

There was a part of me, though, that railed against the thought. A part not content to let my world end again.

Not for a bunch of loud, frightened boys playing men, and not for Davenport, whose eyes had gone so flat and empty she didn't look like a person anymore, just a living reflection of wrath and despair and water.

I saw the black heart of what we were born into, how Fisher and I had each lived alone in our small, secret rooms, and still been able to find each other. Shiny, eight years old and praying for rescue that didn't come.

The help was with us, though.

They were here, living in the shadow of our own everyday, watching over Shiny while she slept, telling Myloria the stories that she put in her tattoos. Now, with the reckoning upon us, there was no line between us and them, no magic that could keep the fiends in the hollow.

I opened my mouth to scream for them, but it was all grit and water. I was afraid that soon, there wouldn't be enough breath left to keep me upright.

They were my birthright though, my legacy. I carried them with me in the same way that Shiny carried heat or Rae the peculiar and careful magic of her own mind, and they were always with me. The chimes, which had jangled so fiercely in the wind, had all stopped ringing. They hung perfectly still as the trees thrashed and beat at the sky.

The boys in the yard were slumped and choking, blue lipped. Their faces had all gone slack, more awestruck and more afraid than I'd ever seen them. I turned, holding on to

Fisher with both arms, clinging more fiercely every time I felt another warm surge of his blood jet out into the water.

The fiends had all materialized inside the house. They stood looking out the glassless windows, more glorious and more terrible than anything I could have hoped to see.

The first to come through the door was the burning woman, wrapped in her white sheet. She stepped onto the porch, shining like a desert sun under the wind chimes. As she passed it, the fire licking up the side of the house went out.

Behind her, a gnarled man and woman came, holding hands. Their skin was gray and twisted like the willow roots that grew along the banks of the creek. Then the hungry man from the hollow, bony and blindfolded, in his black preacher's pants and his white shirt, his teeth filed to points.

The fiends of the Blackwood house stood side by side on the porch.

The coalition had an age of hate and judgment on their side, but my past—my history—was stronger. These were the people who had made me what I was, blood of my family, and every one of them a vision of power. Once, the town had been theirs just as much as anyone's, and now, in the hour of our destruction, the only thing was to give it back to them.

The last of them was the woman I'd seen reflected in the bedroom mirror, her face an empty moon, her eyes like two burning holes cut into a perfect sky. They glowed like comets, and I understood that her blood was the old, savage blood that gave me mine. She was the source of my light.

"Please," I said, water running out of my mouth. My chest kept jerking, trying to draw breath. My arms were shaking as I tried to keep Fisher's ruined chest above the swirls of black poison spreading like fingers through the water. "Please, help us."

The air seemed too high-voltage to breathe. When the first bolt of lightning hit, it lit up the Willows like a crack in the sky.

The fiend of light turned to me with eyes so bright they left a blinding glow inside my eyelids when I blinked. "Will you release her?" she said. "Will you break your star and offer her to us?"

Davenport stood in the middle of it with her arms out from her sides, her fingers spread as the creek churned around her. She was crying now, long sobs that made her whole body shake.

I had always thought the world was good, that everyone could find the beauty in themselves. Everyone could honor, and forgive, and live a full and gorgeous life, even when the hands they'd been dealt weren't easy.

But what Davenport had been born into had taken so much from her, leaving her with just the wickedest and the worst. Her father had given her life, and then taken every scrap of joy or freedom, and even now that he was dead, all he had left her with was a deep, abiding hatred for what she was.

Her power was tremendous, working through her, but it had gone to rot, and without someone to help her and to love her, she did not know how to take it back.

"Yes," I said to the fiend, water spilling out of my mouth. "Yes—whatever she needs. Give her whatever she needs."

The fiend crossed the porch, and when she stepped into the water, the whole creek glowed around her. In the glow, I could see the dark shapes of the fishes, following her as she waded across the yard to Davenport.

The other Blackwood fiends followed her through the flood. They moved slowly, drawing the snakes and hell dogs and all the wild, spectral creatures with them.

When they reached for Davenport, her face crumpled and she gave a small, desolate cry. It was hard to tell if it was terror or relief.

The coalition had all hunkered down in their trucks, coughing and choking, looking for all the world like what they were—cocky boys with their fathers' guns, staring out at the terrible, wonderful history of my family.

The fiends paid not a bit of mind to any of them. They gathered around Davenport, reaching for her, closing her gently in their arms, whispering all the ways they'd come to take her home. She fell against them and they turned in one motion, bearing her away toward the hollow.

DUSK
CHAPTER TWENTY-SEVEN

The yard was deathly still. No one dared to move or speak.

With Davenport gone, the creek had begun to recede. Now everyone lay wet and shivering, breathing in long, choking gasps.

In my arms, Fisher lay motionless.

I shook him, trying to raise his head, to make him look at me. I wanted to stand, to drag him up, but he was heavy in my arms and the poison had seeped inside him. His blood had all run out into the water.

Under my hands, I could feel the shape of his ribs, the dense, fluttering knot of his heart, not much bigger than my fist. He was still alive, but with every beat, his pulse was growing fainter, thinner.

He was slipping away from me, even as I tried to call up the bright, flickering power that could save him. But my body was heavy. My hands were cold and numb. Without Davenport to complete the star, the light that had been so strong inside me a moment ago suddenly felt just as wrung out and exhausted as the rest of me.

I pressed harder and closed my eyes, working desperately to pull the poison out of him, to keep a hold on his heart—reaching for it, finding it. I held it in my mind, pouring all I had left of my exhausted craft into the very center of it.

It seemed so hopeless, so impossible that a life could rest on such a small thing.

Everything was very still.

And then it beat, pushing back against my hand. Blood ran through him, through every artery and vein. I could only pray silently, steeling myself for what would happen when I lost my last particle of strength and the power of the hollow was gone completely. I pressed my forehead against his and waited.

His heart gave another violent jerk and I knew I wasn't the one doing it anymore. It was beating, he was healing, and I started to cry.

I sat in the ruined yard of my ruined house, holding on to Fisher as under my hands, the buckshot began to push its way back out of his skin. Mike Faraday's truck still burned like a signal fire, towering over the Willows.

After a while, the water washed back.

❊   ❊   ❊

Fisher and I lay in the middle of the yard. The blood and the water and the awful chaos of the reckoning had all washed away.

Shiny and Rae were huddled together on the porch. The place under the window where the bottles had exploded was still smoking a little, but surprisingly, the house did not look considerably worse than it already had. Shiny's skin was still a red mess of cracks, though, and she was shivering like her whole body would fly apart.

In the yard, the air was hushed, like the stillness after a clap of thunder. There was nothing but the stillness of it. Nothing and nothing. Seconds stretched out.

I lay in the dirt with my head on Fisher's chest, looking up. The sky was cloudless now, clearing to a pale, watery blue as the sun went down. The ground was freezing, but under me, Fisher was warm. The air was clear, singing with crickets.

"It's over," I said into his shirt. My voice sounded flat, so rough and strange that I wasn't sure it was mine.

The boys from the coalition lay sprawled around us on the muddy ground. They were coughing and spitting, but Davenport's craft had been undone the moment the fiends had taken her, and we were all breathing clear and easy now, in no danger of drowning.

There were a few changed fish flopping in the mud like slimy, spiny monsters, but they were going still. The brambles and the vines were all turning black, sinking into the ground as the light from the hollow faded.

Mike Faraday slumped against the fender of someone's off-roader, staring around at the dying catfish like someone seeing his own nightmares. At Fisher, red and tattered from the shotgun, and at Shiny's raw, cracked skin.

His eyes were dazed and he kept opening his mouth and shutting it again.

Shiny sat on the edge of the porch, letting her legs hang down. "Mike," she said, and her voice sounded tired. "If you say one word . . . I don't even know. Just take your merry band of assholes and get out of my yard. You're lucky right now that it's only your truck I burned down. Next time, I promise it'll be you."

Her shoulders were sagging, though, and for once in her life, she didn't really seem to want to burn down anyone.

Mike stumbled away from the truck and stepped down hard on the thrashing fish. It made an awful crunching sound under his foot, twisting and snapping at his boot, but it was already getting weaker, going still.

"The reckoning," he said finally. His voice sounded dazed, like he had lost himself and was only now realizing it. "It was happening, and y'all just *stopped* it."

But I'd only done the thing that I could, called on the power that we had. The fiends might be strange and full of mysteries, but they were the beating heart of everything we were.

Shiny leaned against the porch railing, wincing. Her voice was husky, and she'd taken back her buck knife from Rae, but she was smiling a little. "I don't know if you know this, but Blackwoods are very good at surviving."

The boys and men from the coalition were all struggling up, getting into their trucks, backing down the driveway and out onto the road.

It confounded me that they could leave us just like that, like they had never felt a fear so great they were willing to burn us. But it was the way of things, the way of people.

336

The town could be nearly destroyed, then pick itself up and straggle on—maybe the same way I could lose years of my life to the cellar and then, when all was said and done, still come home to the Blackwoods.

The same way Davenport had left this place and gone to another.

When Fisher shifted under me, I pushed myself up on my elbows and leaned over him. The spray of glass sparkled down the side of his face and little streams of blood still ran down his cheek, making crooked pathways in the dirt. His shirt was in a state, torn mostly to rags by the force of the gun. The skin around the buckshot wound seeped and bruised but had already knitted itself back together.

"We are not good for the environment, Clementine," he muttered, looking up at me.

I could still feel the light deep in my bones, humming more faintly since the star had broken, as low and tired as the rest of me. "But we're very good at saving the world."

He lifted an arm and set his hand between my shoulders, holding on to the back of my dress. "No, we're not. Look around you—we are terrible."

But he was smiling, and then he kissed me. His mouth was hungry, and he lay on his back with his arms around my waist. The way his lips moved against mine made it hard to care that the yard was muddy or my dress was wet or there were twigs and leaves stuck to my legs, only that he was warm and alive, that kissing me like this was what he was born to do, like we were all there was.

THE TOWER
CHAPTER TWENTY-EIGHT

It was a hot, sticky day, and Fisher and I were in the front hall of the Blackwood house, prying boards off the blackened doorways and throwing them into a pile. It was hard, messy work, but there was no way around it. Without opening up the doors, it was impossible to say for sure that the house was beyond saving.

At first, Myloria had been deeply distrustful of this scheme, but now she drifted around after us, peering into rooms she hadn't looked inside in a decade. The upstairs was flatly unusable, and most of the rooms would need a lot of work just so no one would fall through the floors, but some were only singed and neglected, and it would be nice to be able to spread out.

Fisher kept offering to get various boys from town to come out and help, but Myloria was set against that. It was safe to say that Mike Faraday would probably never be welcome in the house, but Tony Watts and the Maddox brothers had been civil enough, and even said hello to me sometimes in town without acting like I was going to attack them.

Fisher was working at a particularly stubborn board, trying to pry it away from the wall.

"Can you get me a screwdriver?" he said, glancing over his shoulder.

When I came into our bedroom, Shiny was kneeling on the floor with Rae. The two of them were bent over Shiny's sketchbook as Shiny drew out a sketch of a high, crooked tower. The lines were shadowy and old-fashioned, but something in the shape and the round scallops at the bottom made it look a little like the outline of a truck, with a towering pillar of flames rising from the bed.

Her watercolor box was sitting by her knee, globs of paint arranged around the edges of an old dinner plate. She was staring down at the drawing with a kind of quiet ferocity.

The design around the bottom of the card was only half-finished, but I could make out a tricky scalloped pattern, and there at the center, a girl with long white-blond hair and a delicate fairy-princess face, looking sadly at the burning tower, which would always be an eternal second away from falling.

Shiny glanced up, wrinkling her forehead. "I know it doesn't seem right to use her."

"More right than to forget," I said. "I can't think of one other person more fitting."

Rae sat on her knees on the bed, watching as Shiny filled in the flames.

The witch deck was mostly finished now, laid out in a

line on the dresser to dry, and I touched the corners of them, letting the rough edges brush against my fingers.

Shiny had drawn each of us at our most pure and resolute, the portraits of our better selves.

I pulled out the ones I wanted and arranged them side by side. When the Tower was done, the five cards would make the reckoning star, but without Davenport, we were just four people who carried all the mysteries of the hollow—the legacy of our blood.

In most decks I'd seen, the Star was a long-haired woman pouring water, but in Shiny's deck, the Star was a skinny black girl sitting on a red bicycle. Her face was peaceful and kind—not a destroyer or a miracle-worker, but the voice that said the world was good, that secrets could be known and miracles were possible.

Shiny's own picture was of Justice, with a fishing pole in one hand and a lighter in the other, ready to provide or to burn, depending on the judgment.

She had painted Fisher as the Magician. He stood in a meadow, holding an ax. All around him, the field was full of sunflowers, which bloomed in huge yellow bursts all the way up the sides of the drawing, but the biggest, brightest one was on his chest—a splattery ring, painted in gold and black and red.

"I was going to make *him* the Tower," Shiny said, watching me turn the card in my hand. "Because of his tattoo and . . . everything else, really. Anyway, I changed my mind. The Tower might be a strong card, but it's not steadfast or loyal, so I figured I had better make him the Magician instead, since you were the Priestess. She works on him and through him, like the driving force inside things. So . . . you know."

It was the closest Shiny had ever come to saying that we were good together, or that we could be, so I just looked away and smiled.

The picture of the Priestess was no priestess at all, but an unnaturally red-haired girl standing in the dark rectangle of a doorway. She was dressed in a blue nightgown, surrounded by roots, but not touched by them, not trapped. Her eyes were open.

I stood looking at the image of her. Of me.

So much was beyond my sight. There was so much about our past that I still didn't understand, and I wasn't one to tell the future. I could only tell the way the world worked. History was a tangled thing, people were resilient, and the one constant law of the world was that it would heal.

ALL THANKS TO:

My agent, Sarah Davies, who approaches every circumstance with grace and style.

My editor, Jessica Almon, who asked a million questions, supplied a million answers, harnessed the power of Pinterest, saved the day more than once, and took me out for olives when she didn't even know they were my favorite food.

Ben Schrank—the man who steers the ship.

As ever, the brilliant and multitalented team at Penguin Young Readers. They make my books pretty in absolutely every sense and do their best to guide me toward proper comma use.

Maggie and Tess, who never, ever make me do this alone.

My sister Maddy, an object lesson in impeccable principles and a real class act. She totally would have let the animals out of their cages.

David, who reads and reads and reads, even when he should be thoroughly tired of this book by now. Who loves me even when I stop making sense and was a constant advocate for more action, more danger, and more kissing.

The state of Arkansas, where I planted sunflowers, kept tadpoles in a canning jar, had a pet goat named Rover, and rarely wore shoes. My first childhood memories are mostly of various carpets, but my best ones are of the Ozarks. There's magic there, and no one will ever convince me otherwise.

ABOUT THE AUTHOR

Brenna Yovanoff once thought she wanted to grow up to become an editor. Although it turns out she was mistaken, she doesn't regret her days as a slush-pile reader or the fact that she's memorised large stretches of *The Chicago Manual of Style*. Her short fiction has appeared in *Chiaroscuro* and *Strange Horizons*. She has an MFA in creative writing from Colorado State University and currently lives in Denver. She is also the author of *The Replacement* and *Smoulder* published by Simon and Schuster.

WANT MORE
MYSTERY?
MORE
DARKNESS?
MORE
DANGER?

'I so loved
this book . . .'
LAUREN KATE,
bestselling author of
FALLEN

'Eerie and
beautiful . . .'
MAGGIE
STIEFVATER,
bestselling author of
SHIVER

The
REPLACEMENT

BRENNA YOVANOFF

'a dark
tale that
will totally
change your
preconceptions'
THE SUN,
on *The Replacement*

SMOULDER
BRENNA
YOVANOFF

From the author of *The Replacement*

BRENNA YOVANOFF